MAGNIFIED
WORLD

 Random House Canada

PUBLISHED BY RANDOM HOUSE CANADA

www.randomhouse.ca

Random House Canada and colophon are registered trademarks.

This book is a work of fiction. Names, characters, places and incidents either are the product of the author's imagination or are used fictitiously. Any resemblance to actual persons, living or dead, events or locales is entirely coincidental.

Grateful acknowledgement is made to Helen Humphreys for permission to reprint a portion of "Blurring" from *The Perils of Geography* published by Brick Books and to House of Anansi Press Inc. for permission to reprint a portion of "Gravesong" from *The Address Book* by Steven Heighton.

Library and Archives Canada Cataloguing in Publication

O'Connell, Grace
    Magnified world / Grace O'Connell.

Issued also in electronic format.

ISBN 978-0-307-36037-3

    I. Title.

PS8629.064M33 2012   C813'.6   C2011-908182-2

Text and cover design by Andrew Roberts

Printed and bound in the United States of America

10 9 8 7 6 5 4 3 2

"Why will you stall till the stalling's your life?
It's wake yourself now or never be woken."

—STEVEN HEIGHTON, "GRAVESONG"

"You never told me what it was
that became clear; or else I've forgotten.
All I know this moment is that
the magnified world is oddly disappointing
and the sun is going down here,
reeling distance in across the water
to break gold and sudden on
the shoal of shadow outside this window."

—HELEN HUMPHREYS, "BLURRING"

For my family and for EM

PART ONE

BLACKOUTS

One

Toronto, late 1990s

The first time it happened, I didn't open the store on time. I found myself standing on the sidewalk outside the locked door at noon, the Queen streetcar going by behind me in a baritone of metal complaints. It was two hours after I was supposed to have opened and I had no memory of anything after going to bed the night before. The brown canvas shoes I had on were pinching my toes. I'd never seen the shoes before in my life and it seemed obvious that I was dreaming. If I was dreaming, my mother would be there like she always had been. But when I let myself in, there was no one.

Then my father was running down the stairs from our apartment on the second floor and I knew I was awake.

"Where have you been?" he said.

"I don't know."

"What? Where have you been?"

"I don't know," I said. "I don't know."

His mouth opened and I knew he was going to ask me again.

I was lying on the floor. I could see that the bottom shelf of the Fortune and Foretelling section was filthy with dust. It took me a moment to realize I had fainted. My mother was the one who fainted. Who used to faint. I'd never fainted before.

My father picked me up—he actually lifted me up onto my feet, which I didn't realize he was capable of doing. When I wobbled he set me back down again and knelt beside me and all I could think was that it must hurt his knees to be like that. I could see into the collar of his shirt. His chest was that of an old man, an older man than him: a dull red unrelated to the colour of his face, a lattice of grey hair. I didn't want to look.

"Where were you? Are you sick? Where were you?"

"I don't know."

"What do you mean, you don't know?"

"I don't remember."

He seemed to bite down very hard; I could see a tendon in his neck jump. My head ached.

"You don't remember."

"I went to bed. After *A Bit of Fry & Laurie.*" My boyfriend Andrew had come over to the apartment where I lived with my father above the store. He had rented the show at Queen Video and we watched it together after dinner, curled up on the couch. My father walked by in his pyjamas at one point, holding a cup of tea, and said, "That's a good one. That British humour. Funny stuff." Near the end of the video, with my father in bed in his room, Andrew started to kiss the back of my neck. He slid his arms around me and ran his spidery hands over my breasts. His lips on my earlobe sent fizzing little darts of pleasure all over. Then the *shush* of water running came from my father's washroom, over our shoulders, and we moved apart.

We sat in silence while the credits ran, and then I walked him down to the street. It was completely still, without the slightest trace of wind. Andrew unlocked his bicycle from the drainpipe beside the store.

"I've got a tutorial tomorrow at ten and they're turning in their papers, so I'll be a hermit for a while," he said. "I'm sorry. If you really need me, you can call." He looked down and away, fiddled with his light. He'd felt guilty about working since my mother died, about being away from me.

I tucked my hair behind my ear. "No problem," I said.

He looked at me again for a moment, kissed me, then got on his bike and pedalled away. I locked up and went back upstairs, where I washed my face and got into bed.

The next thing I knew I was outside the store in blazing daylight. And now I was on the floor beside my father.

"You don't remember anything after going to bed?" My father's face had gone oddly flat and the redness had drained away, but all he said was, "I'll stay in the store until you're feeling better."

I went upstairs to my room and closed the door. On the windowsill was a card, just sitting there without an envelope. When I picked it up, it was slightly warm.

I'm so sorry to hear of your loss, it said. *With love, Gil.*

I didn't remember putting the card there. I didn't even remember a Gil—was he a customer? A friend of my father's? It sounded like an old man's name. Dozens of cards had arrived after my mother's funeral, mostly politely worded watery-toned notes from my father's colleagues at the university. This card looked no different except for the pained and jerky handwriting.

The canvas shoes had straps that pinched at the top of my instep. They fit so badly it felt like they'd been worn in by someone else altogether. I sat down on the edge of my bed and slid my feet out, wincing when the skin pulled away from the fabric. I carried the shoes to the hallway mat. The foyer was open to the kitchen, and through the windows, the light was unbearably bright.

We called it *the blackout*, like we could have lit some candles and waited it out. *The blackout. Your blackout.* I wanted to know what had happened in the time I'd lost. I asked Andrew and my best friend, Wendy, if they had seen me or heard from me in the missing hours. I went by George's Diner to ask George if I had come by that night. Wendy and I had been going to the same College Street diner since high school because of George, a handsome first-generation Greek with a perfect profile and soft curls that we had both spent our freshman lectures daydreaming about. We were all friendly, though we'd never seen him outside the restaurant.

He leaned out of the kitchen pass-through and put his hand on my shoulder, squeezed. He shook his head. He hadn't seen me. Andrew and Wendy hadn't seen me. I'd been nowhere, it seemed, doing nothing with no one.

George said, "Are you okay?" Then he washed his hands in the steel sink and got back to work.

No one had seen me. I felt like a dog in a telephone pole advertisement. *Have you seen this girl?*

I wanted to know what had happened, but there were so many things I didn't know right at that moment that a little more hardly made a difference; it seemed like water being poured into a glass that was already full. I wanted to know, even if it was bizarre and unbelievable—because wasn't life bizarre and unbelievable? My mother drowned in the Don River with her pockets filled with polished zircon, a not-very-popular gemstone we sold in the store. It's associated with the crown chakra and can be used to stop bleeding. I puzzled and puzzled over the zircon—*was there a message there?*—until I realized that zircon distinguished itself in one way: it was the heaviest gemstone we sold. She must have wanted to be sure, in case her wet wool coat wasn't enough. Although she needn't have bothered— the water was still so cold in early May, they said she probably passed out within minutes. They said she'd hardly have felt a thing, as if the words *probably* and *hardly* didn't matter at all. It wasn't very specific, the accounting. It wasn't very precise.

The police returned the zircon to us in Ziploc bags and I didn't know what to do with it. In the end I put it in a glass bowl on the kitchen windowsill, like it was an urn of her ashes. My father and I scattered her actual ashes in Trinity Bellwoods Park. He was nervous, unsure whether scattering ashes in the park was allowed, so we went on a damp Monday night after sundown, up near the north end where it was very quiet, in the little valley where the drum circle would meet during the warmer months.

I made a note in the store's Excel spreadsheet ledger beside the long, nonsensical item number for the zircon. *Forty polished, unsized stones. Removed from inventory.* Now that was me. Several pieces, removed from inventory.

I went to Dr. Henderson, the same family doctor who'd prescribed me nasal sprays and antibiotics since I was eighteen, who said I was exhausted. That I was still mourning my mother, that the funeral had overwhelmed me, that I was "distressed." He recommended vitamin C, iron-rich foods, a restful schedule. Official scientific diagnosis: a short circuit, a temporary brain fritz. I thought, *You really can't do any better than that, Doctor?* I thought I might as well put some blue calcite, which was supposed to help with memory, under my pillow. That it couldn't hurt. When I got home from the doctor's office, I took a piece of the pale, wan stone from the crystal trough in the store and slid it into my bed. That was in early June: three weeks after the funeral, a month after my mother died, five weeks after my twenty-third birthday.

I'd opened up the store again only a few days after the funeral—it was the only thing I could think to do, the only reason to stand up, wash my face, move my hands. I wanted to open the store, be normal, but in the first few days I found myself glaring at customers when they touched things, bamboo socks and journals bound in grasscloth. She might have touched them last. I wanted to lick the whole store, consume it, keep it. One morning I put on one of her long linen skirts, over my jeans like a dress-up costume. Maybe someone would mistake me for her, some old nearsighted customer. Not that we looked alike. But still. When my father came home through the store, I pulled the skirt off fast, behind the counter before he could see it, the fabric puddling on the floor.

The morning after the blackout, my father and I both got up early and sat down at the kitchen table at the same time. We looked at each other as if to say, *Do we have to talk now* and *If I had known you were going to sit here too I might not have sat here.*

"Everything will be all right," he said. He stood up with much scraping of his chair on the floor—*were they always that loud?*—and put his hand on my shoulder.

I stood up too and he hugged me. I wasn't used to touching my father. I wasn't used to having him here in the mornings; even on days when he wasn't teaching, he usually liked to get up early and go to his office to grade papers or read. Since she died, though, he was around more, taking up more space. I wanted to have the Lucky Charms my mother knew I kept in the back of the cupboard, but I didn't want him to see and tell me I ought to be eating Shredded Wheat or unsweetened oatmeal. We hung onto each other, as if unsure how to get back to our chairs. The window was open and cool morning air ran into the apartment like water from a tap.

A week passed, and I drank a lot of orange juice and ate a lot of spinach and red meat as I had been told to. I got a canker sore underneath my tongue from all the orange juice. Nothing was happening, but my father was watching me strangely, at moments when he thought I wouldn't notice. When he came home, walking through the store, I could feel his eyes on me while my fingers stretched against the bottom of the penny slot in the register as I dug out change for a customer. When I got up to open the door for Andrew in the evenings, I sensed my father's gaze following my back. The canvas shoes sat by the doorway, the cruel straps lolling unfastened, slightly obscene. I knew he looked at those too.

Two

My mother had a stockpile of sayings from a time before her own. She would smile and wave at me with whatever was in her hand—a horoscope scroll, a spoon—and say, "safe as houses," and, "A nod is as good as a wink to a blind horse." She would say, "A mill can't grind with water that's past," like I knew what it meant. If I asked for something outrageous or expensive, she would grin and say, "The age of miracles is past, darling." She told me not to wear polyester and not to apologize to anyone for my taste in music and food. Some expressions I'd heard other people use, some I assumed were things she'd picked up in Georgia, where she grew up. She said all of these things during her up times, because she was like a coin that could be flipped and sometimes it went one way and sometimes the other. During the bad times, she said nothing, and stood behind the counter in the store, staring out the window towards Trinity Bellwoods Park.

Sometimes I would linger in Bellwoods on my walk home from school, ambling around between the widely spaced trees, watching the squirrels, who ran constantly along the branches for no apparent reason or hung face down on the trunks and stared at the ground. There was supposed to be a white squirrel in the park. The idea was, it was good luck to see her, but I never did. I still looked, out of habit, any flash of white making me flinch, hopeful.

When my mother stared, blank-faced, at the door, she'd say she was waiting for customers. Or sometimes she yelled, smacked the back of my head with her palm or swung the side of her fist into my side. Sharp, shocking, not meant to hurt. And then her look of surprise, genuine and raw. Once when I was fifteen I hit her back, in the face, and I could see the outline of my hand on her skin for a second before she put her own hand over it. It was like hitting a dog that has snapped at you. She looked at me with her hand on her face and said, "I'm sorry." I couldn't even remember where she had hit me. Her eyes were enormous in her face. I thought: *Who hit her?* Even though my palm was still itchy-stinging.

Or other things, harder things. One night she'd be fine and the next morning have ragged cuts on her forearms, until my father locked up the knives, the look on his face like a man who has closed his hand in the car door and has to open it and has not yet gotten himself up to it. Sometimes brownish bruises up to her elbows, we couldn't do anything about that, they hardly showed because she didn't bruise easily. They'd bloom faintly, pink to brown to yellow, and then gone.

I learned to feed myself. To do laundry. I would count the change carefully out of the cash drawer in the store, writing down the amount I took, and walk west to the supermarket on Gladstone with the little upright wheeled buggy we used for groceries. I bought Pop-Tarts, Kraft Dinner, frozen Green

Giant vegetables, the pieces of carrot like marshy orange dice. I would write down the amount left over when I returned. I found an extra stepladder in the attic storage room and brought it down to the kitchen so I could reach the higher cupboards. My father would praise my efforts, eat too quickly and leave the table, his stomach making discreet noises of protest as he made his way up the stairs to his study. Sometimes my mother would accept these efforts, mechanically eating what I'd prepared, her mouth a little open. Other times she would be puzzled, almost offended. "What are you doing, darling? I'm making stuffed peppers for dinner." Like she was a regular mother and it was a betrayal to prepare for anything else, any other possibility. I was like a sailor obsessed with the weather, with the slightest change in the wind or clouds, always watching.

For the first few weeks, I forgot sometimes that she was dead; not completely of course, but in little, individual moments, when I would see the yellow zucchini she liked in a store, or smell the rooibos tea she drank. If they were still selling these things, if they still existed, then she must be alive, to eat, to drink. It takes time for your small, intimate brain to catch up to your large, conceptual one. A phrase came to me, something she had said: "Screw your courage to the sticking place." That's what it felt like to walk down the street, to keep my head from drifting down to rest on my chest. Those hard words: *screw*, *sticking*. A mechanical tightening. When I woke up in the morning and remembered she was gone, it was the kind of grief that curls your fingers over.

It took me time to straighten out and get down to the store, but I craved the routine. Tidy the shelves, count the till, check the safe, note what we're low on, sweep the floor, check the window display, put out the sandwich board, unlock the door, turn the sign. I had a list in a notebook, as if I might have to leave instructions. Maybe we would have to hire someone now. Unthinkable, but I thought it. Then un-thought it.

The store itself was one of those places that everyone in the neighbourhood knew. It was a long narrow space with built-in shelves, weathered wooden tables, and a pressed tin ceiling, the real kind, not the tiles. There was a huge, slightly wavy window that ran the length of the storefront. It was a common layout for the early twentieth-century Toronto. The store had come to my mother when she was in her twenties, shortly after she married my father and had me. At some imprecise time in the past it had been a grocery store; you could tell from the way the shelves were built. It was my father who knew things like that, who pointed this out to me, although he'd never seen it or even been in it before he met my mother. By the time she came to Toronto, the store had shifted closer to its present form, selling tarot cards, candles, healing crystals, teas. During the draft, dirty and confused teenaged dodgers slept on mattresses in what was now our apartment, my mother sitting cross-legged with them before and after her shifts in the store, long hair falling almost into her lap, and my father, surely, leaning against the wall, awkward and uncomfortable. Out of place.

She was only twenty-one; he was thirty-five, a series of creases already fanning out from the corners of his eyes. He was the wrong kind of professor for their crowd, he wasn't political, his Ph.D. was in Renaissance literature. Theirs was a City Hall marriage and the photos looked older than they were. My mother was from Georgia, and her parents weren't there. My father's were, looking chipper and bright, their smiles stretched out so their eye teeth showed.

Until I got the call about my mother, their deaths were the only ones I'd experienced, their absences that had felt like day turning slowly and without violence into night. I would have said I knew what it was like to lose someone I loved. I'd gone to their funerals, a year apart, in my grade school, crushed-velvet dresses and cried during the hymns, those sad songs I'd never heard but that seemed somehow familiar. Now I knew that there was no such thing as being acquainted with death.

My mother was friends with the draft dodgers who slept upstairs and she worked in the store sometimes back then, how often I don't know. There were a lot of jobs from that time before she was married that she would mention in passing: *When I delivered the* Globe and Mail *. . . when I was an usher at the Cumberland . . . when I worked for that painter, helping with the egg tempera* . . . The owner of the store liked her, and when he retired, he told her to get together the money and buy the place.

Why not? It seemed to me like that was the way things went back then, just casual and easy—a Toronto that existed before permits and bank loans and historical preservation societies, a city of children whose parents had gone away for the whole of the sixties and seventies. I knew that wasn't right exactly, but that was how it sounded when she talked about it, and now she wasn't around to ask for more details.

I don't know where the money for the store came from, how much it was. She renamed the store with her married name, my father's name, our name: *Pierce Gifts & Oddities*. The name caught my reluctant father up in the store, shanghaied him into a partnership.

When the draft dodgers moved on from the apartment above the store, my mother and father moved in. Pierce Gifts & Oddities did a brisk trade and as the neighbourhood changed, my mother successfully steered us into the booming green and organic movements, stocking gifty items like Palestinian olive-wood dinnerware and recycled silk scarves, moving away from the less popular, New Age stock. But my father seemed to be waiting it out. He expected she would get tired of it and sell it. He didn't think it was an appropriate pastime for a professor's wife. That's how he thought of it, as a pastime. He thought we should be living in the Annex or on Harbord Street, that I should be going to a better school. All of this my mother told me over the years, in her roundabout way, not angry but amused, impish, like someone savouring a punchline.

By the time I was old enough to help out on weekends, my father had learned to float through the length of the store, almost invisible, and soundlessly ascend the stairs to the apartment. He could almost walk through the tables.

I didn't feel the same way as my mother about the things in the store. It wasn't that I believed in them more, exactly, but I was more afraid not to. Hence the blue calcite under my pillow.

She did her tarot readings from memory, occasionally mixing up a card or two, and she laid crystals on her wrists when she was bored, not paying attention. She knew what they were for but she didn't take it seriously. I was afraid of making a mistake, mixing up amazonite and aquamarine, forgetting that the ten of swords needed to be read slightly differently when the spread also contained the nine of cups. I catalogued it all, the things we had, the promises of what they could do. Uses. Theory. I wrote them in my notebooks, and whenever the store was quiet, after I'd tidied up, I wrote them out again. I went through the reference books we carried and made notes as if studying for an exam. The notebooks piled up, filled with lists and lists of uses for this stone or that, this and that herb, tarot spreads and their meanings, interspersed with personal lists of places I wanted to visit, songs I liked, movie stars I wanted to kiss, courses I wanted to take. While we were in high school, my friend Wendy would come by the store when I was working and make lists too sometimes, but she got bored with it. "Making a list doesn't tell me how to get it. 'Visit Paris,'" she read from her page. "I don't need to write that down to know what I need to do it. Money." Then she would wheedle me to go see George. "Gorgeous George," she'd say, her eyes rolled back in her head, hands clutched over her heart.

As time went on, I showed her my lists less and less. By the time we graduated from the University of Toronto, where I had avoided not only my father's classes but his entire department, I was working full time at Pierce Gifts & Oddities, and my notebooks were stored in a file box under the counter. Wendy applied to internships in public relations and magazine publishing, hoping to make good on her English degree. My own degree, mostly consisting of shaky Bs and Cs, was in history, and after graduation I put the cardboard tube with my diploma under my bed in a box of old books.

In the store, I made my notes on the stock in an official-looking binder: organic skin care, alternative healing therapies, foretelling aids, yoga and fitness accessories. Occasionally my mother would offer up strange, unsolicited bits of information to customers. Copper for blood problems, worn over a vein, preferably in the crook of the elbow. Almond oil for pregnant women's bellies, mint for concentration. These were things she just knew, but that I had to write down. Her smile was pleasant and soft, and slightly absent. Around her the store was stuffy and bright, a sweatbox in the summer, and in the front you could see a powdering of dust motes in the sunlight.

As the nineties revved up, the neighbourhood changed. Galleries and cafés moved in, bringing a new kind of customer: art students, designers, people who charged Bay Street executives exorbitant prices to have their offices feng shui'd. Our stretch of Queen Street started to change slowly from a street of fabric stores and butchers to one of upscale restaurants and designer clothing stops. We spent some money on a new, nicer sign, a flowing script of white paint on an indigo background, and floodlights to illuminate it at night. My mother and I would go over the supplier catalogues, or go down to trade shows at the Metro Toronto Convention Centre, and every season she was in love with the smell of a new organic shampoo or the smooth gloss of bamboo candlesticks. In the store, she would sit silently reading her own spreads over and over, occasionally getting up to round the store, touching this polished stone or that silk scarf, as if she never got sick of something being only beautiful. That softness was what people wanted in her; even if they were just buying a yoga mat, they wanted her to be serene, like it said something about them as people, their decision to shop there. She never made them feel stupid for what they believed rocks and candles could do or for wanting credit for saving the world when they bought reusable coffee cups made from corn oil. And it helped—they helped, somehow. It was as if their expectation, their unthinking acceptance, cast a spell of protection. She never had a problem in the store while there were people around. Pierce Gifts & Oddities was a circle of salt. And all the time, my mother stood behind the counter, turning ·smoothly when the bell over the door chimed, always looking as if the person walking in was the only person she had been waiting for.

Three

It was in the store that I was keeping my secret. The bottom drawer under the cash register was full of scraps of paper for making signs, extra rolls of price stickers, a bottle of Dead Sea Mineral hand cream I had taken out of inventory but never paid for. Underneath all of this was the card, an ordinary greeting card. The one I'd found on the windowsill in my room after the blackout. From Gil. *I'm so sorry to hear of your loss. With love.* It hadn't meant anything to me at the time. On top of it was another card, in the same spiky, frantic lettering. Like someone trying to disguise their handwriting. It had arrived addressed to me, the day after the first one. It was a card of the sort sent out by charities to people who had donated small amounts to their effort. A white border, a stolid Canadian scene of lake and granite, pines and sky. In black permanent marker on the outside: *Maggie may tell me a story.* And inside: *Maggie may catch a redhanded story. Much love, Gil.*

The words were strange to me, like a nursery rhyme I couldn't place. *Red-handed* was hot, the word itself seemed to burn my fingertips as I sat on my stool, tracing the letters with my index finger. I didn't know a Gil, had never met a Gil. I had asked my father, cautiously flippant, if he knew a Gil. He looked up from the kitchen table, where he was reading the book review section of the paper.

"No, I don't believe so. Why do you ask?"

I shrugged and picked up the milk carton, filing it back into the fridge. I didn't say anything.

"Is he from the history department?" I heard my father's question, but I had already ducked into my room.

As the days went by, more cards arrived. *Gil*, I thought to myself sometimes when I was alone in the store. It was such a short, wet little name. I stored the cards in the drawer. *Gil*. I thought of him as being made of paper, like the cards themselves. In my mind he was just the outline of a man, like the paper dolls endlessly holding hands that my mother would sometimes cut out of crinkling wrapping paper for me on Christmas.

After we opened up again following the funeral, some of my regulars came in to pay their respects after reading the obituary in the *Globe and Mail*, the short one my father had written and sent out—another baffling, correct task he'd undertaken after her death. I didn't realize until then how many people read that part of the paper. I never had.

Carol Pierce née Woodham of Toronto, originally from Savannah Beach, GA. Owner and curator of Pierce Gifts & Oddities. Beloved mother of Margaret and wife of Christopher.

I liked the word *curator*. There was a dignity there, a small offering. I wanted to thank my father for it.

The older women, many of whom had known the store before my mother took it over, were the most anxious to offer comfort. One woman reached across the counter and slipped her hand into mine the first time she came in after the funeral. It felt like plastic drinking straws wrapped in silk.

"Your mother's spirit is here," she said. "It always was. She's protecting you. Not a ghost, a spirit. Benevolent. Do you feel her?"

I nodded, but I had a hard time ascribing those qualities to my mother. Benevolent I could understand. But protective?

"It's a good day to get this then." The customer held up a midsize crystal ball that was speckled throughout with air bubbles, like someone had exhaled into it. "I've been waiting for the right day. Sometimes it's hard to tell."

I rang her through. "Thank you. For what you said about my mother."

"Never mind, Ducky." She took the bag. "What you need to do is breathe it out. A little at a time."

I had no idea what she meant. *Breathe it out.* I gave an experimental sigh, checked myself over mentally. *Nothing different.*

"That's the spirit," she said. Then she left with the little bag stowed safely in her purse.

I thanked all the customers who said things like that, things meant to comfort me, and I shelved self-improvement books and healing candles and stuck them with price tags from the price-tag gun after rolling the numbers into place. It was strange to be in the store without my mother; even when I had worked alone, it was always her store. She was always coming back, any minute. She could only go so far. I made a new display for the Green Housekeeping section and didn't have her to ask if it looked all right and so it never did, each bottle, box and book seeming slightly skewed.

She would like the cards from Gil, the words. Sometimes I fanned the cards out in my hands, as if displaying them. She would like Gil, whoever he was.

I wasn't used to working in the store every day. Monday was our closed day, as was the Queen Street custom, but my mother had usually handled the busy Friday and Saturday shifts. I found myself cancelling on Wendy and Andrew more often. The way I phrased it, I was tethered to the store. I didn't say I'd rather be here. Summer had pushed its way into the city, the puffs of air through the opening and closing door grew warmer. A few days after the blackout, Andrew arrived forty minutes before closing and announced he was kidnapping me.

"It's twenty-five degrees. Toronto is out there having a veritable orgy. People are wearing next to nothing. It's wall-to-wall hot pants."

"It's June. There's plenty of nice weather to come," I said without pausing in my reorganization of the incense section. The smell was heavy, cardamom mixing with vanilla and ylang-ylang. I was alphabetizing, working up from the bottom.

"I made a picnic," he said, pivoting to show me a bulging backpack. "Picnic."

"It's not six yet."

"There's no one here," he said, and then, "Okay. We'll wait. The bread might get a bit hard. But it will be fine." He stored the bag under the counter.

I moved the rosewater beside the raspberry, making sure the angles aligned. I heard the soft slap that meant Andrew had hauled out his ever-present stack of papers. Marking maybe, or notes on his own work. He was teaching courses while he worked on his Ph.D. and was constantly swamped by pages and pages of faulty reasoning and hasty research. He also taught an evening workshop in creative writing. He liked to snicker over the bad poetry, but was offended when I did the same. "It's different," he would say. "I'm their *teacher*. I want them to improve."

The skree of a highlighter made me realize I needed to put on some music. Soft classical or world music was what my mother had favoured, but lately I'd been listening to the radio, singing along to '80s pop songs I hadn't known I knew. I spun the dial and moved up to the *P*s. Peppermint, Pine, Pumpkin Pie.

"Maggie," said Andrew. "The bread. There's still no one here."

"Okay." I turned the ocean-scented incense box upside down to mark where I had stopped. I went about the end-of-day procedures while Andrew waited, shuffling his papers, pressing his thin body against the counter when I passed back and forth.

"I'm in the way," he said.

"You're not."

"I won't say a word until you've battened down the hatches. I promise."

I had my head in the safe, where I was storing the till. "It's fine. Did you get that nice bread?"

Andrew liked a particular baker's bread that he bought fresh in the Annex. I think it made him feel like one of the Romantic poets of his subject area—he liked to tear chunks off and smear butter on like he was half blind. I don't know how he could stay so thin, the way he went through it. When we first started dating, I'd tried to be helpful by bringing groceries to his apartment, which wasn't an apartment at all, but a fresh-bricked new townhouse in a row of identical siblings. The bricks were pink, the doors were white, and the little lawns had been replaced with parking pads bordered with hardy foliage. The townhouse had been purchased for Andrew by his parents, who lived in the suburbs and rarely visited, and had been decorated by his very capable mother. She favoured blond wood, neutral sofas and glass tables, none of which were visible beneath Andrew's strewn papers and books. Occasionally silent casseroles would arrive in Pyrex baking dishes, or bread from his mother's bread-making machine, which Andrew would eat with methodical disdain. I quickly found that my offerings of Dempster's and Diet Dr Pepper were no more appreciated. Andrew would poke at the plastic wrappings. "How can you eat this stuff? It's full of preservatives. I thought your mother was big on organics." After a while I stopped spending much time at Andrew's place. He seemed to prefer coming to the apartment, taking the stairs from the store two at a time, eating dinner most nights with my parents and me. He and my father liked to talk shop; though he was still in his Ph.D., he counted as a junior faculty member, a holy emissary to the same bad-wine and sweaty-cheese university parties that my father loved to hate. Sometimes Andrew would show up at the apartment in a self-consciously bad sports coat, his thick, pale hair brushed back from his forehead. A good, high, academic's forehead. He would walk over to the campus with my father for a professors' party with Styrofoam cups and screw-top wine and come home quiet and happy, like he was reliving it in his head, pleased with himself. It might be another two or three years before he finished his degree, but everything was pointing in the right direction. "Andrew," my father had once said, "knows how to line up his ducks."

We locked up and crossed to the park, entering through the towering white limestone gates.

"You know these used to be part of the university. There was a college here that was knocked down and absorbed into U of T."

"I know." Andrew loved any trivia to do with the university and I'd heard most of it before. I turned and looked back at the store. It was still only five to six. There was a man outside the door in a dark cap. He looked up and down the street, then made a box with his hands and peered in through the glass.

"There's a customer," I said. "Andrew. Somebody wants into the store."

Andrew was retying a shoelace, finishing with a practical double knot. He turned to look.

"There's no one there, Maggie." He let his hand hang beside mine, just touching. "I got the good bread. And snap peas and grapes. Potato salad. It'll be nice."

I looked back while we walked, trying to see where the man had gone. I had an irrational fear that somehow he had broken in. He was nowhere to be seen.

All the picnic tables were occupied, so we sat on a dry patch of grass. The park was full of people playing Frisbee, walking dogs, playing ball hockey on the cement of the net-less tennis courts. I resisted intoxication, the vivid springiness. Toronto as a city celebrated good weather like a civic holiday, the first hot days of the year getting everything but a parade. The park was as populous as a small town.

"So do you want to talk about it?" Andrew was ladling potato salad onto paper plates. He looked somewhat amphibian whenever he sat without a chair; he was tall and long-limbed, thin and pale. His body seemed to get away from him in such a desk-less posture.

"About my mom?"

He was studiously intent on his serving. "I meant the blackout."

"Well, I don't really know what to say. Considering I was blacked out for the whole thing."

"I'm just trying to help. If you want to talk."

"Sorry, yeah. I just don't know what to say."

"I mean, is it safe for you to be working alone?"

"I hadn't thought about it." I had a grim vision of the gaping register drawer, the front window smashed to bits.

"I worry about you." He handed me a straining paper plate. "There are other things you could do now, now that—well, I mean, you have options."

"What do you mean? Like hire someone part-time?" The idea of someone else standing in my mother's place behind the counter was unthinkable.

"I just thought, now that your mom is gone—may she rest in peace—you could do . . . whatever it was that you would have been doing. Normally."

"Normally? This is what I do."

"Well, you have a degree. An undergrad, at least." He looked up, smiling as if we were sharing a joke, and said, "What, are you going to spend the rest of your life working in the store?"

I stabbed my plastic fork into an overcooked cube of potato and it crumbled.

"I'm sorry," said Andrew. "That was stupid. I'm sorry."

"You and my dad, I swear."

"Maggie. Let's just forget it."

We sat and ate while a couple of teenagers sat on a bench across from us, kissing. Every minute or so they would break apart and look up and down the path. Once in a while the girl would drag her sleeve across her mouth.

"What were you like as a teenager?" I asked. Andrew and I had been dating for almost three years and I had asked him all those get-to-know-you questions before. But I felt the need to be reminded, as if I were starting everything over now as Maggie-who-doesn't-have-a-mother. Andrew blushed pink.

"You know, I was focused on school. How about you?"

"About the same, I guess. Same as now, I mean." He put a grape in his mouth and I asked, "Do you think you could ever kill yourself?" He swallowed all at once, choking a little. "I don't know if I could," I said. "I don't mean like Mom. I mean like if you were in a situation where you had to, like if you knew the location of the bomb and the enemy captured you or something. Or you were shipwrecked and no one was coming and you were going to starve to death, or you ingested some completely unstoppable poison and wanted to put yourself out of your misery. I just don't know if I could—" I pulled my index finger across my throat.

"Maggie. Please stop."

I sat there, stunned at what I'd said. "I'm sorry."

Andrew had put himself behind me and I turned my head and leaned into him, his bony shoulder digging into my cheek. The teenagers kissing on the bench were staring at us, silently, critically. I thought, *Dr. Andrew Kaplan*. In a few years, he would get things in the mail and they would say "Dr." on them and it would be for real. Just like my father. My mother used to say, "Paging Dr. Pierce" when she was annoyed.

I let the tension in my body go, the way the relaxation tapes in the store said to. *Imagine your pain is a dark bird taking off from the top of your head.* That one had always troubled me. Wouldn't the bird hurt your head? Claws and all that? I slumped against Andrew, burrowed against him, into his pale corona of promised success.

"I'm sorry," I said. "Please forget it. I'm just not myself these days. I don't know why I said that." My eyesight swam for a second, darkness gathering in the corners like staticky snow on a broken television.

Then Andrew's solid presence disappeared and I overbalanced, I was oriented into my body all at once like a toddler stuffed into a snowsuit, I was standing, falling, I hit the ground. My hands went out instinctively, met concrete instead of grass.

Andrew was there beside me, picking me up, and car horns were blaring.

"What happened?"

· We were halfway across Queen Street, crossing back to the store. I'd fallen, my kneecap connecting with the streetcar track, my palms scraping on the road.

"What happened?" said Andrew, again. He pulled me to the south side, and I sat down hard on the curb, one hand cupped over my sore knee.

"I don't know," I said. "Did I pass out?" *We were there. And now we're here.*

Pale eyebrows stitched together, Andrew said, "Are you all right?" and then, "Is this like before? Is it"—he transitioned into a stage whisper—"*a blackout*?" He took my hands and turned them palm up, frowned at the scratches.

I said, "I'd better go in and disinfect these." Andrew fished my keys out of my pocket and unlocked the door so I wouldn't have to do it. I stepped through first, and flinched. A shadow from the vegan-leather purse display had flickered and I'd been sure—just for a moment—that someone was there. The image of the man in the dark cap peering into the store flashed through my mind. But of course there was no one.

"You did, didn't you. You blacked out again."

"Maybe it was sunstroke. It's so bright today."

I went up the stairs first, Andrew following. In the kitchen I held my burning hands under cold water, then dabbed them with calendula. The bottle was almost empty, I would have to get another one from the store.

When I was done, Andrew wrapped his arms around me. "Is there anything I can do?" The staginess was gone from his voice.

I was shaky-tired, as if I'd been exercising. "I just need to lie down," I said.

Together we went into my room, lay on the bed on top of the comforter. There was an invalid feel to lying down in the daytime, the light obvious behind the curtains, the room still warm from the sun.

"What did I do?" I said. "You were there, right? Did I—talk, or anything? Was I weird?"

"What do you mean?"

"I can't remember. From the picnic to the street. The last thing I remember is saying what I said—the thing about killing yourself. Asking you if you thought you could do it."

"And nothing else until we were crossing Queen?"

"No. So tell me what happened."

"Nothing really. We finished the food, the kids on the bench left so we sat there once they were gone. We talked a bit about my classes. I was telling you about a conference I have to go to in Halifax—do you remember that? Halifax?"

"I don't remember anything."

"I don't see how that's possible. You were fine—completely fine."

I shook my head. Then I said, "I feel like reading. Something old. My hands still hurt though."

Andrew shifted. "Do you want me to read to you?"

I nodded and he got up, went to the sparsely populated bookcase beside my door.

"A kids' book," I said. "Or something like that. Something nice."

He came back and sat up against the pillows beside me with his long legs stretched out.

"'Chapter One,'" he said. "'Lucy looks into a wardrobe.'"

I lay back, resting. I knew just how Andrew felt, to be that conciliatory, that concerned. *What do you want, how can I help, what do you need?*

Andrew kept reading, and sometimes he stroked my hair, softly, hardly a touch at all. At the end of the chapter, he pulled my shoulder and rolled me towards him. He wiped my eyes and nose without disgust and dried his hands on his shirt. I fell asleep and woke to a twilight gloom, to him softly opening the door.

"I have to go get some work done," he said.

"Thanks for staying with me, before."

"No problem. I love you."

"I love you too."

I stayed awake long enough to hear him speaking in low tones to my father, in the kitchen, but sleep pulled me back down, the quiet groan of their conversation disappearing into the night.

The next day I was still feeling bad for what I'd said to Andrew in the park. What was I thinking? It had sounded flippant, horrible. Maybe the blackout was stress-induced—could that happen? Maybe I hadn't blacked out, exactly, maybe I was remembering it wrong. But underneath all my worries was another little voice. *Maybe it's your turn now.* And then, *It wouldn't be so bad, would it? Andrew did a good job taking care of you.* My mother had never blacked out as far as I knew. But it was Andrew's grim worry, my father's watchfulness, all too reminiscent.

I lay in bed in the morning. Part of me was dismissive. *I could never be like her. I'm the one who took care of her, I'm the one who was there. I'm not the sick one.* But waves of guilt came over me. What, was I too good to be like her? Too strong? Had she been tripped up in some way that I could be sure to avoid? She was beautiful, beloved, she looked like Joan Crawford in hemp lip chap. How was I any better than that?

I couldn't stand to think like that anymore, and I couldn't fall back to sleep after going to bed so early the night before, so I got up and dressed. My father's bedroom door was open, the bed neatly made. I could hear the occasional creak of the third floor, he must have been working in his upstairs office. I listened for a few minutes, heard nothing else, and then wolfed down a bowl of Corn Pops with milk. I went quietly up the stairs, my feet bare. His office door was shut, but the door to our third-floor storage room was ajar.

The storage room was a large, plain space where we kept both overflow from the apartment and extra stock for the store, and it was full to the slanted eaves of the roof. Other than when hauling stock up and down, I was rarely in the storage room. It was understood to be my mother's space. She had a system of organizing the right-hand side of the room, the things unrelated to the store, that neither my father nor I were privy to. There were boxes and boxes of old books and papers, photos and disused board games, and who knows what else.

My hands were on a box without my knowing how they got there. I pulled it out, sat down on the floor. There were old traffic tickets, short and polite letters from my Georgia grandparents, sewing patterns, tarnished jewellery, photographs, crumbling dried roses, movie stubs from *Ghostbusters* and *Any Which Way You Can*. I looked in vain for something, any small thing, in my mother's smudged handwriting. I wanted to see her backwards loop at the bottom of a lowercase *f*, the smearing along each word from her awkward, overhand writing style. The roof seemed to exhale, pressing downwards. My mother would never write anything ever again. Everything she would ever say to me was in this room, in the boxes of random junk she chose to keep. There were things I still didn't know about my mother, basic biographical details I'd never pressed her about. I thought there would be time. And I was scared to ask anything she didn't volunteer, because couldn't there be something that was dangerous to ask? So many things were unexpectedly dangerous for her. But here was a room of her. There was a fat manila envelope in the bottom of the box and I could see photos and papers sticking out. Some of the pictures were black and white. I took it out.

The bones in my ankles and knees ached from sitting on the floor. I slid the things back into the envelope and set it on the floor, then packed up the rest of the box and returned it to its place on the shelf. Part of me wanted to stay in the storage room and rummage through every scrap. But what would be left after that? Once I'd seen everything, where else could I go to get something of her? What if I discovered something only to black out and never find it again, never even know what I had missed? I checked to make sure my father's door was still closed, then headed down to the store, taking the envelope of photos and papers with me.

The sideways morning light desaturated everything on the first floor. I stored the envelope from the attic in the bottom drawer under the cash register, filed behind my collection of Gil's cards. *Don't forget it's there. Don't forget.* How could I ever say that to myself again without wincing?

Opening wasn't for another two hours, so I climbed up the rolling ladder with rags and Orange Glo and dusted the shelves and the mouldings, relieved that the hot sting of my palms from my Queen Street wipeout had faded to a hardly there ache. I swept the floors, dusted the tables, made sure the scarves and bags were hung evenly, folded smoothly. I finished alphabetizing the incense. I felt like someone was chasing me and I could stay just ahead of them if the store was tidy enough.

At ten, I lugged the sandwich board outside and flipped the door sign to OPEN. No one came in, and although there was nothing left to clean, it was good to be alone, not speaking. I was starting to distrust what might come out of my mouth. But once the first group of customers arrived—teenage girls skipping school—the spell was broken. I joked with them, sold them organic lip gloss and a little zodiac compatibility chart on which to find their boyfriends' sun signs. Everything was suddenly fine.

The store was busy all morning and nearly everyone who came in bought something. An old British man even bought the didgeridoo my mother had ordered in a fit of optimism, later admitting we would probably never sell it. It was a good day, and I put on the radio and one of the customers sang along, *I want to know what love is*, in a breathy, beautiful voice. After she left, taking with her a package of lucky red envelopes and a Chinese zodiac chart for the Year of the Pig, I turned up the volume and was dancing myself around the whitewashed tables, one hand out like someone was holding me, when the bell over the door chimed and I turned around to see a man standing in a sheet of dusty sunlight.

"Well, darling, all you need now is someone to dance with," he said, and he smiled with his lips pressed together.

I dropped my hands to my sides, embarrassed.

"Can I help you find something?" I stepped forward.

He looked about my age, but wasn't dressed like most Queen Street twenty-somethings, wearing instead tweedy slacks with a rumpled white shirt. Underneath a brimmed wool cap he had dark hair, curling at the back of his neck and behind his ears. He was dressed too warmly for the summery day, but he didn't seem uncomfortable, even in the stuffy store. Instead, he was moving around appreciatively, the way you do in a hotel room. *Yes*, you say to yourself, *this will do nicely.*

"I've been meaning to come in here for a long time," he said finally, not bothering to turn his head and help his words carry to me. There was a slight slipping to his voice, an accent worn thin. Southern? "I was very sorry to read about Carol."

"Thank you," I said. I didn't want him to start in on how she had been released from her physical body and was a part of the universe now. Though he didn't look the type. He didn't look like he should be in the store at all, but he seemed somehow familiar, like a small-time actor or a long-forgotten waiter.

He finished his circle of the store and held a jade carving in his hand.

"You must be very strong," he said. He had a high voice for a man, almost girlish, and rough, dry-looking skin on his face. I wondered if I should recommend one of our organic lotions. Aloe maybe. Eucalyptus. I was examining him; he had a very deep groove from his nose to the top of his upper lip, which gave him a bit of a sneer. I realized I was staring and grabbed a bottle of rose oil off the table, unscrewing and re-screwing the lid purposefully.

"How much is this?" he asked, opening his hand. In it he held a little jade angel figure. Most of the figures we carried were animals, dozens of little tigers and horses and eagles made from healing stones, but there were a few other things—a few flowers, a globe, a creepy onyx skull, and the requisite parade of angels. They didn't sell well; most of our sales came from organic skin care, green cleaning products, natural fibre underpants and T-shirts. But I was attached to the carvings and had a little zircon cat I kept in my bedside table.

I knew how much the jade piece was, but I took it out of his hand and looked at the price tag on the bottom, because it irritated me when customers wouldn't turn things over for themselves. Through the lens of the glass base on which the angel stood, the finely mottled colour variation of the jade was magnified, beautiful.

"'Eight dollars,'" I read, and I pointed to the tag for his benefit. Privately I was surprised he'd picked an angel—they usually sold to women of a certain age: slightly breathless, watery-eyed. The angels made from white and pink stones sold the best. I didn't think I'd ever sold one to a man, in fact.

"You're very pretty," he said, and he was close enough that I could smell him a little, a smell like soap and cloves, with an undercurrent of something slightly stale.

I stepped away and got behind the counter, shutting the little hip-height cupboard door behind me.

"Jade is a good choice," I said brightly. "It banishes worry. It's good for stress." I worked alone enough to know the principles of keeping a strange man under control. Remove yourself, smile, chat, pretend nothing is happening.

"Don't worry, darling," he said, moving to the opposite side of the counter and sliding his wallet out of his front pocket. "I'm the last person you should ever worry about."

"That's nine twenty with the tax," I said. Under the counter was a bottle of bear spray I had bought at Mountain Equipment Co-op years ago. It was as good as mace.

He counted out exact change and put it on the counter rather than in my hand.

"Thank you very much," he said. "I'll come back soon."

I braced my hands on the counter after he left and let my head fall forward, stretching my neck. I returned to rotating all the bottles label-out on the shelves, lining them up. My mother had never bothered with it, but I couldn't stand for them to be mismatched. Even just since the morning's cleaning binge, everything was askew.

The bell over the door rang again and I looked up quickly. It was Wendy, pulling a silk scarf from around her neck. She put her purse behind the counter and turned up the radio.

"Madam Shopkeep," she said, doffing an invisible hat to me and hopping onto the stool behind the counter. She slouched spectacularly as always.

"You're going to look like a hunchback in a few years," I said.

"Yeah," she said without straightening up. "Most likely. So. I went out with whatshisname again."

"Don't tell me. You're going to be Mrs. Whatshisname?" I clutched my heart. "Are you here to register? We've got everything the modern bride needs."

"Ha ha, very funny. You know who I mean, though, right? The one with the turned-out toes, remember? The Pigeon Man."

"Oh yeah. Mister Pigeon. How is he these days?"

"You know. Okay. He showed up in a suit, an actual honest-to-god suit, with a vest no less. I felt like I was at his funeral all night. Regarding the men of Toronto: I despair. It's official."

Wendy leaned over and crossed her arms on her knees. Her sweater was rumpled from her posture and her hair was dark and lank in her eyes. She had that sort of skinny body that looked posh when she was dressed up and trying, but on days where she didn't care she looked more like the checkout girl in a small-town 7-Eleven.

"How are you feeling these days?" she said, and it was a completely different voice than the one she'd been using up to that point.

I was alarmed by a sign of weakness in Wendy. "I'm fine," I said. I thought about telling her about the cards. *No, not yet. Those are private.* I realized I'd paused too long, I had to add something. "I had another blackout yesterday. I think. Just a short one."

She looked down, chewed on her lip. "Are you okay now?"

"I guess so. I fell. But my hands don't hurt anymore. Just my knee."

"Maybe you need to take some time off," she said to the countertop. "Just a little time. You could hire someone."

Taking time. Time being taken. "Lying in bed watching soaps isn't going to change anything."

"I'm just trying to help."

"I know," I said, and Wendy looked pained. "You can change the station if you want," I said.

While Wendy fiddled with the stereo, I came out from behind the counter and checked on the tables. Sometimes they seemed to become messy on their own, even though I could swear I had watched each customer browsing. I squared stacks of tea and turned a split quartz up on its end to better display the toothy crystals inside. When I got to the stone animals I hesitated. There was a bright circle in the fine layer of dust. Just the size of the jade angel. I moved a sodalite owl to cover the spot.

"Can I buy these?" Wendy was right behind me, holding up a box of scented soaps. "They smell so damn good. Smell, smell them." She held the box to my nose and the scent of rosemary bloomed in the air. It was a green smell, spicy and homey.

Wendy withdrew the box and slipped her wallet out of her purse. "Staff discount, right?"

"Of course." My voice came out rough, like the top half of my breath had been scraped off. I cleared my throat and rang her through, looking at her across the counter. She was as close as he'd been, the man with the jade angel.

"Let me see those again," I said, reaching for the soap. Wendy handed them over and I pressed the box to my nose, breathing deeply. I could almost feel the flat rosemary needles in my mouth, bending against my teeth, the smell heady and warm. It was what jade might smell like, if it had a scent. It made me think of the nature scene on Gil's card. Pine needles, granite. The customer's rough skin. His high voice, thin, like the upstrokes of a hastily written note.

"So—can I have it back?" Wendy reached out, took the soap from me.

I stared at her for a moment. "Oh, the soap. Sorry, yeah of course."

"What frequency are you on today? Did one of your customers bake you some brownies or something?"

"No," I said. "I just got distracted. Forgot what we were talking about."

Wendy packed the soap away as I shut the till and keyed in the code to print out the daily totals. "Definitely quitting time," she said. "It's past six, you can close up."

I nodded, folding the long receipt into an envelope.

I stepped out onto the sidewalk and picked up the sandwich board. It was still bright out, like the middle of the day. Above my Everything from Auras to Zodiac! on the board, someone had sketched a message with a clean finger in the dusty surface: *The truth will set you free.*

I pulled the board inside and locked the door. Ten to one it was some religious nut. We dealt with it every once in a while, graffiti like *Witches will burn!* or *No God above me*, because of the tarot cards and the few other New Age–y hangovers from the old store. Mostly, though, the neighbourhood was easy-going, happy as long as the drunks in the park kept to themselves. The truth will set you free? Pretty tame stuff, really.

I rubbed the message out with the side of my fist and slid the board away.

Four

The girl at the desk had me sign a sheet that asked whether or not I wanted to have "reassuring physical contact such as hugs and handshakes." I did. When I finished with the forms I handed them back, getting my hand tangled in the elastic that bound the pen to the clipboard.

"Sorry," I said as I extricated myself.

She smiled and took the forms, but didn't say anything. I returned to my seat and waited. I was in CAMH, the Centre for Addiction and Mental Health, a low-slung hospital building a couple of blocks west of the store, waiting for my first appointment with a psychiatrist.

After the second blackout, I'd gone to Dr. Henderson and asked him to help me find a therapist. I hoped he wasn't insulted to hear that his prescription of vitamins and rest after the first blackout hadn't quite cut it. He just nodded, mumbled something about "in your situation . . ." and gave me a referral for a Dr. Malik at CAMH. He'd tried to get my mother to see a psychiatrist—I knew this in the amorphous, gossipy way of family knowledge where things are known without being explicitly said—but she had slipped sideways through these recommendations, resisting in her irresistible way. During the good times we hadn't wanted to press it, to remind her of the darkness. And in the bad times it seemed we were past that already, well past.

When I told my father, he put his hand on my shoulder and said, "I think that's a wise choice." Then headed back up to his office on the third floor.

When the receptionist called my name, I gathered up my purse and notebook before I trotted over to the desk.

"Dr. Malik is ready for you," she said. "Please follow me."

We went down a little hall into the hospital proper, over-lit and painfully clean.

"Right in here, dear," said the receptionist. She walked into the room in front of me, handed the forms to the doctor, and left. He flipped through them for a moment and put them inside a green file folder on his desk.

"Hello, Maggie. Would you like to sit down?"

"Hi. Okay, thanks." I felt shy, gangly, ridiculous. I thought, *It's silly that Andrew will be called "Doctor."*

"Is this your first appointment with a therapist, Maggie?"

"Sort of. The police gave me a phone number I could call, a counselling thing. I called once. But I hung up."

"It's nice to be able to see the person you're talking to," he said. When I didn't reply, he said, "Losing a parent is an incredibly difficult experience, and when the passing is self-inflicted it compounds and complicates our feelings." The word *suicide* reverberated unspoken.

I nodded. I wanted to appear intelligent, but I couldn't think of anything to say. Dr. Malik looked athletic, big but fit. His brown skin was very even in tone, like someone on television. There was a photo on his desk of a child waving from a small sailboat, wearing a bright orange life jacket. When I still hadn't spoken after a minute or so, Dr. Malik went on.

"We can experience a lot of conflicting emotions. Grief, and also guilt. There can be a sense of relief sometimes, to know that someone who was troubled is now at peace, which in turn can make us feel guilty, since we don't expect to feel relief in a sad situation. We can feel adrift if much of our energy has been directed to caring for our loved one. We can feel lost. Does any of that sound familiar?"

When he spoke, the crease between his eyebrows deepened. I focused on the crease. *Occupational hazard. You have to look a little sad all the time. You can't go grinning at your patients, can you.*

"Yeah," I said. "That's very— That's a lot to process."

"Why don't you tell me a little bit about your mother."

"She was a lot younger than my dad." Why was that the first thing I said? How could I say that like it was the most important thing about her? I said, "She knew a lot of things, how to help people." I suddenly felt I didn't know enough about her, not nearly enough.

He was making notes and I wanted to see what he was writing.

"Why don't you tell me a little about the memory loss episodes you've had? That must have been scary."

I didn't like that he said *scary*. What you would say to a child. *Terrifying. Frightening. Unsettling.* Did he not think I could differentiate?

"I just . . . go away. I'm there, but I'm not there. I mean, I do things, I just don't remember. And then when I come back into myself, it's like a snap. There's no space in between for me, just this moment and then—bang—this next moment, but it's later for everyone else. It goes a little dark at the edges, but it's all so fast."

"The edges." He wrote something down. "I'm going to tell you a possibility from my point of view, Maggie. You don't have to say anything today. Is that okay?"

"Yes."

"It's possible that your blackouts are a manifestation of the loss you feel about your mother. The human brain is an incredible network, and one we still don't fully understand. The way we react to extreme stress, well, our understanding of these things is not perfect. There is something called fugue state, but it is extremely rare. What you are experiencing may be unique."

You're making it up. You're doing it on purpose. You're a liar. I could feel the heat of my face and knew I was flushed; I tried to breathe it out.

"Dr. Malik. Don't you think if I was going to forget something, in order to make myself feel better, I would forget my mother's bad times? Or how it felt when I found out that she was— Why would I forget *a picnic*? Or whatever it is I was doing when I got those shoes."

"I'm not accusing you of anything, Maggie. And I don't have the answers to those questions. That's what we're here to try and work through. But I don't believe in withholding information from my patients or in thinking one thing and saying another.

You're an intelligent girl, and I wanted to share one possibility with you." After a moment he said, "We can talk about something else for a little while if you like. What do you think?"

I nodded. He asked about my job, about the store, about Andrew and Wendy.

"They're good, they aren't part of the problem."

"I think it's great to have a support network like you have. Why don't you tell me about Andrew?"

"He's a nice guy."

"How did you two meet?"

"At a book launch."

"You don't hear that one all the time," he said. "My parents met on a blind date."

I nodded, squeezing the well-padded arms of my chair. Dr. Malik was painfully likeable. I wanted to draw my feet up and sit cross-legged. I thought of Andrew folded up at his desk at home, adding little marks and ticks to young girls' poems about the loss of their virginity. I frowned and Dr. Malik said, "Are you still with me, Maggie? Here, why don't you have some water." He had a pitcher and paper cups on his desk. *Low overhead—ply the crazies with tap water*. I stood up to receive the cup and had a low-blood-sugar moment, my vision going black and spotty. I took the water and sat down, held my head in my hands. My notebook was open on my lap and my vision swam as I looked at my own handwriting, the tidy letters.

The valley, the river. The Don is a misfit stream: a river that is too small to have eroded the valley in which it runs. It's been there for a million years. Andrew taught me this, years ago on a bike ride east along Queen Street.

Her shoulder bag lay neatly on the grass, a book beside it. She must have wanted something to read on the way. Not a book from the store, but from the library, a murder mystery. The card in the back pocket with her name on it, a date in the future. I returned it later to the City Hall library, walking through those big wooden doors with their goalie-stick handles, pretending to be the same as anyone else in the city.

She must have taken the streetcar and then walked down the stairs from the bridge to the river path. There are two landings, two places to pause. And there's an arch over the bridge, right in front of the staircase, as if it's marking the spot. I had never really noticed the arch, it was just part of the city, just more metal, but I noticed it when I went to meet my father there that day. The arch is high, way up above the passing cars, with a clock in the middle and words—it took a second to read them. At first I thought it said river step in, river stand in, *like an invitation. When I saw it in full though, I read,* THIS RIVER I STEP IN IS NOT THE RIVER I STAND IN, *and it sounded to me like one of my mother's sayings, something that made perfect sense for a moment and then slipped away from me. Like the last thing she said, left stretched above the street for me. And I'm failing to understand. I stood and looked at it for a full minute until someone brushed past me on the sidewalk. Then I headed down the stairs, the river spreading out to the left, dirty and green brown. She hated to get dirty. She wore rubber gloves to garden, to make sure none of the soil would get under her fingernails.*

I left the store unlocked when my father called and told me to come. I had never left the store unlocked before. When I got back from the river and realized what I'd done, I was stunned. But nothing was stolen, nothing was moved. Still, I felt like someone had been inside, touched everything, moved something, one hidden thing that I would never notice or be able to fix. Like a before-and-after game from a kids' colouring book. Something that would just always be off. How could I have forgotten to lock the store?

At the river, I stood on the path with my father and a police officer, a little bit back from the edge of the river, where there was a concrete ledge and a drop of four or five feet to the water below.

There were five of them, although maybe some of them weren't exactly police; they were the police-like people who are sent to places where people have died in unusual ways. Not that they were outlining things in chalk, it wasn't like television. What would they have outlined? One of them had on a grey sweatshirt, like a runner. I was on the path with my father and his face was a little crumpled. The Don was higher than normal but I could see things: I saw a grey sock, empty cigarette packages, a child's hat. There were cyclists going by on the path, rollerbladers, people looking curiously at us and then sharply away. Wendy was with me, she had come with me from the store. So it was Saturday. It was a Saturday, yes.

"What did you feel right then, Maggie?"

The light was different. I looked at the clock—forty minutes had gone by since I drank water from the paper cup, which was overturned and empty, near my foot on the carpet. Had I read my notebook aloud to Dr. Malik? The private things I'd written after it all, private things about her? I couldn't believe it. I looked at Dr. Malik, trying to focus—what had he just said?

"What did I feel?"

"When you were at the river. Did they know she had passed at that point?"

"Yes. I never saw her in the river. They had already—got her, when my father got there. That's why they called him." My voice was breaking although I felt calm. The glands in my neck felt swollen, and an ache was radiating from my cheeks to my chest.

"So you knew what had happened when you got there."

"My father told me."

"What happened right after he told you? What were you thinking? Just tell me anything that comes to you. About what you felt."

"The book."

"You felt like the book?"

"No, I felt the book. My mother's book. I picked it up and felt it. The cover wasn't real cloth—it was fake. Paper, made to look like cloth. There must have been a jacket—but it was gone."

"And then what?"

I shrugged.

"Was it something you'd rather forget about? Does it hurt to talk about it?"

I shook my head no, and then nodded it yes. Dr. Malik picked up my hand and squeezed it, his hands dry and smooth, with ragged nails. I wondered what he would have done instead if I had checked the box for *no physical contact*.

"Maggie," he said. "We don't have to hurry; you can take your time. Do you want to take a break?"

"Yes."

I walked to the south end of the hospital grounds—*the campus*, they'd called it at the hospital, like I was a student again. How embarrassing to fail. What was I supposed to be studying? Myself? My mother?

It wasn't far to the south end, but it was warm even for June and I was sweating inside the light summer jacket I'd bought when Wendy and I went shopping at the outlet stores north of the city. That was years ago.

Dr. Malik had said, "You felt like the book." The thing was, I did, I did feel like a book when I was standing on the path with my father, and afterwards, back in the store, after we opened up again. Not the inside of the book, not the narrative, but the outside, the colours of them. Green, dark orange, brown cracked leather. The soft unravelling of cloth covers. And then there, and there, the blank spaces on the shelf where books ought to be, where someone had forgotten to return them. Missing time. Blackouts. Episodes. Whatever I ought to call it. Trouble, like my mother had. Something had slithered off her onto me.

When I got to the southern fence, I stopped and sat in the grass, which was cool but dry. It wasn't a tall, chain-link fence meant to keep us nut-jobs in, but a little half-fence, iron with industrial black paint, like the edge of a city park. Stone flowerbeds were sprinkled with plastic bottles, streetcar transfers, cigarette butts.

I wondered when the next one would come. Maybe I would be somewhere different afterwards. Maybe I would start walking back to the hospital but a step that started on the little footpath would end in Mexico or Las Vegas or Rome. I didn't want to move. I wondered how I would ever move again. *Get up, darling.* I stood and looked at the building and started walking. As long as I didn't take my eyes off it, I would make it back. That was the deal.

Once inside, I took off my jacket and went back to Dr. Malik's office. His door was closed and a man was standing outside, half turned, like someone waiting but trying to seem casual. He was tall and dark-haired, with a neatly trimmed beard. I stood back for a minute, where he couldn't see me, and flipped to an entry in my notebook dated earlier than the one I'd looked at with Dr. Malik.

The first couple of days after going to the river to meet my father, I slept ten and twelve hours a day, as if I had the flu. I tried not to think about anything and read old books from a box half filled with stuffed animals in the storage room. My mother appeared again and again like a kick in the chest and I forced her down, for now, just for now. The store was closed.

Sometimes my father was gone to the funeral home, but most often he was there, and he would open the door to my room every hour or so without knocking. He made bland food like peanut butter and jam sandwiches or boiled perogies and offered it to me from the doorway. I wanted to be up and helping him, but it was like the gravity in the apartment was stronger, pulling me downward, and the longer I stayed in my room the more ashamed I felt for leaving him alone. Andrew came each night, usually just to sit silently in the armchair at the end of my bed, sometimes reading to me, an indulgence that made me feel childish, cocooned. Sometimes he was in the kitchen, talking to my father, but I didn't get up to listen. I wasn't involved in planning the funeral at all, but at the last minute my father asked me to read some scripture, obviously embarrassed by the request.

"They thought it would be appropriate," he said. I didn't know who they meant. I took a bible from the store's Standard Religions section, noting it carefully in the ledger.

The funeral happened in a church I had walked by but never been in; the minister was a colleague of my father's who worked in the Religious Studies department. A lot of the people there were customers — I knew faces, not names. My father had sent the obituary to the local free paper as well as the Globe and Mail. They shook my hand very hard, especially the older people, as if I would find it bracing. The floor of the foyer was a mottled grey marble that hurt my feet.

"Who was that one?" Wendy asked after an old woman had departed from the corner where we stood. Wendy had posted herself beside me all day.

"No idea. She is always buying herbal teas for her daughter. She's nice. She's a Taurus. That's all I remember."

"She smelled like a car air freshener." Then, after a moment, she said, "I'm sorry. We don't need to talk. We can just stand."

Wendy being polite made me feel horribly lonely. I wanted her to be her usual self. She hadn't even gone out for a cigarette.

I looked around. Only two or three people remained, milling around and admiring the church. Andrew approached Wendy and me and stood without speaking. I wanted him to take me home,

I wanted to take a taxi, I didn't want to walk. He was like a wooden chair and I wanted that.

But it was Wendy who said, "I'll take Maggie home," looking up at him. He was nearly a foot taller than her. Together, they steered me towards the door and I shambled down the wide shallow steps.

Looking over my shoulder, I saw my father standing alone by the main doors to the sanctuary. A man approached him and said something, holding out his hand. My father didn't shake it and, after a moment, the man put his hand in his pocket. The man said something else and my father shook his head. I couldn't hear his response, but he looked irritated, animated, more like his usual self. The minister approached and put his hand on my father's shoulder. He spoke and my father nodded, his body limp again, his expression sagging into the same one I'd seen all week. He put his face in his hands. I'd never seen him do that. The man I didn't know backed up and then turned, leaving my father with the minister. The man was a little younger than my father, tall and dark-haired with a neatly trimmed beard.

Now he was wearing a doctor's coat over a crisp dark shirt. Closing my notebook, I stepped forward and he saw me and flinched, clearly surprised, but his expression immediately smoothed into a smile.

"Hello," he said. "You must be Dr. Malik's patient."

"You know my father," I said. I got the impression he knew exactly who I was and I didn't like him pretending not to. "I saw you at my mother's funeral."

"Oh yes, of course. I am so sorry for your loss." He ran one knuckle along his jaw like he was touching someone else's face, not his own. "Carol was a very special woman," he said.

"Thank you," I said. Why did it seem as though everyone had known my mother, all these people I'd never met or heard of? What else had I missed? I was annoyed and wanted to get back to Dr. Malik. If I stayed in the hallway, I thought I might take this tidy man by the shoulders and shake him until he told me every word she'd ever spoken to him, every little thing she'd done. It was a want so bad it shocked me.

Trying to compose myself, I looked meaningfully at Dr. Malik's door, which the man was blocking. For a moment neither of us moved, but then he stepped aside.

When I walked in, Dr. Malik said, "Sometimes I find the fresh air helps me feel more collected. Did it help?"

"I think so." I sat down.

He did his very small sad smile with the crease between the eyebrows.

"I'm sorry," he said, and a little chime sounded. "Time's just up now. Will I see you again on Thursday?"

"Sure," I said. I wanted to smooth his eyebrows apart, to send him home to the little boy in the sailboat. I was wasting his time, going off on blackouts right in the middle of his therapy sessions like a complete idiot, fantasizing about assaulting hospital staff in the hallways. "Thanks, Dr. Malik."

I gave him a big smile and backed out of the office. He stood up and followed me out.

The bearded man was still outside, and Dr. Malik looked surprised and said, "Hello, Aaron."

"Hello, Rajeev." They looked at each other and at me. Dr. Malik said, "This is Maggie. Maggie, this is Dr. Rosenberg."

The bearded man held out his hand, as he had to my father. I shook it. "It's nice to meet you," he said. Looking at Dr. Malik he said, "Now, I'm not trying to poach your patients, Rajeev, but I feel I should mention Wooster House to you, Maggie. It's a facility that I run out in Port Credit. It's a place for people in your situation—we call it a grief management facility. It's a very supportive place. You might find some people you can relate to there."

Dr. Malik smiled but didn't look pleased. His sad crease was back. He said, "We have several options to explore before we think about residency. Maggie is working very hard."

"Of course," said Dr. Rosenberg. "I just want Maggie to be aware of all her options."

Dr. Malik put his hand on my arm and said, "I can walk you out."

I was glad of the light pressure of his touch. I didn't say any-thing to Dr. Rosenberg, but I looked over my shoulder at him briefly as Dr. Malik and I walked back towards the waiting room. He was standing still outside Dr. Malik's office, watching me go.

Wendy was in the foyer when I went back out.

"Andrew called me," she said, standing up. "He asked me to come by, thought you might want some company. I nearly fell asleep waiting for you, I'm wiped out." She reached out and hugged me, going up on her toes. "Man, sometimes I wish I worked in the store too. Get up at nine every day."

"You know me—less than eight hours of sleep and I'm a crazy person," I said, and there was a silence while Wendy looked surreptitiously around the waiting room. *Crazy.*

"Sorry," she said. "I have to check with my boss on something, that reminds me." She had a cell phone her job had given her and she spoke into it in a low voice. At one point she said, "Well, is there any evidence?"

The publicity firm where she worked sometimes helped politicians and movie stars ride out their scandals and win back the adoration of the public with careful copywriting. I didn't bother asking, since she was never allowed to talk about any of it.

When she hung up, she looked at me and said, smiling, "Sometimes I think this job is turning my soul black." The plastic of her phone, still in her hand, bore the greasy imprint of her cheek.

"Well, the wages of sin are reduced student debt," I said.

We walked out the glass doors onto Queen Street, and turned towards home.

Five

I did return to Dr. Malik later that week, and I tried my best to listen to what he had to say. I liked him. I liked the photo of his little boy. Most of the time he didn't say much, unless I'd been silent for a long time and then he would ask me a question. He asked me about my mother and father, he asked me to tell him about our vacations, our family dinners, our fights and holidays. He wanted to know all about the store. After a while I felt like he was being a bit nosy. I wasn't used to talking about my mother, not about the private things. I wanted to curl around her bad spots the way people on television curl in around a bullet wound, a stabbing. But also I was realizing, as I had in my first session, that I didn't know enough about my mother, that I couldn't answer all the questions correctly. I had thought I knew everything, I had spent my whole life watching her. But when I tried to talk about her earlier life, about her history, I found myself coming up blank. I couldn't believe I had never asked these things. Why had my parents gotten married? I had counted the months, and though it was close, I didn't think it was because of me. Why had my mother moved to Canada from Georgia? How had she ended up at the store? Where did she learn everything she knew about the cards, the stones? What the hell had I spent the past ten years—longer—talking to her about? These thoughts buffeted me during my therapy sessions and I would lapse into silence.

When this happened Dr. Malik asked other, less personal things, like whether Wendy was close to my family, whether my parents liked Andrew, whether we ever talked about getting married or moving in together. I would sit with my notebook in my lap, sometimes doodling geometric shapes or writing down scraps of this and that, and try to answer him.

The truth was, I always suspected that my mother didn't like Andrew. She hardly said anything at all about him, though she once observed that his aura was very cool.

"It's not necessarily a bad thing," she said. "Like a grape. Like a green grape."

Andrew had smiled at her, uncertain. We were eating dinner; it was the first time I'd brought him home. In the silence that followed my mother's comment, my father asked how we had met. Andrew said he had asked me out after we met at a book launch that Wendy dragged me to.

"Good man," said my father. "'Be bold, be bold, and everywhere, be bold.'"

Andrew smiled. "The Faerie Queene," he said. "I had some good times with Spenser at McGill." My father's area was the Renaissance, and the comment won Andrew instant approval.

"I don't mean cool as a bad thing. Auras are complicated," said my mother, as if the conversation hadn't moved along.

"Let's not get into all that nonsense at dinner," said my father.

"It's nothing." My mother was making rings on the table with her cup. "It's not nonsense," she added quietly.

"It's nonsense."

"It's only nonsense if you take it seriously," she said.

"What is my aura like?" I asked.

My father speared a green bean. "Don't answer that, Carol," he said.

"Like a piece of paper," she said. "Thick, soft paper."

I looked down at my food. "You think I'm boring?"

Andrew said, "This is delicious. Especially the potatoes."

My father sighed loudly. "Do you know what the saddest part is?"

"What?"

He looked at her. "You really could have had a wonderful mind if you'd applied yourself. You were as smart as a whip when I met you."

My mother gathered her hair into a dark rope and put it neatly over one shoulder. "I was a very young girl when you met me," she said.

"Don't go blaming me."

"I'm not blaming you for anything. I am very happy with my life."

"Well." My father pushed his plate away. "This big bad wolf has work to do." He gathered a file of papers from the sideboard and went up the narrow staircase that led to his office and my mother's storage room.

"Don't pay any attention," she said, and just then, the footsteps on the stairs stopped.

I glanced at Andrew, who looked frozen. Then he called out, "Nice to see you, Dr. Pierce."

I took his hand, excused us both, and headed down to the store, leaving my mother alone at the table.

"I want to show you something," I said, leading him to the table with the stone animals. It was a bit messy, so I turned them all—jade, hematite, onyx—in the same direction. Then, feeling foolish, I turned a cat to face the eagle beside him.

"Watch out," I said, wiggling the cat figure. "Watch out."

When I was younger I used to assign personalities to all the different stones. Red jasper for fighters: warriors and knights. Black and grey onyx for priests and thinkers. Sunstone for ladies, unakite for jesters, sodalite for royalty. Jade for wanderers, tiger's eye for lovers. On and on.

I picked up the cat and clinked it gently against the eagle. "Run for it," I said. The sound was like glass tapping glass. To Andrew, I said, "I used to play with these all the time."

He looked at me. We'd only been on a half-dozen dates, we hadn't slept together. He'd kissed me a few times, tentatively, his lips tight but skillful. He was much taller than me, and sometimes I found it harder to read his expression than other people's, as if the extra few inches of distance diluted their meaning.

Then he leaned over and picked up a moss agate horse. He galloped it across the table. "I'll save you, milady," he said, and his serious face broke into a wide grin.

I stepped into him, raising my arms and sinking my fingers into his pale hair. The voice that was always in my head, observing, said, Be careful, he's already seen her go a bit off. Don't let your guard down too much. When we broke apart, I pressed my forehead against his chest, and took the little stone horse in my hand. Just a little, I told the voice. I'll be careful.

I didn't tell Dr. Malik any of this. I didn't want him to think I was crazy.

After my third session with Dr. Malik, I bumped into Dr. Rosenberg in the hallway again.

"Maggie, nice to see you again," he said. "How are you?"

"Good," I said. "I mean, well."

"Have you given my suggestion any thought?"

"The residency place? I can't go anywhere. I have to run the store, it's been busy lately."

"Wooster House," he said. And then, "Of course. I remember how much Carol loved that store."

I got the impression he knew how badly I wanted to ask him about her, but instead of dangling anything else he said, "I see you've got a journal with you. I seem to recall you had one last time I saw you as well. Is Rajeev—is Dr. Malik—having you journal as part of your treatment? It's an excellent idea."

I frowned. "No, not exactly."

"Ah, well, please don't let me stick my oar in—but it might be a valuable exercise. I encourage bereaved patients to journal, especially in situations of unexpected death."

"Funny how that's a verb now," I said, and he looked startled. "You know. *Journal. To journal.*"

"Yes," he said without smiling. "Well, just a thought." He backed up, picked an invisible piece of lint from his collar. "Of course, I'm not your doctor. I don't want to interfere with Dr. Malik's line."

"No," I said, as Rosenberg dipped his smiling head at me in dismissal. "I'm sure you wouldn't."

He left me alone in the hallway. Two women emerged from an office nearby, and I turned and went out to my bike, locked up on the north side of Queen Street. It was after seven o'clock in the evening but the summer light was still bright. I headed west to the grocery store, stopping once to check the air in my tires. Moving felt harder than I expected, slower, like I was going uphill even when I wasn't.

I'd hardly had a meal since the funeral that didn't originate in a box or tin, other than what Andrew cooked. My default mode for eating was the easy convenience food that I'd gravitated to when cooking for my parents during my mother's low times, the sort of things Wendy's mother served when I went over for dinner in junior high: Hamburger Helper and Lipton soup, soda crackers with little winking crystals of salt on them. All-American convenience food was safe, hyper-normal, set against my mother's more exotic dishes, her cuisine a weird blend of Southern traditional and ultra-modern harmony with the earth: syrup peaches after bulgur and steamed bok choy.

I decided to try cooking something myself tonight. Even using one of her recipes. That would be okay. I couldn't survive on sodium and aspartame forever. I both wanted to picture her cooking and couldn't bear to. She had made all of my birthday cakes, my father's too. I'd light the candles, and she'd say, "Don't forget to drown it," and I would turn on the tap and soak the smoking match, then throw it in the trash. When I was younger, she explained how carelessly disposed matches could burn down a house, conjuring images of ominous wisps of black smoke, raging fires leaping from Georgia garbage pails, men in white pants and undershirts passing buckets of water along a line. She must have been speaking from her youth in the South, where things like fires and floods and runaway horses could ruin lives. Things that couldn't happen in Toronto.

I got to the grocery store before eight and locked my bike to a post nearby. Inside, I loaded my basket with quinoa, tangerines and apple cider vinegar. I went to the fish counter and asked for six scallops, which I'd never prepared myself. They looked like yellowed marshmallows, the misshapen homemade kind. I had everything else I needed at home, so I paid the clerk, loaded up my bike and set off east along Queen towards home. I hadn't been on my bike much in the spring, and my legs were still winter-weak. The burn up the back of my thighs felt good; my grocery bag was jaunty in my wicker basket. At Ossington, right outside CAMH, the light changed to green and I pressed down on the pedals, pushing myself up off the seat, rushing forward. The dimness of the sky above the sinking sun rushed with me, closing in.

I couldn't move or breathe. Light was coming at me strangely, at bizarre angles. I was lying on my back on the road and several people were crouching over me.

"Oh my god, oh my god," said a freckled woman. "Did you not see me? The light was yellow, it wasn't red yet, I swear. Oh god I'm sorry. Are you all right? Are you all right?"

Without sitting up, I recognized where I was from years and years of walking the same few blocks. I was lying at the intersection of Queen and a little street called Niagara, just east of the store. East of the store—I had overshot it, gone straight past.

"I can't move."

"Oh my god," the woman wailed.

An older Asian man was on his knees beside me. He picked up my hand. "Can you feel that?" he said.

I could. I closed my hand around his. "Yes."

"I'll help you stand up if you want to try." He got one arm under my shoulders, reached the other across my front. I leaned forward, found I could move. He got me on my feet and I unbuckled my helmet.

"I think I just got the wind knocked out of me."

"You rode right out in front of me. I was turning left and I swear—I swear—the light was yellow, not red."

"I called nine-one-one," said the man, who still had one arm around me. As if on cue, the wail of an ambulance opened up, drowning out the woman's repeated explanation.

"I'm sorry, I think the sun got in my eyes," I said to her, to get her to stop.

She handed me a piece of paper. "My information," she said.

"My bike. Where's my bike?"

The man took his arm away, held his hand up near me for a moment in case I was going to fall, and then pointed. "It's right there. It's pretty mangled. It's a good thing you were wearing a helmet. You went over your handlebars, landed right on your back. That must have been some sun, you went right into her hood." He was looking at me strangely.

I turned away, looked where he pointed.

My beloved ten-speed had been dragged off to the side, in front of the appliance store. It looked awful, the front wheel compressed and twisted. The bag of quinoa was on the ground nearby, unbroken. The rest of my groceries were nowhere to be seen.

Now that I could move again, I hurt all over. My left hand was crumpled up on itself in a sickening way. The back of my head throbbed, like someone had punched me where my spine met my skull. Then the paramedics were there, checking me over and putting me in an ambulance, and the man came with me.

He had a cell phone and he said to the paramedic in the back with us, "Is it okay if I call someone for her?"

The paramedic was checking me over, smoothly, not panicked, her hands quick and focused though her face looked tired. She had tight black braids pulled into a ponytail and she wore gloves.

"Sure, thanks," she said, without pausing.

"Do you want me to call your parents? Or are you a student? Is there someone in town?"

My head throbbed more intensely, as if someone were slowly submerging me in hot liquid. The pain crept upward until even my jaw and forehead ached. I opened my mouth to say something to these two strangers, but then my vision blurred. The next thing I knew I was in a hospital bed with the curtains drawn. My father was there with his hand on my shoulder.

"I hate to wake you," he said. "But they said we can go home. I'm going to go fill your prescription downstairs—they've given you some Tylenol 3s—and you don't have to come back to get your hand checked again until next week." His face was a storm cloud of unasked questions.

Ask me! I wanted to shout.

Instead I said, "Thank you for coming," and reached out for his dry and papery hug. I could feel the pulse in his neck, pressed against mine, and it seemed much too fast. How much more could we all look out for each other—him worried about me and me about him, and anyway it was too late because we'd both already screwed up being worried: we had worried wrong or not enough about her, hadn't we? And so I pushed the thought of his too-fast pulse away and watched him walk out, heading for the pharmacy.

A moment later someone else walked in, much younger with dark hair and a rumpled white shirt. His hand was closed around something.

"Looks like you might be the one who needs this," he said, and opened his hand. It was the jade angel, the man from the store. He had a bit of a beard now, which made him seem older and slightly foreign. He looked worn out, his mouth with its deep dent at the top was purplish. "You sprained two fingers on your left hand," he said. "And you're banged up but otherwise fine. That second time, that was just regular passing out. So just one blackout to worry about today." He stopped smiling. "You're going to be okay. You're lucky, darling." Again I heard the Southern inflection swimming up in his voice.

"What are you talking about? What are you doing here?"

"Bad choice of words, maybe. *Lucky.* I would suggest you give up cycling for a while, though."

I glared at him. "Who are you?" I closed my eyes and my headache returned. I was still groggy; I wondered if they had put me on something. There was an IV taped into one of my hands. The other was wrapped in an elastic bandage.

"I went by the store. You weren't there. I—telephoned around."

"Telephoned who? Why are you here? What do you want?"

After a moment of silent contemplation, he said, "I want to talk with you."

"What? How did you know about the blackouts?"

"I'm an old family friend."

"Of whose family? Mine? I've never seen you before. I mean I've seen you, but—I don't know you."

"I'm writing something," he said. "Your mother—well, you and your mother are important to my work. I'm writing something of a family history. I've been through her hometown, in Georgia. I need some more information."

"Get out of here," I said. "Don't come into my store again or I will call the goddamn police." I pressed the button for the nurse.

He rubbed his beard. It was likely he had hair on his chest, a dark furry patch of it. *Why think about that? That's an insane thing to think right now.*

"I need your help," he said. "You tell me everything you can, and I'll write. I've already started."

"Look, I don't mean to be rude, but you don't know me, or my family, and I don't want to talk to you."

"I need your help," he said again. "And you need mine. I can help with the blackouts."

"How? I mean—stop. Go away, please." I wanted to scream for the nurse to hurry but I was afraid. What if he choked me?

What if he had a knife? He didn't seem dangerous, or even crazy, except for what he was saying. Except for that small thing. There was instead something appealing about him, something almost attractive. But then, what did I know about sanity, given my current situation?

"This wasn't the right time," he said. "I'm sorry." He put the jade angel in his pocket and walked out.

A moment later my father returned, carrying a paper bag. I was sweating onto my pillow, my hair wet behind my neck. *A dream. A hallucination. Stress.*

"Are you ready?" he said.

He waited while I changed back into my street clothes; the knees of my pants were ripped out, unsalvageable, destined for cleaning rags for the store.

When I came out of the little washroom, he looked at me and I looked at him and I wanted someone else to be there with us, even a nurse or a doctor or another patient in the empty second bed, just someone so we weren't so utterly alone together, because it was too much to be all there was for him.

I said, "I'm ready," and we went out into the hallway together. The nurse, heading towards my room, looked at me for a moment and then turned back.

In the taxi on the way home, he folded his hands in his lap and said, "I'm worried, and I don't know how worried to be. I don't know what's going on. I don't know how to help."

I wiped my hands on my torn pants and didn't say anything.

"I know you must miss your mother very much," he said, more quietly. "I know how close you were. And I know—I know that I am not a perfect substitute by any means. But I want you to know you can talk to me. About things. Your—troubles."

I knew I ought to be grateful. I wasn't so self-centred that I didn't see how carefully rehearsed, how painfully memorized my father's speech was. How he must have run through it in his head in the pharmacy, in line to get my pills. But it gave me a queasy feeling, like seeing the skin gape when you slice into your thumb by accident.

"I don't know what's going on," I said.

He reached over and squeezed my upper arm, and I looked at him. The choppy moving light from the street fell on his hair, grey now for some years. It used to be like mine, a fox fur red-brown. For the first time I could remember, I realized he was a handsome man, that he had been and still was. You don't think about your father like that normally; it was a strange thing to think, but true. He was angular, with thin lips and a big head, the sort of man who wouldn't look unnatural on a ship if he were only a little taller. And as he took his hand off my arm I was ashamed to realize I had hardly ever looked at him before.

"We'll figure it out," he said. "I'll get going with some phone calls. What you need is the right doctor. Obviously Dr. Henderson and Dr. Malik missed something."

But he was looking at me like he'd looked at her, a mixture of exasperation and terror. I wanted to tell him I was all right, that he didn't need to watch me, or hide the knives and scissors. But maybe he did. I didn't know what happened during the blackouts. Why would they happen at all if it wasn't to make way for something awful? And at the same time I was indignant. Hadn't I been the one who'd stuck to her, all day sometimes, to monitor and soothe? Hadn't I been more than responsible? For him to treat me like that, like her, after I'd been so good, done his job, let him cloister himself away in his shabby university office, let him ignore it, duck through the store as if visiting temporarily, wasn't fair.

I said, "Dad, do you know who Dr. Rosenberg is?"

"Rosenberg? He's a psychiatrist. An American, up from Vermont or Connecticut or someplace in the sixties. How do you know him?"

"He works at CAMH, I think. I met him after one of my appointments with Dr. Malik. He seemed, I don't know. Not like a psychiatrist."

"He has some non-traditional practices, as I understand it."

"He was at the funeral. I saw him."

"He knew your mother. And me, I suppose. Not well—he was one of the fellows who hung around the store too, for a while. A draft dodger, I think. There were lots of people passing through back then." Then, as if he'd been goosed by an invisible lawyer, he added, "He's quite well-known in his circles, though, I understand. And he was at Cambridge, I think, later, in the seventies."

"He runs a place in the suburbs. It's a grief management facility." I made quotes with my fingers.

"He mentioned it. At the funeral." He was looking somewhere past me, out the window, but then he swung his focus back. He said, "If there's anything I can do, Maggie. Please do ask me."

I nodded, trying to give the action a healthy vitality. *I'm okay! Nothing to worry about here!*

When we got home I went into my room. On my desk with the mail there was a new card. I pulled it out and saw that it had a cartoon fish on the front. Inside, he'd written, *I love you even though you're trying to gill me.* And below: *Get it? Love, Gil.* I still hadn't told anyone about the cards, not even Andrew. After the taxi ride, Gil's card was like a pop song on the radio, like a kiss. I held the card like it could warm my hands.

Two weeks later, I took Gil's fish card with me in my purse to the hospital to get an MRI. I thought of it as a good-luck charm, the cartooniness of it, the lightness, a contrast to everything that had been happening.

After a referral from Dr. Henderson, my father had pulled strings, impressive strings it was implied, to get me in so quickly. In for what? I hardly knew what an MRI was. And what strings did he have? This was what was needed, he said, in order to move forward.

I spent a long time waiting at Mount Sinai before they called me in. The room was very bare, removed from the main part of the hospital. A woman with an astonishingly round face took me over from the man who had escorted me from the waiting area. Once inside, she shook my hand and asked me to undress behind a curtain in the corner. The curtain wasn't fabric, but plastic, like a shower curtain, and it smelt of cheap tennis shoes. There were no windows in the room. I put on the hospital gown and came out.

Outside, my new bike was locked up. I wanted nothing more than to run out to it and pedal home as fast as possible. I was still riding, though my father had expressed his disapproval about it. The new bike was a fat coaster, more work and more stable. Andrew and I had picked it out as soon as my wrist bandage came off, and he bought me a new bell as a present. Unlike my father, Andrew was taking an approach of absolute normalcy, for which I was grateful.

On the way to the hospital, I had ridden up the sidewalk of University Avenue past the U.S. Consulate, with its understated but serious security. Concrete pillars and planters studded the walkway out front so no one could drive their car into the building, and in a little box like a parking lot pay booth, a guard sat with his automatic rifle. You couldn't see in, but I knew he was there and I pictured him as handsome. Dark blond hair and sunglasses. Big white American teeth behind a hard, closed mouth. As I biked by, I thought about a bullet going into my head. I could see it, a dull pinky bronze, pressing on something important in my brain. No blood.

I thought about just making a break for it and jumping on my bike, my naked bum winking out of my gown every time I pressed down on the pedals, all the way down University and west along Queen.

The woman nodded at my gown, a greenish grey the colour of lichen, as if to say, *At least you can dress yourself*. She sat me down in a one-armed desk pushed against a wall, and injected me with a contrast agent that made my arm ache.

"Sit here until I come back," she said. I sat. When she returned, she said, "I have to ask you one last time if you have any metal implants or a pacemaker." She smiled as if to acknowledge that she and I were both smart enough to know better but that the process must be followed.

"No, nothing."

"Okay then, we're ready to go. Do you have any questions, anything?"

I shook my head.

"It's perfectly safe. You have nothing to worry about."

"Wait," I said. "I do have a question." She gave her head a little wiggle meaning *go ahead*. I asked, "What are you looking for?"

She looked surprised and started to ask me something; I could tell it was a question by the shape of her mouth, the tilt of her head. Then she changed tack and said, "Tumours, abnormalities, pressure or blockage, blood pooling, nerve damage—basically anything that could be contributing, physically, neurologically, to your"—here she paused and jutted out her chin—"condition."

"Oh."

She helped me climb onto the padded narrow slate and gave me a pair of earplugs. After I put them in, her voice came through, muffled, making me sleepy.

"Remember to close your eyes when I tell you it's time. People get claustrophobic with their eyes open."

I closed my eyes right away. I lay there for some time, and the woman arranged my arms at my sides.

"Relax," she said. Then, after a while, "It's time," and I was loaded smoothly into the machine.

A moment later there was a loud, clattering noise, audible even with the earplugs. It went on and on; I felt like my brain was being shoved around by it. I couldn't tell how long I was in there. Sometimes the colours behind my eyes would change, black-red, black-green, black-orange, like the aura of a sick person, shot through with darkness. I had a list in my notebook of all the aura colours and what they meant. Black: a lack of forgiveness, hurts from a past life, illness, blockages, hidden feelings or thoughts or memories. Secrets. Or nothing: some people interpret black as a hole in the auric field, a non-aura. I opened my eyes, looked around the spaceship-like interior.

"Please don't move," said a voice, muffled through the earplugs.

I thought it was the woman, but I couldn't be sure. I closed my eyes again.

I imagined my father and Andrew and Wendy standing outside the machine, peering into my brain like it was a diorama.

Oh, there it is, Andrew would say. *Right there—can you see it?*

Like a bruise on an apple. Wendy.

I knew it, says my father. *Well, better this than if she was just making it up.*

Or crazy, says Andrew.

Wendy, looking from one to the other, says something, but it's drowned out by the noise of the machine.

I squeezed my eyes more tightly closed and managed to will the image of the three of them away.

Six

I liked working in the store. Sometimes it seemed more like home than the apartment upstairs. I didn't have to wear a name tag or dark slacks, the way Wendy had to when she had worked part-time at the Royal York Hotel. The light came from old chandeliers we'd found at a store in Parkdale, not from harsh fluorescents. There was a softness to the days, even the annoying days with jackass customers. It was like wet wood, that slight give. After blacking out on my bike, though, I found myself wanting to lie down a lot, wanting to stay in bed. I felt safest lying down, as if the blackouts might sweep over me and keep on going if I could make myself slippery enough, aerodynamic enough, so that nothing could catch. I thought maybe I could see it even, a dark thing that would sail across the ceiling of my room, searching for me. Something eyeless and snoutless. I thought about the things I did during the lost time, the bizarre normalcy. It seemed laughable—surely I was supposed to be doing sinister things, spectacular things, if my brain was going to all the trouble of wiping them away. Why black out the mundane?

I began to have trouble counting change for customers. I got dizzy when I moved from sitting to standing. I started to take more time off, asking my father to cover for me. He put aside his coveted summer research time and took my place, standing poker-straight behind the counter. Sometimes he would come down to the store even when I hadn't asked, stand there rocking on his heels a little, folding and unfolding his glasses, looking around. He offered to man the counter so I could catch up on inventory or ordering and receiving. He brought me coffees and cookies from a café and told me to go eat in the park, get some sunshine—he would hold down the fort. But when I came back he'd be frustrated, bewildered by some small thing, how to enter a discount after totalling a sale, or unable to find something a customer wanted. Still, he kept appearing, half smiling, looking for all the world like a man searching for an address on a street where he'd never been.

I told Dr. Malik about the blackout with the bicycle at one of our twice-weekly sessions. He remained his calm self, continued to probe gently into my feelings about my mother, my thoughts about the future. I would come home from our sessions feeling blank, as if bathed, and spend the rest of the evening with my mother's things in the third-floor storage room, mindlessly cataloguing it all, making pages and pages of notes. I bought new notebooks when the old ones were full. I got hand cramps the way you do writing an exam. My handwriting, instead of deteriorating, got better, tighter, neater. I didn't make notes just about what I found, but also about things that popped into my head, my mother's sayings, little moments that drifted into my field of vision. My mother helping a store owner down the street sweep up broken glass when his windows were smashed. *Bring a knife to a gunfight.* Her clumsy swipes while playing tennis in the park with my father. *A rising tide lifts all boats.* The time she accidentally spit the ginger candy into a customer's purse, the bright sudden blush, the laughter. What if the blackouts changed and started reaching backwards, taking away the memories I already had? I wrote things down to keep them safe. I wanted to keep it all in one place, to keep her in one place. I bought an entire box of Paper Mate pens. Even in school, I had never written so much. If the man in the hospital, the jade angel man, had inspired me by talking about his writing, I didn't admit it. Surely writing about my mother wasn't bad. I'm sure Dr. Malik wouldn't have had a problem with it, if I told him. Dr. Rosenberg had suggested it, after all. And so what if the odd customer had the same idea? Even crazy people can have good ideas. *Even a stopped clock gives the right time twice a day.* I tried not to think about him while I sat in the hot, stuffy attic in the evenings, telling Andrew I had inventory to do, putting Wendy off with excuses about fatigue, overdue library books, flattened bike tires.

Three days after the MRI, I woke up feeling like I had the flu. My neck was tender, my arms and legs ached. I put on my dressing gown and went into my parents' room—my father's room—and asked him if he could watch the store for the morning. He was reading a magazine in bed, wearing a T-shirt so white it looked brand new.

"Of course," he said, pulling his blanket up higher. "If you need to rest, absolutely. I don't want you to exert yourself."

"Thanks, Dad." He was still lying on his own side of the bed, the far side. My mother had slept beside the door.

He turned back to his magazine and I went back to my room. After I closed the door, I could hear him get up and go into the washroom. I sat on my bed with the door closed until I heard him head down the stairs to the store. When I lay down, I could see the tops of the trees through my window, swaying a little. *When the trees move there's enough wind to sail by.* Who told me that? I couldn't remember.

I had a book from the library to read, and there was a Tupperware of celery in the fridge, just waiting for me to add peanut butter and Cheez Whiz. I would be okay for a while.

A few minutes later, I heard a knock on the apartment door. No one ever knocked on the apartment door. There was a back door at the bottom of the stairs, a passage that led from the back alley to the apartment without going through the store, and gave access to the garage and my father's rarely used Volkswagen. There was a broken back step my mother had jumped over to get to her garden; it had needed fixing for years. My parents weren't handy, and they were always forgetting about it since we hardly used that door. It was always locked. But now some-one was knocking at the interior door, at the top of the stairs. Had someone come through the store? Was my father knocking for some reason?

I wrapped myself in my dressing gown again. I didn't even remember opening the door, but suddenly there in the frame was the customer, the jade angel man, looking nervous and clean and vaguely displaced.

"Pardon?" I said, even though he hadn't spoken. There was the deep cleft over his lip, the too-warm wool cap.

"Hello, darling," he said.

He took his cap off and his hair was somewhat tamed, neatly parted on the side, and I could picture him combing it, running the comb under water and cocking his head to one side. It must have been a picture from a movie I'd seen, a fragment left over from a forgotten whole. *Who uses a comb anymore*, I thought stupidly. *I mean, really.*

"What are you doing here?"

"It's me, Gil," he said. It was a little after ten in the morning, which was when the store opened for business.

"Oh," I said, rolling my dressing gown more tightly closed. "Yeah, I thought you might be."

He nibbled on his thumbnail, and then pulled his hand away with a deep intake of breath. "Nail-biting is a terrible habit," he said. He didn't sound apologetic.

I fiddled my fingertips along the edges of my thumbnails involuntarily. "The cards," I said.

"I thought you'd like them," he said shyly.

"So," I said. "What now? Do I call the police?" *Do I call the police? If I do, should I call 911 or look up the non-emergency number? It's not really an emergency, is it? No one's broken the law, have they? Would I get in trouble for calling?*

"I'd rather you didn't."

He looked much neater than before. I sucked on a stray strand of hair.

"Do you think I could come in?" he asked. "If it's not inconvenient."

"Definitely not," I said. But I felt oddly rude, as though I were ignoring social propriety.

"Right. Well, I can understand that. I thought I would ask, though."

I should hit him with a frying pan and call the cops. Why am I talking to him? Is it safe to leave him to get the frying pan? Do I have a clean one? Does it matter if it's dirty? My mind was whirling, but I found it hard to take the panic seriously. He still didn't seem crazy to me. Maybe he could use a round of vitamin C supplements, but he had a generally sturdy build, a peasant-ish air of resilience. He was wearing a pale yellow shirt that buttoned up with Western style snaps. I couldn't imagine anyone crazy wearing yellow or having those snaps — the fun little click they made, it was too fanciful. Being crazy was a serious business, as I was coming to know all too well.

There was a silence while I readjusted my robe.

"It must be really difficult," he said. "With the blackouts. You feel like you can hardly step outside your own house."

"Look, I don't know how you—"

"Maggie, Maggie," he said. "Don't you understand? Don't you even understand what they are?"

He frowned and his forehead wrinkled. It was oddly attractive. He seemed to have stepped closer without my noticing.

This was the moment when I needed to close the door. It wasn't safe not to. But I didn't.

"I can help you," he said. "If you'll help me. I can give you what you need to stop the blackouts."

I said nothing, and after a moment he let out a puff of air.

"Look," he said. "This is my number. Call me when you're ready. Not before that. I need you totally committed, I need all of you. Halfway would be a disaster, for both of us." He handed me a slip of paper.

"You're crazy," I said, but I took it. We stood staring.

"I told you," he said. "I need some information for my book. Things about your mother. I need—another point of view. When it's finished, I'll give you something to stop the blackouts. And you'll be able to get on with things."

He moved and I ducked down, covering my head with my arms. His hand near my face. I thought he was going to hit me. He stayed perfectly still, his hand hovering, and finally I rose up like a fighter coming warily out of a crouch.

He ran the flat tips of his fingers along my jaw from ear to chin, barely touching. His fingers were held tightly together. The first thing I thought was, *Did I wash my face this morning?* as if that was important. There was a feeling like all the blood in my heart had zinged down my legs and back up again.

"You have no idea—" he said, stopping suddenly. His girlish voice was soft.

I almost reached out before I came back into myself, jerked my face away from his hand and stepped back through the door. I watched my body slamming it closed, decisive, responsible.

Then I slid the deadbolt and melted down onto the floor beside the shoe rack, with my back against the door and my robe mashed up under me. A bright pearly grey nothingness thundered around in my head.

Sometime later, I got up off the ground and dressed. When I opened the door there was no sign of Gil in the hallway. I went down into the store and found my father, who was reading a book at the counter, head down.

"Dad," I said. "Was there someone here?" I kept my voice low; there were customers looking at vegan cookbooks in the back of the store.

"Plenty of people," he said. "It's been a good morning."

"A young guy. Dark hair, kind of curly?"

He shrugged. "Maybe," he said. "Are you waiting for someone?" He frowned and seemed about to ask something else, and I cut him off.

"I didn't tell you, but I had a blackout. That I didn't tell Dr. Malik about."

"Another one?"

"I mean, I had one during a session with Dr. Malik. When we first started."

"During?"

"Yeah." I nodded. "In his office. Forty minutes. I didn't go anywhere, I was just sitting there in his office, but I'm scared of—I don't want to—" I made myself meet his eyes, briefly.

I couldn't say anything else out loud. The rush of water, the deafness. A jade angel on the bottom of the river.

"You're going to be fine," he said, but he was leaning forward, his shoulders curved over like he'd been hit in the chest.

"I'm sorry I didn't tell you."

He put an awkward hand on my shoulder. "You told me now. That's a lot better than—a lot better than it could be."

The bell over the door went and three middle-aged women came in.

"Do you tell fortunes here?"

I stepped forward. It was a relief to get away from what I was saying to my father. "We don't, but I can refer you to someone good." I had a friendly relationship with several city psychics and often sent them business.

"Oh pooh. Not even a little reading?" They were giggling like teenagers. They all had big leather purses in non-leather colours: pink, green, yellow. They made me think of champagne.

My father said, "Aren't you going to rest?" and the women looked at him as if he were talking to them.

"I'm fine now," I said. "You can go. I'll take over. And can you check the back door, make sure it's closed?"

He looked at me and then the women, nodded and headed to the back.

When he was gone I said, "For twenty bucks I'll give you all a basic reading. One card each. The immediate future."

The women drew up to the counter as I got behind it. I took out my mother's deck from the drawer and shuffled it.

"My mother used to do this with playing cards," one of the

women said. "It's all from the same culture, it's all Gypsies, it just got broken up."

I held the cards out and instructed them each to pick one.

"Now lay them out." The first was the four of wands. The woman with the pink purse. "Wands are creative, physical. Generative." When I said *physical* the women all laughed so loudly I had to wait a moment to continue. "This is a good card. You see the wreaths? That's bounty. This is good for houses, for marriages—foundations. Are you renovating? This would be a good time to do it."

The woman clutched herself and said, "My god." The green purse woman said, "Jessica, did you hear that? The back deck! This is just perfect!"

I turned to her next. She had turned out the ten of pentacles.

"Oh wow," I said. "You ladies are having a good day. This is a really, really good card. I mean, no card is exactly good or bad. But this one, it would be hard to make it bad." I looked up at her. "Prosperity. Good, lasting prosperity, something you can have and pass on."

She and the other women clapped their hands with only the palms touching, their fingers bent back. Little bursts like wind-up teeth chattering.

The woman with the yellow purse nudged her card forward.

"The star, reversed." I didn't say anything for a moment. I pictured the list in my notebook. I'd studied the cards, watched my mother read spreads for customers. I knew what it meant. Sometimes my mother would skew these readings a little, since they were unofficial anyway, a couple of cards at most and we didn't declare the money. We sent anyone who wanted a full reading to the professionals. I'd ask her afterwards about her fudged interpretations, wanting to make sure I'd memorized the cards correctly, and she would just smile, say that people didn't really want to know anyway, so why not make it nice.

But I would want the truth, if it were me, even if I didn't believe. I would want to know. And this card was clear.

"Lack of perception," I said. "Loss. Illness." The woman's face was still half caught in laughter, her mouth slightly open. "False hope."

The three women stared at me for a moment. "Jesus God," said the first one. "Congratulations on spoiling our day."

The woman who had pulled the star looked at her. "It's okay, Jessica. It's just for fun." She smiled, but it was weak.

"Forget about it," said Jessica. "Forget about her." This meant me. She looked at me. "Didn't anyone ever tell you a white lie doesn't hurt anyone?"

"Jessica," said the woman again.

"Well, what would it have cost her? Nothing. She could have made up something really nice and our Toronto trip would have been that much better for it. You don't deserve that kind of treatment, Elaine."

She threw a twenty-dollar bill onto the counter and the three of them hustled out, but I felt hot all over.

The customers with the vegan cookbooks came forward, wanting to buy them. I tried to smile, reaching out to receive them. My hands worked for me, automatic pilot.

It wasn't the reaction to the reading—I had read cards before and had had every unexpected reaction from tears to cursing— but the last thing she'd said: *You don't deserve that kind of treatment, Elaine. Elaine, you don't deserve that.* I slipped the books into paper bags stamped with *Pierce Gifts & Oddities*, ran a VISA card through our system, handed over a pen for signing. *When the trees move there's enough wind to sail by.* I'd just been thinking that up in my room, and now this woman came in, saying *Elaine.* I had known an Elaine; she was the one who told me about the trees. I hadn't seen her for years. I took my most recent notebook out from under the counter, flipped back to the beginning and started to read.

Seven

*T*he stone animals never sold all that well. People liked crystals but they liked them anonymous and polished, not shaped into monkeys and jaguars and sparrows. Not watching. Even the angels sold only sluggishly. We hardly ever had to reorder the animals, whereas every two weeks like clockwork I would pull open the plastic net bags of unshaped onyx, sodalite, quartz, and pour them into the long wooden trough with its little square compartments. All of our signs were hand-lettered by me; my mother used to do it but she was left-handed and inevitably smudged the ink, leaving the lettering smeared and sad. I was right-handed with neat printing that went straight up and down, with no tilt to either side.

It was my mother, though, who came up with what to write. She knew what each crystal ought to be used for. For heartbreak, for digestion, for clarity, for rest. I made my lists and tried to keep up, to remember.

People were shy when they looked at the crystals, like they were in a doctor's office poking through brochures. No one wanted to be seen looking at what they wanted, like the wanting itself was shameful.

My mother was good at this; she would float over, hardly seeming to notice the customer, as if she had merely decided to stroll around the store and suddenly remembered—oh yes—what a lovely crystal *selection we had. She would never ask what they were looking for but instead would reach out and palm one of the stones, saying, "I use the citrine in the mornings. If you keep it on a windowsill, it will absorb the sun." And she would lay it against her cheek, cool and smooth, and the customer would be nodding, reaching for it, wanting to be as serene. She wasn't a showman, she didn't wear scarves and earrings and let her long dark hair suggest vague, Gypsy knowledge; instead she would laugh lightly with the customers, as if the very idea of needing the stones, of heartache, or poor health, or pain, was somewhat silly but worth indulging, like a craving for bubble gum or ginger ale—harmless, fine. Shoulders eased down as she spoke, eyebrows smoothed apart, and bags that had been endlessly, nervously hitched up hung loosely, relaxed. Her favourite stones— garnet, amethyst, rose quartz—almost always sold out.*

Occasionally my father would come down, saying he needed a break from marking, or he would come through the front door, home from his office on campus, pushing ahead of him an air pocket of academic impatience, crisp and bright, like it was always autumn near him. He would stand in front of the crystal display sometimes, let his narrow fingers trail through the stones, reading the signs silently. The stones were always cool to the touch, but they warmed if you held them long enough.

When I was ten my father told me my mother had to go away. She was going to visit her parents, who I had never met, mysterious people in Georgia about whom I knew very little. I imagined them to be the source of my mother's idioms, that they probably spoke in code, and it was this secret language, which sounded like English but wasn't, that she occasionally slipped into. I worried I wouldn't be able to understand her when she came back.

She left in the winter and was gone for what felt like forever, and my father hired one of his students to look after the store, a heavy-set girl named Elaine who had the longest eyelashes I had ever seen. You'd think you had felt a breeze when she blinked. No one called her a babysitter but she cleared out the little backroom where my mother did the ordering, brought an armload of pillows down from the couch in the apartment and made me a little nook. I was delighted by this and I would come home after school and burrow into the pillow pile and watch the tiny rabbit ears–topped television Elaine had produced from somewhere.

"You alive in there?" she would call out sometimes from the counter. "Or am I going to have to deal with a zombie kid?"

"I'm a zombie now!" I yelled back, sometimes taking the time to lurch out, arms stiff in front of me.

"Oh, too bad I have this anti-zombie laser," she said, hefting the price-tag gun. "I would hate to have to kill such a cute zombie. Are you sure you're a zombie?"

All of this, at ten years old, I found unbelievably hilarious. I don't remember evaluating Elaine, or even meeting her for the first time. I only remember her there, shifting her weight on the stool behind the counter and singing pop songs under her breath, Michael Jackson and Journey and "Don't You Want Me" by the Human League. She would close up the store precisely at six and go down the street to buy herself something for dinner. In the spring before school ended for the year, I would go with Elaine and sometimes she would buy me a custard tart from one of the little Portuguese stores, flaky and gelatinous, slightly burnt on top, utterly delicious.

After dinner, if my father wasn't home yet, Elaine would take me to the park and teach me to turn cartwheels, or twine her fingers together and give me a boost into the lower branches of a tree. She was graceful, with large breasts that she covered up with scarves and jackets. Sometimes she wore little black lace gloves like Madonna, who was just coming into popularity. She taught me to braid my hair and make thin, flat bracelets of embroidery floss, in the colours she favoured: red, hot pink, black, white. I wanted to make one for my mother but I thought the harsh colours would be too much for her, might burn right through her wrist. And also I didn't know when she was coming home. When I asked my father or Elaine, they said, *soon, soon.*

But then one day my mother was there again, looking exactly the same. She had acquired an ankle bracelet that had a tiny bell on it and when she walked around the store or the apartment, it jingled quietly, like a cat's collar. After she unpacked, the first thing she did was take down most of the photos hanging on the walls, old black-and-white photos that I liked, where she was very young and very pretty, smiling widely. My father watched her do this and said nothing. She went to Kensington Market, to the watery-eyed old blonde women from whom she bought her clothes, and got colourful fabric hangings. She put them up where the photos used to be and said, "Isn't this a pretty state of affairs." I said, Yes, they were pretty, and she and my father looked at each other over my head. Those photos went into the attic storage room, those photos my mother couldn't stand to look at anymore after coming back from Georgia.

It was early summer when she got home and Elaine stayed on for a little while, arriving in the morning after I ate breakfast and taking me on the streetcar to High Park or St. Lawrence Market, places that felt far at the time, and alarmingly special, like Christmas coming over and over. This must have been my father's idea, or Elaine's, because it was clearly not my mother's. I could tell from her mouth, from the shape of it. Not a frown, just the wrong shape. It was one of the signs. Or her skin, sometimes it looked slightly grey. The greyer it looked, the more I watched her. There were certain mannerisms, a dullness of the hair, a softening under the chin, that were important to notice.

One evening soon after she got home my mother projected photos from her trip on a white sheet we hung over the kitchen window. I helped put it up, feeling important as I pushed the copper-coloured tacks into the unmarked wall. It was one of her ideas, and she had spent considerable time and money getting her photos converted to slides, borrowing the projector from the university with my father's help, and picking the order in which the photos would be displayed. I didn't know why these photos were okay and the other ones, the ones she'd stored away when she came home, weren't. Throughout the slide show the sheet bulged slightly because the window behind it was open a little, to let the cool evening air in. It looked like a sail filling and emptying, distorting the images.

We all sat at the maple-wood kitchen table, which was the same colour as Elaine's hair. My father struggled with the projector and the slides for a while, cursing softly under his breath. When it was up and running, my mother stood, impressive in her white summer dress, and held the button that shuttled the slides through their circular track.

She pointed at the images on the wall and said: magnolia; Spanish moss; Little Wendy, the bird girl. Most of the photos were devoid of people. This last was a statue of a girl a little younger than I was, wearing a dress that looked to me like a nightgown. She held out two bowls, which my mother said were bird feeders, and her head was cocked to one side. She looked sad.

"That's in Savannah," said my mother. "In Bonaventure, a cemetery. She reminded me of you."

And it scared me because the girl's eyes were not detailed; she looked blind. I drew closer to Elaine, who was sitting beside me.

The next slide was a photo of my grandparents, my grandmother with a cloud of dark hair while my grandfather's steel-grey curls peeked out from under a soft cap above his still-black eyebrows. He wore a linen suit and the two of them leaned on the railing of their front porch.

My grandfather had worked at a clay company when my mother was a child and he worked there still when she went to visit. She was just over thirty and her parents were not yet sixty. At the clay company they exported kaolin, used to make paper and porcelain. I didn't understand how any one thing could be used to make two such different materials, and that night, during the photo slide show, I had to be reminded what porcelain was, and I was embarrassed for this to happen in front of Elaine, who had, as my father said, "A mind like a steel trap."

During the war my grandfather was kept home with flat feet, asthma and thick eyeglasses. It was hard to reconcile these ailments with his physical self, short but well formed, strong-jawed, seemingly resilient. Some men were ashamed not to go, but my mother said that her father kept himself to himself and didn't give a fig what anyone else thought about him. *Didn't give a fig* I remembered long after, and when I finally ate a fig many years later, I thought of my grandfather.

My grandmother, a respectable woman, never had a job, but canned and boiled and sewed and cleaned and knew a dozen uses for lemon juice and stored the correct vegetables in boxes of sand in the shed. She was soft and round in the photos, but had been tall and thin as a girl, taller than my grandfather, and after she had my mother the doctor said no more, her back would not stand for it. So my mother was an only child in a town with eight and ten and twelve children to a house. She was a poor student and disappointed her father by putting aside *The Sun Also Rises* and *Moby Dick* and *A Tale of Two Cities*, which he read at night with his glasses off. Her parents were quiet people, firm people, who went to church and prayed before meals but not in crises. My grandmother would say, "If you want something done right, you have to do it yourself," and seemed to think this extended even to God.

All of this my mother told us, breezy and even-toned, while she flipped through the photos. Elaine looked down as if checking to see if her lovely breasts were still there, and didn't look up for most of the evening. If my mother's personal stories made Elaine uncomfortable, my mother seemed not to notice.

That same summer I met Wendy, when our parents enrolled us in swimming lessons. Elaine, who was still inexplicably around, drove me down to Sunnyside Park in my father's Honda. I had taken swimming lessons before with the school, in the over-bright indoor pool. The high ceiling and clean whiteness of the room made me think of an unplugged refrigerator. I was a weak swimmer, a belly-flopper, but my mother took a rare stand and said I had to learn.

Outside in Sunnyside pool, I found it nearly impossible to keep my head above water, and I envied the strong thighs of my classmates, who stuck their hands in the air and kicked the eggbeater for the required two minutes while I choked on the over-chlorinated water. There was one other weak swimmer in the class: Wendy, who went to my school but was in the separate, gifted class. She was small and scrawny and I was tall for my age but uncoordinated, and between us we had a hard time with pretty much every task. Sometimes after class when we wrapped ourselves in towels that pictured Bambi or Mickey Mouse, I would look out on the lake, its wrinkled surface gleaming in the sunset, and wish we were swimming there instead. I thought it would feel softer than the pool water, colder, more watery somehow. I tried to explain this to Wendy as we sat on the grass sharing pieces of Juicy Fruit and Doublemint gum, folding the pieces over on our tongues and singing the jingles. Already Wendy's mother had decided Elaine could take over ferrying Wendy to and from lessons, since we lived just down the street. I looked out at the lake and asked Wendy what she thought of it, if she wouldn't rather be out there.

"What's the difference?" she said. "Water's water and we're rotten swimmers either way." Then she asked me to tell her about the crystal ball she'd seen in the store.

My father said it was too polluted to swim in the lake near the city, although some families still unrolled picnic blankets and spent the day swimming and building sandcastles back then. He was ahead of his time with environmentalism, composting our food waste in a jerry-rigged trash bin in our tiny backyard, doing it right so the soil that spilled out the bottom looked like melted chocolate and made my mother's half-hearted garden grow like an English heath.

Sometimes Elaine would go sailing during our swimming lessons and meet us afterwards looking wind-blown and flushed. She sailed at the Boulevard Club down the road, a big red-roofed building, where her boyfriend had a small, sleek boat.

When she told us this, it was the first I had heard of a boyfriend.

"Oh," she said, "Alan's not exactly a boyfriend, he's more of a family friend." She was a girl who blushed easily, who had that see-through sort of skin. "We just have a lot in common. A number of small things. He's very bright." Her speech always seemed more formal after she came back from sailing, as if she'd been in school.

"Do you go on dates?"

She shook her head. "I don't know," she said. She herded Wendy and me into the car, our damp skin sticking to the leather below our shorts. The feeling of peeling my legs off the seat, the stinging satisfaction of it.

After we dropped Wendy off, we pulled my father's car into the detached garage behind the store and got out. Elaine never wore a seat belt even though I knew she had seen the television commercials: *Seat Belts Save Lives*. The recklessness seemed out of character.

As we walked out of the garage, she said, "Did you have fun today?"

"I hate swimming," I said. "I'm awful."

"Just give it time," said Elaine, but she seemed not to be listening to herself. She looked down at me and smiled like she was only just noticing me.

We rounded the corner from the alleyway and stood on the corner so she could hail a cab.

"You're a cool kid, Maggie," she said, looking west down Queen Street. When a taxi stopped, she said to the driver, "Just a second. You can run the meter," and turned to face the store.

She stood still for a moment and put a big smile on her face. Then she pushed me through the door ahead of her.

My mother, who was always watching the door, was looking down.

"Hi, Carol. Here she is."

"Thank you, Elaine." She didn't look up.

"Well, my cab is waiting. Better jet." She turned to go, and I said, "You're cool too, Elaine." I wanted her to take me to the park. I wanted to practise my cartwheel and feel the slight head rush that came with it. I had taken one of the animals from the store and wanted to give it to her, but I felt restrained, as if giving her something from my mother's store, and certainly in front of her, would be a betrayal in some way. The zircon cat was in my pocket. No one ever bought the zircon, I didn't think it would be missed.

"Bye, Maggie Mags," she said. "I'll see you soon." She went out and got into the green and orange taxi and was carried away.

It was late for the store to be open; even though it was July, dusk was setting in, so it must have been after eight.

"How's Elaine?" my mother asked. "Is she teaching you how to curl your eyelashes and paint your toenails?" And even though those were both things I would have liked to learn, I rolled my eyes and said, "No, of course not." I sat down on the stool, which my mother never seemed to use.

She softened and she pulled me, stool and all, closer to the counter. "How do you like swimming outside?"

"It's okay. I wish we were swimming in the lake."

She shook her head. "It's not safe," she said. "Make sure you don't go too close to the shore."

"Elaine goes out on the lake."

"Does she? She swims?"

"No, she sails. With her boyfriend, on his sailboat."

"Her boyfriend." She seemed to think very seriously about this. "Have you met her boyfriend, Magpie?"

She used my nickname, but there was a strange wheedling tone I hadn't heard before. I was worried about my answer and thought about lying. After a moment I said, "No," which was the truth.

"I wonder," said my mother slowly, "if she made mention of this boyfriend to your father. I wonder whether it slipped her mind." She smiled and made a *poof* gesture with her hands, her fingers spreading outwards to signify Elaine's forgetfulness. "I wonder. It's not like your father to enjoy being third on a match."

This phrase meant nothing to me. "Third on a match?"

"It's just an expression."

"What does it mean?"

"It means just what it says."

I nodded, looked down.

"It's from the war," she said. "It means someone else got to something before you did."

"The war?"

"If you needed a cigarette, you had to light a match. By the time the match got passed to the third man, the trench would be lit up like a Christmas tree. Third on a match—*zip*! A Frenchman would shoot you, right between the eyes."

This was utterly unlike her. *Zip*. Too many words, all at once, and too fast. She never talked about violent things. The stones can pick up that kind of sludge, she'd say. Especially the quartz. Why occupy yourself with ugly things? Or as my father would say, not realizing he meant much the same thing: *Inelegant thoughts are for inelegant minds.*

"They said in class that the French were on our side. Why would a French person shoot you?" I said. I wanted to be clear on this. Even for my mother, with her endless idioms, this was confusing.

She said, "You are so literal-minded sometimes."

I didn't know what she meant and I knew from her tone she'd forgotten it was me she was talking to. I knew it was an insult, whatever it meant.

She looked at me and said, "I'm sorry, darling. I've still got some lemon cake upstairs? Why don't you go get a piece? It's poppy seed, just like you like?" And she was trying very hard because every part sounded like a question.

I didn't want cake. I wanted a custard tart like Elaine bought from the Portuguese place. But I'd eat the cake, of course. Of course I'd eat the cake. I would screech my finger across the plate to get the crumbs, and my mother would say, "Dinner table," meaning "That's not polite," but she would secretly like it. I would do anything I could think of. Otherwise someone might get shot.

"Who are the other two people?" I asked. "If Dad is third on the match? Is Elaine one of them?" And she didn't answer for a long, long time, so I said instead, "We have to dive for the brick tomorrow." The brick in question was a bright yellow rubber-covered brick, and Wendy and I had been dreading the test. We knew perfectly well that neither of us would last that far down, and that we would flop awkwardly in, try to get down far enough, wave our hands through the water in hopes of making contact, and come up empty-handed. I'd been dreaming of the brick for a week. In some of my dreams I saw it resting peacefully in the shallows of the lake, but most of the time it was glaring up through the too-clear water of the pool.

"What brick?" said my mother. Then she rolled her hair into a rope and threw it over her shoulder, a trick she did unconsciously and that signified she was about to move. "Don't worry, honey," she said. She moved me out of her way in a firm but absent-minded manner and headed to the back stairs. "I have to talk to your dad for a minute," she said. "I'll be right back."

Elaine was gone one day in the fall, after I'd already returned to school. I asked my father if she was coming back and he seemed irritated by the question.

"No, she's not coming back," he said. "She's getting married."

"Isn't she still in your class?"

"No, she's not."

"Where is she now?"

"She's moved away. They moved to New England."

"Where is that?"

"America."

I thought about this. "Is it near Grandma and Grandpa?" I thought of Elaine trailing through the magnolia trees, the Spanish moss hanging down, leaving her dappled in sunlight.

"No, Margaret," said my father. "America is a big country."

He only called me Margaret when I was in trouble. I was confused; what had I said? Normally he liked when I asked questions; he liked to teach, it was generally a way to get him in a good mood.

He said quickly, "Why don't you run down and get your mother? You can watch the store for a minute, can't you? You're good at counting the change, I saw you helping your mom the other day."

And I went, because I was being granted a reprieve, because his voice was lighter than before, and because I didn't understand the feeling that was radiating from him.

In the store my mother was behind the counter. There were two customers, a man and a woman together, who were picking up tins of tea and reading the labels, and I stood behind the back table, turning the animals the right way and waiting for the people to leave. I hadn't given the zircon cat to Elaine but I hadn't returned it either.

The rule was to let customers browse as long as they wanted. When they finally left and we were alone, I went to my mother, who was standing behind the counter, and told her that Dad wanted her upstairs.

"I bet he does," she said, and she didn't move to go.

"I can watch the store," I said. "I know how to do it." The wall cabinet behind her was open and a box of rose quartz was spilled inside. I wanted to scoop them up, put them back, close the cupboard. But I couldn't bear to go behind the counter. I could smell my mother, her spicy ginger shampoo. She made it herself.

She didn't say anything, and I said, "Where is Elaine?" Immediately I knew this was the wrong thing to say and that somehow in saying it I had hurt my mother.

She came out from behind the counter and I moved away from her. Not too far, because I felt guilty, but I felt a premonition of something bad. I wanted to run; I wanted to tear down to the lake and see if I could spot Elaine, sailing off in the distance. I assumed she was on a boat.

"This is my store," said my mother. "They can't take it from me." She was gripping the counter so hard that her knuckles were stretching apart under the skin. The store was closed and the lights were off, but the glow of the street lamps on Queen Street lit up her face. It was streaked and wet. "I never wanted her to come. I wanted to take care of you myself. I could do it—I can do it." She went down on her knees and pulled me close. I let myself be pulled. "You're the good thing," she said. "You're the good thing in a bloody, bloody world. Why would you make it worse? You could never make it worse."

And it wasn't the first time I'd seen her cry, and it wouldn't be the last time, and when she stopped, she shook me, hard and rhythmically. I stayed limp in her arms and waited for her to finish. It hurt my head, which snapped back and forth, and my arms and shoulders where her fingers dug in. The store seemed bigger then, emptier. After my mother came home from Georgia, the pillows that Elaine had brought down for me had been returned to the couch and the little television had disappeared. I tried to think about nothing.

Finally my mother let me go and hugged herself hard, rocking back and forth. "I'm sorry," she said. "I'm sorry." She shook her head. "I had to come back to you. How could I not come back for you?"

When my father came down, I hated him for not having come sooner and I looked at him and saw that he knew it. And yet neither of us wanted to leave her there on the floor.

"Come on, Carol," he said and he sounded bone-tired. And although he was a slight man, he lifted her up and carried her to the apartment. She looked like a dead thing; she didn't even hold her head up.

"Lock the store, Maggie," he said from halfway up the stairs. "That's enough for tonight."

I went to the door and turned the sign on its hook: OPEN, CLOSED.

It was hard to breathe, like I was swimming and could only inhale on every other stroke. Wendy and I had both failed the brick test in the summer. Wendy cried after and Elaine had hugged her and told Wendy she was pretty, like that meant the test didn't matter. Wendy and I had been eating lunch together since school started, meeting outside her gifted classroom door and walking arm in arm to the lunchroom with our Thermoses of soup and little square sandwiches, hers on cloudy Wonderbread and mine on crunchy twelve-grain whole-wheat.

I turned the lock on the door and felt it click, then slid the chain in place. Something was different here than in other houses, something that had to do with bread and the soreness in my neck, but I didn't know what exactly. It was something to protect, to gather around the way a pearl gathers around a grain of sand. It was an answer to a question that hadn't been asked, like Elaine telling Wendy she was pretty when it seemed to have nothing to do with what was happening. It was a direction to always be looking in.

PART TWO

THE
JADE
ANGEL

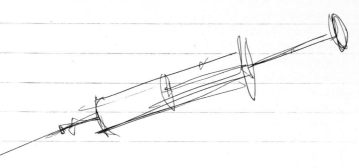

Eight

He was sitting at one of the wooden picnic tables in Trinity Bellwoods Park, watching a crowd of people who were practising tightrope walking on a cord strung between two trees. The cord was slack and swaying as a girl in purple tights reached out to a man who wore runner's shorts over striped stockings. Their feet spilled over the cord as they shuffled towards each other. I held my breath although they were only a few feet from the ground. We'd arranged it on the phone. I'd held onto the scrap of paper he'd given me in the apartment doorway, folded and unfolded it a dozen times before I made the call.

"That's something," he said, nodding to the tightropers.

I stood with my hands in my pockets. I was vaguely embarrassed to speak to him in public. He looked the worse for wear since our encounter in the hallway and his unkempt appearance gave him the aura of possibly being a pervert. For the first time he was wearing a T-shirt and shorts. His naked arms and legs seemed too personal, which was a stupid thing to think, but they were all sinew and hair and bone and I couldn't stop staring.

"I guess so," I said. "They're here a lot." I watched the walkers join hands and prepare to move around each other. They swung from side to side and the man jutted one arm out for balance.

"I've never seen them." He squinted up. "You can sit down, darling. I think I've shown a level of dedication."

I sat down beside him, looking ahead. "So. You say you can help me. Give me your best pitch."

"Well, I can help with the blackouts. Once I get what I need. But helping me helps you too. You're trying to sort through things, right? Get things into order?"

I thought of the notebooks, my scrawlings about Elaine, about my mother. The boxes in the attic. "I guess that's part of what I'm doing."

Gil snorted. "Part of. You don't have to play your cards so close to your vest, darling. This bargain is good for both of us."

"Tell me again."

"You talk to me. Tell me everything—about now, about before. I take what I need for the book. It will help you with your little project, I'll finish my work, and best of all, in no time at all, you get to live blackout-free."

"And what is this book? Will it be for sale or what? Why are you writing it?"

"It's kind of a history of the area, a sort of family history. I just need some context from you. It's research, it might not even end up in the book. Once it's done, we can worry about the logistics. I thought you'd be more interested in the blackouts."

"Well, what stops them? What is it you're going to give me?"

"Now, now. You run a store. You know business doesn't work like that."

"Look, you seem like a nice-enough guy, but I have a boy-friend. I shouldn't even be here."

"All right, I understand that. But you are here, so obviously something bigger is at work."

"You mean fate?"

"No. Me." Relenting, he added, "The book. The blackouts. All of it."

"Oh," I said. "Suppose I did take you seriously. Just as an experiment."

"We can start from there."

"I mean, what would it involve?"

"Well. The relationship between writer and source is intense. You would have to be honest with me. You're not a very honest person sometimes, it seems to me."

"Oh thanks. You're really winning me over here."

He shrugged. "If you want me to go. If you were disappointed to find out the cards were from me—if you can honestly say you have no interest in talking to me—"

I cut him off. "I guess it would be nice to have someone to talk to, about her. Someone uninvolved. You could come by the store. Near the end of the day, and I could—tell you things. On nights when Andrew doesn't come over, or before he gets there."

"That's a good start." When I didn't respond, he said, "I know it's asking a lot. But maybe a leap of faith could be a nice change of pace."

I looked at him, critically. He wasn't bad looking, in a Back-up Mobster #3 kind of way, but he wasn't exactly a heartthrob. I thought of Elaine, with her tawny hair, sitting in the same park, practically on the same bench. The door. Had my father checked the back door—was it locked when Gil came to the apartment? I forgot to ask him after the tarot card women rattled me.

"How did you get up to the apartment? When you came to see me."

"Through the store. I've been in there before, remember?"

There was a yell and we both looked over to see the male tightrope walker lying on his back on the grass, glaring up. The girl grinned down at him, crouched low on the swaying rope.

Gil stood up. "We could start now. No time like the present."

I thought of the bowl of zircon, the stones she'd had in her pockets. There was a scale in my mind, weighed down on one side with the zircon. I put Gil's book on the other side, prayed it would balance.

"Okay. So. How do we start?"

"We've already started," he said.

"And what should I be doing?"

"What you would normally do. Just be yourself. And talk to me."

"About what?"

"Everything."

"Everything?" I leaned back against the top of the picnic table, felt it dig into my back. I was thinking of body hair, dental floss, snot and urine. "I don't know."

"Calm down," he said. "This isn't a tabloid. I'm not trying to catch you with your pants down. Just talk."

"And you can make that into something?"

"I can only promise I'll do my best. It's not a tame animal."

The park seemed impossibly big at that moment, like any

number of people could be in it—millions of people. Gil's knee bumped against mine and I flinched away. I thought of Andrew's checkmarks on his students' papers, which were backwards because he was left-handed. My mother was surprised when I told her he was left-handed, like her. She said she didn't think he had it in him.

"I had this backpack," I said. I waited for him to respond but he didn't. "I thought I might be going somewhere."

His leg touched mine again, our knees bumping together, the skin stretched thinly. Our bones were almost touching. I took my notebook out of my bag.

I was sixteen when I started working properly in the store. Wendy had her part-time job at the Royal York Hotel, washing dishes, and she talked about it a lot to the other girls who sat at our lunch table—the dim glamour of the ballroom after everyone was gone, the handsome waiters. She showed off the dangling earrings she bought with her paycheques, swishing her head back and forth. I'd always helped out in the store, but I wanted something I could show to other people.

Also I wanted money, money of my own like Wendy had. Not for earrings; instead I had an idea that I needed to be ready for an emergency. I bought a medium-size hiking backpack from Mountain Equipment Co-op and stored it under my bed. I'd found and had been rereading some of my old books, from what I called "when I was little," and one of them was My Side of the Mountain. *I had a mixed-up idea that I might suddenly need to fend for myself, for even the basics, and I filled the backpack with silver solar blankets* that folded into tiny squares, water-purifying tablets, various collapsible cooking implements, a second-hand Swiss Army knife. I made long lists in the notebooks of everything I would need. This theme of sudden isolation and survival turned up again and again in the books I was reading—kid detectives escaping from the villains and spending days in the woods, or princesses possessed of anachronistically feminist tenacity tying bindles to their backs and fleeing bad marriages.

After a while, though, my father noticed what I was reading and gave me a hardcover copy of Joyce's Ulysses. He did this ceremoniously, like it was a secular bat mitzvah, as if I should be flattered by this invitation to the adult world. Taking My Side of the Mountain, by then woefully well thumbed, from my bedside table and replacing it with the Joyce, he said, "You can do better." Instead of reading Ulysses, I went to Book City and bought a copy of The SAS Survival Handbook. "Almost everywhere nature provides the necessities for survival." Almost everywhere, I noted. Almost.

At that point, my father was still hopeful. The Joyce wasn't the only book he gave me. He was still crossing his fingers under the dinner table that I was just a late bloomer, that any day now I would fall onto his side of the fence, keep him company among his books, the right kind of books.

My mother didn't care what I read, but she gave me the promotional bookmarks publishers sometimes sent to her along with their catalogues. This season: Think Yourself Well! Accessing the World Spirit! Organics for Everyone! She herself left her mystery novels open face down, scattered around the apartment and slipped under the counter in the store. My father would find them, fold down a corner and close them, mourning the cracked spines.

"If you're going to read it, you should respect it," he said one day, ostensibly to me but in fact to my mother, who was sifting flour into her blue ceramic mixing bowl.

She said, "They don't have feelings, Chris. Besides, it means I like them. It means I'm trying to make them last." She tapped the sieve against the bowl, clink-clink, and said, "It's not like you to be so touchy-feely." She smiled at him, showing her right incisor, which was pushed forward in a manner that made it look a little fang-ish. She was shy about it normally. My own teeth were small and straight, like my father's.

I turned to see what my father would say in answer to that. I was interested in my parents in a way other teenagers were not. I wasn't interested in finding their faults or exposing their hypocrisies with door-slamming bouts of self-righteousness. I was interested in the two of them together, speaking to each other, and whenever this happened I would pay attention, I had to pay attention. I did have some nagging questions of fairness—this was what my friends were concerned about, such as why their mothers could smoke if they weren't allowed to. I wondered why I had never been to Georgia. I envied the secretive allure of wild horses, house fires, enormous creaking verandas wrapped around massive wooden houses—my hidden, Southern grandparents.

Anyway, all this was a luxury—grandparents, mysteries, fair-ness, answers. I was concerned with necessities, with banking my small paycheques that felt large at the time, and filling my emer-gency backpack, honing my list. Binoculars, first aid supplies, two compasses, waterproof matches. If someone had asked me what

I was doing, I wouldn't have had an answer, but I felt compelled.

My father had no answer that day for my mother, who began creaming butter in another, smaller bowl. After that conversation, though, she didn't give me any more bookmarks. She kept them for herself and really tried to remember to use them. One day after school I saw my father smile and pick up her bookmarked Agatha Christie, left sitting on the kitchen counter. She still wasn't good at remembering to put them away. He ran a finger down the uncracked spine and I felt a shiver of embarrassment, as if I were seeing him touch her in an unbearably intimate way.

Gil had a notebook like mine, the kind with the black-and-white mottled cover that you could get at Shoppers Drug Mart and most corner stores. He put his pen down on the bench of the picnic table and shook out his hand like it was cramped.

"Anything else?" he said.

"About the emergency backpack? That's about it. I liked having money. I saved more than I spent, I still do. My mother used to pay me with cheques that said *Pierce Gifts & Oddities,* the kind we pay suppliers with. But now my father just writes me a cheque from his personal account. He's says it's all the same money anyway."

"This is very good, darling," said Gil. "Why don't you let me take a look at that notebook of yours as well. If there's more like that, I can certainly use it."

I hesitated a moment and then handed it to him. It was private, but so was what I'd just read to him. His promise of something that would end the blackouts was too tempting.

"Could you even lift the backpack?" he said. "Once you got all that stuff in?"

I said, "I made myself put it on and walk around my room sometimes, at night. When my parents were sleeping. If I couldn't walk for long, I had to get rid of something. That was the rule." The backpack was still in my mind. I could feel the heaviness of it, in the bright grey light while I walked around my room with it on—the midnight street-lamp light.

He said nothing as he stored my notebook away in his bag. When he straightened up, he leaned over and kissed me on the mouth. I pulled away and looked at him. He met my eye and his expression was calm, clear, like he was scoured of anything unnecessary. He leaned in again and this time I didn't move away.

I should feel guilty. Do crazy people not feel guilt?

Gil pulled away and said, "That was just friendly, of course." He gathered up his pen and notebook and said, "I'll be seeing you soon."

Then he set off up the main path towards the playground and the Dundas Street side of Bellwoods. I felt as if I'd been running. The groove above his lip, the curls of hair behind his ears. The kiss had been silly, we wouldn't do that again. It was just symbolic, like a handshake upon accepting a job. This was just talking. Like Dr. Malik. Just more talking. What could it hurt? What could happen had already happened. She was already gone. Talking was all that was left, and surely nothing could come of it. I headed back to the store, one foot in front of the other. The straps of the backpack seem to dissolve from my shoulders. The muscle between my neck and shoulder seemed to loosen slightly. I felt I could breathe better than I had in weeks.

Andrew and I were sitting at his kitchen table later that evening, sorting stacks of photocopies he had made for his research. It was early July, our third anniversary, and we had dinner planned. Things like anniversaries still happened, still had to be celebrated. I'd arrived early to find Andrew working at home and offered to help.

We sorted the papers, plucking out poems from his students that had migrated from his bookbag. Snippets occasionally jumped out at me. *One of his best-known works,* Lamia, *or the possibility that Byron might have known* were mixed up with *her breasts like bowls of cold porridge* and *verdant, vibrant, vivid fields of lonely, lucid beach glass.*

I was debating telling him about Gil—not everything of course, but something. I wanted to. I wanted to show Andrew that someone found me interesting, and that all this could have happened without his having any hand in it.

"I had the strangest customer the other day," I said. "It was really funny."

"All your customers are strange."

"This guy was different. He wanted to know about my mom."

"How is that funny? That sounds odd. And inappropriate."

"No, I think he's just not all there."

"You're too nice for your own good."

"Anyway, it turns out he is a writer."

Andrew immediately relaxed. With a few exceptions among the Beat poets, he was quite certain that all literature worth the paper it was printed on had been written by D-Day. I might as well have told him Gil was a professional nose-picker.

"Well. More power to him," he said, and he laughed a small, low laugh, as if he were allowing himself, just a little bit.

"Yeah. The funny thing is, he wants to write a book about me."

Andrew rubbed his chin unconsciously, leaving a smudge of ink. He had a habit of buying cheap pens from Honest Ed's that invariably ended up leaking. "What?"

"Funny, eh?"

"I think it's creepy. Just make sure you don't tell him anything personal. He sounds like a stalker. Maybe you should stay here more often."

"I'm safe at home."

"Of course. But I do worry about you, being alone in the store."

"At home there are two locks. The store and the apartment. So really, we're safer staying there. I mean, technically."

"Are you trying to make me worry?"

I put down a stack of poems, which I had been gripping too tightly. "I don't know why I'm being an asshole," I said.

"Maggie," he said, shuffling papers. It sounded like a question. He put them down, looked at me.

"I'm sorry," I said, and I was. With Andrew there, Gil seemed like a story I had made up, a childish one.

I left the papers on the table and went and lay down on the sofa. Andrew joined me, sitting up so I could put my head on a pillow in his lap. There was a silence, and the moment teetered in that place where we would either break apart awkwardly or come together, close and closer. We hadn't slept together since before the funeral, more than two months. Andrew hadn't said a word. I thought, *Maybe it would help, maybe that's what I need. To smash up against a headboard for a little while.* In the comics I read as a kid, one knock on the head gave you amnesia and the second brought your memory back. A stray football, a carelessly opened locker, hasty passion between survey course English papers, though I didn't think Archie had ever tried that one. *Why not, why not anything now, why not remember you have a body for a minute?* But I didn't want to take my clothes off, as if some deformity might be revealed.

I opened my mouth to speak, but before I could, Andrew said, "We should get going. Our reservation is at eight."

"Oh," I said. "Right. Let me go get ready. Should we take a cab or the subway?"

"We're celebrating. Let's take a cab."

We got our coats and walked down to Bloor Street and waited for a cab to come by. Finally I saw one, orange and green with a light on top. Andrew stepped into the street and waved two fingers, like a stewardess pointing out exits on a plane. The cab pulled over and we climbed in, weaving along Bloor and then down through Chinatown, towards the lake.

"So that strange guy," Andrew said. "Did he have a name?"

I was looking out the window. I liked being in a taxi and was irritated that Andrew was talking.

"I don't know."

"You don't know if he had a name?"

"I don't remember. It's Gil. That's it."

"Better memory than you thought, I guess."

I turned and looked at him. His face was stuck between defiance and apology, like a child who lets a swear word slip in front of a parent. I turned back to the window.

We arrived, and all in silence, we paid the cab driver, entered the CN Tower and ascended in the softly glowing elevator. Andrew gave his name to the host in the revolving restaurant without looking at me.

When we sat down, he said: "It's just a matter of time. You're going to leave me."

We were both embarrassed to be surrounded by happy vacationers and couldn't remember whose idea it had been to come. We didn't usually go in for tourist spots, or even proper restaurants. We had spent our last anniversary at a bar in Parkdale, where a man lying on the street had grabbed my skirt so hard that it came down to my knees.

"This is about Gil, isn't it."

"Oh, no trouble with the name this time, I notice." I didn't say anything. "And no. This has nothing to do with him. Although it's funny how you brought him up like that."

"I didn't."

"You did. You just did."

I rubbed my eyes; I felt tired. Then I remembered that I had worn dark makeup for the special occasion.

"Is it ruined?" I stared into my soup spoon, the curved reflection making the purpled eye sockets look all the more cavernous.

"It looks like you got mugged. It looks awful." He dipped his napkin into his water glass and handed it to me.

As I mopped at my eyes, I realized to my horror that there were tears running down my face.

"Oh great," I said.

"Are you crying?" Alarm.

"No. Yes. A little."

"It's not that bad. It's so dark in here people can hardly even see. It's fine. Just wipe off the underneath part and no one will even notice."

But now I was sobbing, great big hysterical sobs that drew the surreptitious glances of everyone in the restaurant. Andrew looked even paler than usual and sat frozen in his seat. I felt freakish, as if my hands and mouth, my arms and legs, were somehow obviously and horrifyingly wrong and everyone could see.

"Sorry," I managed to say. "I'm really sorry."

"Hey, hey, it's okay." Andrew grabbed my hand on top of the table. "I'm not mad," he said.

I promptly stopped crying. I stared at him and at his hand, latched onto mine. It was all bone and tendons, dry skin, the fingertips almost flat. Neat and sparse. Andrew believed in neat and sparse. He didn't mind that I was still riding my bike around the city. He believed that everyone was as healthy as he was. And he understood making lists, he got it, the joy of a sharp pencil-point dotting the numbers, nailing them down. He wanted everything to be neat and so did I. If I had been more like him in other ways, how different would things have been?

"Right," I said, the damp napkin still wrinkled in my lap.

Andrew was trying to keep his face neutral, though I could recognize the look surfacing. The look of a man who has won an argument, proved a point. We ate the rest of our meal talking about the university, the store, his students, Wendy, my father.

When we got home to my apartment I crawled into bed in my underpants and blouse, wanting to sleep. Andrew lay beside me in bed. On the other side of the thin wall, my father clanked around in the kitchen, even the tea-making process sounding moody and fitful, precluding any pressure on Andrew and me to rouse ourselves to anniversary romance.

Andrew was turned away from me, and I watched his flanks go up and down for a while. In what seemed like minutes, he was asleep, one arm turned up to the ceiling, resting in a crook above his head. The skin on the underside was even-toned and soft, like it had been smoothed away until almost blank.

I lay there listening through the wall to my father's tea-making noises. *Was he sleeping less these days? Should I be paying attention to that sort of thing?*

But I was already taking care of someone: that familiar anxiety, the constant checking up. Maggie who had struck a bargain with Gil, who had to shove her hands in her pockets to keep from shaking answers out of Dr. Rosenberg. I was stuck watching over her. And I was unfit; at times a part of me wanted to see what she would do next, what Gil would tell her, what she could get away with. At other times, I wished I could drop her off in Dr. Malik's office and pick her up down the road, when she was fixed. Get her out of my hair.

It was Monday, so the store was closed. I called Wendy at work and asked her to meet me at George's after she finished. I got to the diner just before six, slid into a booth, and called a hello to George as he pushed through the swinging doors to the kitchen. George's was a tiny place on College Street with five booths lined up against the windows and six more seats at the counter. His cooking area was open to the restaurant, immaculate behind a high counter and framed by shutters he painted every year. At the register in front of the kitchen pass-through sat the latest clerk. They were always girls from George's Greek Orthodox Church and they rarely spoke much English.

I said hello to the girl, who stared up at me silently from her chair. I waved, feeling idiotic and patronizing. She waved back.

Then Wendy pushed through the door, calling out, "George, my love, I'm here!" and he poked his head out and said, "Honey, you're going to have to be more specific."

"So what's up?" she asked.

"Nothing much. Andrew and I went out to the restaurant in the CN Tower, the one that spins. Revolves."

"Oh, that sounds good. I had a hell of a day yesterday, had to flip a coin to get out of driving to the airport to pick up some director. Thank God I won the coin toss—and on tails too. Somebody up there likes me."

I was, as always, amazed to hear Wendy speaking about her job, which was adult in a way that left me feeling as if time had passed while I wasn't looking. She took out a package of cigarettes, tapped one out, and jerked her head towards the door. We went outside and stood on the apartment stoop beside George's. Wendy flicked her red plastic lighter, inhaled.

"Anything else fun at work?" I asked.

"Not really, it's torture. I should just quit."

"Want to run off and become showgirls in Vegas?"

"Maybe," she said, descending into giggles.

"I'm thinking of leaving Andrew," I said.

Wendy flinched, cut off in her laughter.

"Why?" Then: "Are we really getting into this or just sort of? Because I only have a few cigarettes left."

"I don't know. Just sort of."

"Okay then. Here we go. He's a good man, he'll have a good job, he doesn't cheat, doesn't hit you, doesn't drive like a maniac, gets along with your dad and that's no easy job, he doesn't dress like a clown, he's not an artist of any kind, he's good in bed, balding does not run in his family. And, he's stuck by you like glue through the whole thing with—everything. So what's the problem?" She dropped her cigarette away from her mouth but held onto it. "Andrew might not be Prince Charming, but who is?"

I looked at the cigarette pinched between Wendy's fingers and realized I couldn't tell her the truth. I took a breath to say, "It's not that," but the words faded away in my mouth, unspoken.

"What is it?"

Wendy didn't let me get away with things, or she didn't used to. Lately she had eased off, treating me like an invalid, walking on eggshells. I should have been relieved to be manhandled, but now all I wanted was someone who would believe me, who would help me believe Gil's bizarre claims. Who believed in all kinds of fantastic otherworldly things. Who was that in my life? Even my mother hadn't really believed. Was I turning into one of my nuttier customers? Since when did I think about this kind of thing? I thought of the jade angel, the church from the funeral.

"He's writing a book about me." This was as close to the truth, to Gil's truth, as I was willing to go.

"Who?"

"His name is Gil."

"And you're going to fall for that? Writing a book? Everyone in Toronto is writing a book."

"Fall for it?"

"Maggie, come on. I know you're going through a bit of a slump, but another guy is not the answer. You're going to kick yourself later."

"Slump?"

"Stop that. Come on. Break up with Andrew if you want to, but do it for the right reasons."

"I thought we were doing the short version of the discussion."

Wendy puffed out irritated air, dropped her cigarette and ground it under her heel. "Look, I have to finish some work, but why don't you just sleep on this and we'll talk more tomorrow, okay?"

"Tomorrow?"

"I said stop it. I hate when you do that."

She reached into her purse and pulled out a silk scarf. She wrapped it around her neck, then pulled it off and tried again.

She looked at herself in the glass of the storefront, pulled it off a second time.

"Don't leave, Wen. You just got here. Are you okay?"

She yanked on the ends of the scarf, arranging it so it wouldn't fall into the scoop of her tank top. "Just think about this, okay?"

"Don't go," I said.

She made a little half-turn as if to go, but then she opened the door and we went back inside.

At the table, we sat for a minute, then Wendy called, "George, can you make us a roast beef sandwich?"

I said, "Any news on the romance front?"

"Oh, you know Toronto. They all just get drunk and want to play the guitar for you."

"Nothing good?"

"The last date I had, I let a girl from work set me up. He wasn't so terrible, but he had a really bad head-to-body ratio. You know? Either way—too big, too small—it throws everything off. He did like photo booths, though. That's got some charm."

"But not the great twentieth-century romance?"

"He had aristocratic hands. Really nice. You don't see that every day."

I laughed and the counter girl looked over.

"I'm trying to look on the bright side," said Wendy.

I told her about the three women with the Easter egg–coloured purses, the bad tarot card. The other Elaine.

"Oh yeah, Elaine," said Wendy. Her voice was utterly neutral, light and simple, and then George brought our sandwich and Wendy blew him a kiss. When we were done she tapped another cigarette out, looked at it, and then slid it back into the package.

"Getting a little better, right?"

"What?"

"Only one. And with coffee even. Maybe I should get the patch."

"We've got some herbal stuff at the store. I don't know if it works, though."

After another cup of coffee, she said, "I do have to go now. But call me, okay, if you're going to do anything." She went and put her elbows on the kitchen ledge, called a "good night" to George, and left.

Sitting at the table, finishing first my own coffee—warm—and then the dregs of Wendy's—cold—I doodled in my notebook: spades and clubs, a spiky maple leaf, geometric patterns.

"Where did Wendy go?"

I looked up, startled. George was standing beside the booth, holding the coffee pot. "More?" he said, hoisting it. His apron was off and he was wearing flat-front slacks, dark brown and fashionably cut. I hardly ever saw him below the waist. We usually chatted through the kitchen pass-through.

I realized I'd been biting my thumbnail and put my hand down. "Home, she said."

He poured more coffee into my cup. "You guys seem like you're going through a bit of a rough patch." When I went to protest, he said, "Hey, don't worry, don't worry at all. Friends have their ups and downs just like men and women. Maybe she's going through some stuff."

I said, "My mother died. In May."

"I didn't know. I'm so sorry." He sat down beside me. "Anything I can do?"

"No. I'm okay."

I could feel his thigh against mine, hip to knee. I had known George for almost ten years, through half a dozen paint colours in the restaurant, but I had hardly ever touched him. I didn't know that much about him. I didn't even know how old he was. His black hair had thinned recently, but he wasn't even thirty-five yet, I'd bet. *Gorgeous George* we used to say. We put his name in our notebooks for MASH, the fortune-telling game. One day when I was in first year, I walked in to see him sporting a black eye. When I asked about it, he said, "I got divorced." I hadn't known he was married.

"George, do you think I'm pretty?"

"Sure. Of course. You and Wendy both. Cute as can be."

"Thanks."

"I can't imagine losing my mom," he said. "A mother is a holy thing. She takes care of you even when you're grown, even when you don't know it. You take your time. You're young for that, for losing a mother."

I couldn't see George's expression because we were side by side, but his voice was loose and easy. I saw a wedding band on his hand, which was resting on the table.

"You remarried," I said.

His hand twitched and he fingered the band. "No," he said. "No, I never did." He stood up then and put his hand on my shoulder. "Hang in there. The worst part is over."

"Right," I said. I tried to add "Thanks," but I couldn't keep my voice even.

George just nodded and picked up the coffee pot. "I'll see you soon," he said.

Nine

My father was sitting at the kitchen table when I got home from George's. The radio was on low.

"How was your day?" he said as he got up. He gave me a kiss on the cheek. "Are you hungry?"

"I'm fine. I'll just get something to drink."

"I made some iced tea. It's not very sweet, though." He was still standing up, and he wiped his hands on his pants. He was wearing a grey tie, tightly knotted.

I poured myself some iced tea and sat with my hands wrapped around the short, sweating glass.

He stood by the window and picked up a glass from the sill. The liquid was lighter than the iced tea, the same colour as the ginger drops we sold in the store. Scotch, I guessed.

"So how is your therapy going? Or do you not talk about it? I don't know how it works." He sipped the last of his drink and took the bottle of scotch from the cupboard. He poured a scant finger into his empty glass.

I drank down the rest of my iced tea, which had a slightly dusty aftertaste. "It's okay, I guess. How is work?"

"Actually, I'm working on a new book."

Startled, I straightened up, banged my elbow on the chair. "A book?"

"Didn't I mention it? Rabelais. It's just another biography, of course, but I'm hoping I can add something. Sort of a linguistic approach rather than deconstructionist. It's nice to be working in French again." He shrugged apologetically, knowing I'd hardly gotten past *le crayon est sur le livre* and *puis-je aller à mon casier?*

"That sounds good, Dad. I hope it goes really well."

He put his glass down. "Do you want to see the manuscript?" He added immediately, "There's not much to it yet. You know how slow I am on the computer." He wiggled his fingers in a typing motion.

"In your office here?"

"It's upstairs, yes."

I stood up. "Sure." I wasn't often in my father's office. Like the storage room, it had a gabled ceiling, and my father had built shelves himself so they just fit in, heavy with books and old typewriters. There was one large window above his desk and an old, beige word processor. I touched the corner of his desk when we walked in. It was recently dusted.

"So where is your manuscript?"

"Oh," he said. "Here it is," and he ran his thumb along the edge of a small stack of printed papers. "So much work for such a little pile."

"I'm sure it will be really good when it's done."

"Maybe, maybe." He had sat down in his chair. "So how are you these days? Is your hand feeling better now?"

"It's okay. A little stiff sometimes." I wished we would go back to the kitchen.

"Do you have any plans now? For the future?"

"Plans? What do you mean?"

"I thought, maybe now that—I know it's difficult—thought you might want to get your own place, or move in with Andrew, or what have you."

"Do you not want me to live here?" He looked small in the chair. His hair was a brighter grey, almost silver, as if he'd put a rinse in it, but I couldn't imagine my father doing something so frivolous.

"That's not what I meant at all," he said. "I am only trying—" He shook his head and seemed to stop, but then he wrapped his hands around the edge of his seat, beside his thighs in their creased dark slacks. He was dressed up, I realized. *For this talk?* I felt something like pain radiating from the bottom of my rib cage. "Your mother made sure I never had a chance with you," he said. "Mean old man." His face looked grey, pulled down. There was a pleat on his jaw line, one on each side. "I wish you could have known her when I met her. She was selling god-damn jewellery on the street outside the store. I thought I was such a beatnik but she saw right through me. It was different then. You didn't get points for working hard, it all had to seem effortless." He moaned, and it was a guttural sound, a sound that embarrassed me, prickling my skin. He was speaking more quickly than usual. "I never thought she would do it. I never thought she would do anything. She was just there, she was always there."

I didn't know if he meant marry him or kill herself. What had he thought her incapable of?

I saw them as they must have been once: a professor, young for his job but not young, not anymore, not compared to her. And her, blissed out and beautiful, smiling her absent smile. Lily of the field, no toiling or spinning to be seen, if you don't want to look. I'd seen photos of her, beads in her hair, little sunglasses, a bright shirt tied up under her breasts, the long skirt. Bare feet, the whole bit. He must have taken the pictures. I never thought of that; I thought they had simply arrived from the country of the past like a guidebook, complete and utterly true. Here and there a photo of him, fourteen years older than her. Shirt open at the neck, tie stuffed into his pocket, headband tied on like a third arm, extraneous and unbelievable. There were always spreading blotches of sunlight in his photos, the few photos there were of him, zinging through the lens to bloom on the film. Bleached out even in the moment.

He wasn't likeable the way she was, he wasn't young when she was. I didn't want to think about what things were like for him—it wasn't a surly, childish desire not to pity him, but a wild, panicked desperation to block out anything he might be thinking. I could feel it, physically, in my chest, as if thin cords were being pulled, cutting into me. I wanted to shut him out.

It wasn't a time I had ever asked about, or thought about. Were there friends then? He didn't have any now, only colleagues at the university. No one came to our apartment; he didn't drink beer with other men or bowl or golf. He'd done everything he was supposed to do; he was a success in his field. But all my mother had to do was stand behind the counter and she was adored. I had always thought I was more like her, because I didn't get his work ethic or braininess.

I knew he was looking at me, but I couldn't look up. He opened the top drawer of his desk, the one that had a keyhole. I'd never seen it open. Inside I saw another bottle like the one downstairs, empty. Beside it was a wooden box. The box he took out and put on the desk.

"I never told you about this," he said. "We used to fight about it. She didn't like it." He opened the box, which had a hinged top. Inside was a gun, an old-fashioned revolver with a thin snout. I stepped back.

"I wanted her to keep it downstairs. I thought, around here, at night, with those nuts down the street, you never know." He seemed to have forgotten I was, myself, one of the nuts from down the street. "But she wouldn't have it anywhere near her." He peered at me again. "Do you hear what I'm saying? I tried to give your mother a gun." He stressed the last word. "I really didn't get it. I thought it was all that hippie-dippy bull-shit: don't want to hurt a fly. I really loved her, I really really love her."

He took the gun out and my expression must have been horrible because his mouth twisted up on one side in an uncontrolled way. He put the gun back in the box, and the box in the drawer, which he locked.

"I never even bought bullets," he said. "That's the kind of man your father is."

I had a sudden vision of myself, ministering to him. Cooking him something hearty, trimming his bright hair, a pair of sewing scissors at the back of his neck. Carefully, carefully; I wouldn't knick him. Sweeping his office, tucking a blanket around him.

But when he put his head down on his arms, I took my opportunity and fled down the stairs. I went all the way to the ground floor and ran out through the store, barely pausing to lock the front door. For a moment I stood on the spot, just outside the store, unmoored. I wanted to run full force into someone, to see if I could knock someone down. I wanted to feel the bruising wall of a chest, unmoving. Gil's chest, slightly damp: a breath of dark hair, rough skin.

Across the street in the park, people sat on the grass, the benches. They shared Slurpees from the 7-Eleven or, furtively, slim bottles of wine in paper bags. Here and there a lighter flared in the dim light, people smoking cigarettes and surreptitious joints. And then there, a face illuminated, dark curls and the deep groove above his lip somehow visible even from far away. He was the one bright point in the dark that was more than night, suddenly descending. There was a feeling in my chest like a bloom of light. *Get to him.* I started to run.

Gil and I were sitting on the floor in the little backroom of the store. His sturdy legs were stretched out in front of him, the knees and ankles narrow with dramatic bones, like something made of driftwood.

"How did I get here?"

"I was in the park. In Bellwoods."

"How did you find me?"

"I don't have a lot of other things going on these days. Besides, I said I would come see you at the store, remember?"

The ceiling creaked overhead and I flinched.

"So this other doctor, this Rosenberg, he knew your mother?"

"And my father." The image of my father's head on his folded arms went through my head like sheet lightning. "I don't know exactly how well or anything. But he knew them."

"Well, it's obvious what the next step is then, darling. You get rid of your nice-guy therapist and get in with the one who knew Carol. Get some information from him."

I closed my eyes. I didn't even remember starting this conversation. I had a feeling like the overlap between my mind and body wasn't quite precise, a drunken expansive feeling. "Yes," I said, "I don't like him. But I think he knows something."

Gil got up, helped me to stand, and then went to the door. Just inside he stopped expectantly. When I didn't move, he hugged me, pressed all up and down against me, and I could feel the sliding muscles under his shoulder blades, the soft pressure of his stomach pressed against me.

I went to my next session with Dr. Malik and did it quickly, before he had a chance to say anything. Throwing him over for Dr. Rosenberg felt like a breakup. Poor Dr. Malik and his little eyebrow crease. I thanked him, apologized, tearing nervously at the rim of my usual paper cup of water. *I appreciate everything you've done for me. But.* And he was so kind, all slow nods and

If you feel it would be beneficial. And so I made the phone calls, set up the new appointment, and turned up at Dr. Rosenberg's office on Monday evening, ten minutes before seven.

His office was smaller than Dr. Malik's, and there was a rattan basket chair with a thick cushion for me to sit in. I sat down, eyeballing Rosenberg. As before, his black beard was carefully trimmed and his fingernails were very tidy.

"Welcome, Maggie." Before he sat down, he shook my hand by grasping it tightly, no movement.

I wondered if he had his beard trimmed professionally. Or maybe he was a beauty school dropout prior to medical school. He looked more like a hairdresser than a doctor anyway. I kept my lips clamped together until he settled into his chair and spoke.

"I was a little surprised to hear from you."

"I liked your suggestion about keeping a journal. I do it and— it seems to help. I thought maybe you could help—more."

"More than Dr. Malik?"

"Just more," I said. "You knew my mother. I thought you might understand better."

"Before we get started," he said, "I need to make something clear to you. I knew your mother. Not very—not well, but I did know her. Even if you're not participating in the residency program at Wooster House, we still need to discuss this if I am going to treat you." I started to protest but he went on. "Then again, I feel I am uniquely qualified to deal with unusual manifestations of grief, which might describe your recent experiences. Particularly problems associated with memory.

However, if you're uncomfortable in any way, just say the word."

"So you did know her."

He shifted like a man trying to fart discreetly. "A long time ago, yes. I was a war resister and your mother—well, we both ended up in Toronto. I spent some time in what is now your store. If you feel the personal connection is too—"

"When was this?"

"Before you were born. Late sixties, early seventies."

"What was she like?" I had trouble picturing the two of them. I could see my mother, I knew what she looked like from photos, her long dark waves parted by her tanned shoulders. But I couldn't imagine Rosenberg younger than he was, certainly not casual, sitting cross-legged, headbands and peace beads. He'd have been as poor a fit as my father.

"Maggie," he said. "I don't want you to think of me as your mother's friend. I want you to think of me as your friend. And also your doctor. Your friend and your doctor. I can be both."

"She used to sing little songs when she was bored. Did she ever do that when you knew her?"

"What I mean, Maggie, is that we're here to talk about you, and your feelings. There is an impulse sometimes, to try and hoard information about a person we've lost, as if we can reconstruct them. But getting information from me isn't going to make anything easier. It might make things harder. We're here to manage your grief, and in your special case, these blackouts."

I was irritated. "You're not going to tell me anything about her?"

"Did you have any blackouts before she passed away?"

"No. Never." I couldn't believe he wasn't going to tell me. How could knowing things make it harder? Knowing things was what I needed—what were the blackouts but the opposite of knowing? I had an impulse to leave that very minute and go read over my notebooks, to call Gil and tell him our plan wasn't going to work.

"No amnesia? No fainting?"

"Never until the first time, when I fainted in the store." Mulishly, I added, "My mother fainted sometimes. Once she hit her head on the floor and had to get stitches."

"How did you feel about that? Were you scared?"

"My father was there."

"And you weren't scared because he was there?" When I didn't answer, he said, "It's important, though, Maggie, that I confirm you're comfortable having me as a therapist despite my having known your mother. You can change your mind any time. The important thing is that you know you're in a safe, impartial place."

"I'm fine. It's fine. Really."

He relaxed into his seat and pushed the pleats on his slacks into a straighter line. "Mount Sinai sent the results of your MRI. There was a very slightly increased activity level in the posterior region, and a decreased level in the anterior, but nothing that worried me. I think that the traditional psychiatric approach is not what will be most effective here. Are you open to trying some alternative methods?"

"So it was normal? The MRI?" I didn't know whether to be relieved or not.

"There was nothing that worried me. Now. Have you ever heard of something called the Journey Technique? Sometimes called the Mental Walk?" I shook my head no. "It's a memory technique. What spaces are most familiar to you? Is there a place near your home you go to a lot?"

"I go to the park a lot, when it's nice."

"That's perfect. Think of the park. There's a path, yes? Think of the landmarks you know along the path. Picture them clearly."

I thought of the white stone gates, the flowerbeds, the community centre, the playground, the north valley, all of it unfolding before me like I was there.

"At each of those landmarks, you can place something. Something you want to remember. Then when you need to remember, you walk along the path. In your mind. And you see the things you're trying to memorize."

"I don't understand. What's the point of this?"

"The point is that your memory is controlling you. This will help you control your memory."

His voice had gone quieter. I wondered where in the States he was from. Wherever it was, he'd done a job to get rid of the accent. If anything, he over-enunciated, his *T*s too crisp, like little flicks against your ears, almost British in inflection. I remembered my father said he'd gone to Cambridge. I wasn't picturing the walk through the park anymore. Instead I wondered what Dr. Rosenberg had eaten for breakfast, what time he had gotten up, if he was vain about his education. He struck me as a man who wouldn't sweat during sex. He wasn't effeminate, but he was prim.

He was eyeing me. I felt like he could read my mind. I tried to think of something banal, but all I could picture while he stared was Gil in the dim store. *He must know something about her. Tell him he can help you. He'll eat it up.*

"What am I supposed to be memorizing?"

"Why don't you try with these?" He took out a deck of Rider-Waite tarot cards, new and still wrapped in plastic.

I unwrapped them and shuffled them into a random order.

"Let's try twenty cards," Dr. Rosenberg said. *Twen-tee.* "Picturing the images in an exaggerated way can help with the memorization."

I counted them out, placing them along the path in my mind. A huge empress at the gates, three enormous pentacles heaped in the flowerbed, ten wands leaning against the swing set, and so on and so on. The time went by slowly. I got distracted by the meanings of the cards. Pentacles for the body, the home, health and money. Cups for emotions, visions, illusions. Swords for thoughts, speech, communication, the mind. Wands for passion, ambition, desire, career. Creative endeavours. I shook my head as if that would help clear it. After a few minutes Rosenberg held out his hand for the cards and I passed them to him.

"Now go along your path," he said, "and remember what is what."

I tried, attempting to reconstruct the picture I had built while looking at the cards. On my first try I got eight right. He made me try again and I got ten.

"Fifty percent," I said. "I guess Mensa won't be wooing me anytime soon."

"It's a very good first attempt," he said. He tented his fingers in his lap. He said, "I'm writing a book."

Another book. I stifled the impulse to laugh. "A book. What is it about?"

"I'm interested in the intersection between memory and grief. And also in alternative spirituality, things you're familiar with through your mother's store. Have you ever heard people talk about the statistically proven benefits of prayer? It was quite a breakthrough when they first published those papers."

"If you don't mind me asking, why are you telling me this?"

"I want to be honest with you. I'm interested in helping you, Maggie, but you might be able to help me too. All the people in my personal group out at Wooster House have agreed to participate, anonymously of course, in particular sections of my upcoming publication. The blackouts you're suffering are truly unique, and combined with your background, the store. Do you believe in the items you sell?"

I pictured myself, shot straight on, face blurred. *Subject's use of tarot cards, jade figurines and bizarre interpersonal relationships creates winning healing formula. It's a scientific breakthrough!*

"I don't know if I believe it all, exactly. But I think it's good to know it. I think it's better to know it than not to."

He leaned forward onto his elbows, then seemed to catch himself and sat back, smoothing his tie. "That's very much of interest to me. I remember your mother had quite an encyclopedic knowledge of much of the stock at your store."

"She had a very good memory. Better than mine."

"I think we could really help each other," he said. "Of course, I do think you ought to consider our residency option. With your blackouts, I have serious concerns for your safety if you continue to operate independently."

"I'm okay, Dr. Rosenberg. I appreciate your concern. I would like to meet again, though, here in the city."

He nodded. "Well, just remember you have options." I went to stand up but he said, "Why don't we talk a little more before you go? Since I took up quite a bit of our time with the exercise."

"Well, I have to meet up with my boyfriend soon."

"Why don't you tell me about Andrew."

"I already told Dr. Malik. Didn't he send you stuff when I switched to you?"

"I've read your file."

"So you know. He's my boyfriend. Pretty basic."

"What is your relationship with Andrew like during this difficult time? Are you sleeping together?"

I stared at him. "That's kind of personal."

"I don't want to make you uncomfortable, of course, Maggie. But sex is no more personal than any other expression of the self. Sex is a part of the whole person, and it's nothing to be ashamed of."

"Oh, well then," I said. "Sign me up as the town bicycle. I'll express myself like a house on fire."

"Humour can be a deflecting tool." He said *humour* as if it were in little quotes. "That's enough from the peanut gallery," my father would say when I was talking too much on car trips.

"No," I said. "I haven't been in the mood."

"And there is nothing wrong with that, of course. Sex and death have a strange connection. Sometimes the presence of death can leave us erotically charged, eager to remind ourselves that we are very much alive. Sometimes it kills the sex drive altogether. Body confusion is very common in these situations. I'm sure you know that in French 'little death' is a euphemism for the orgasm."

Rosenberg was a little flushed. He was either embarrassed or excited, I didn't know which was worse. *Oh wow. I'm in therapy with a Cambridge-educated shrink and I'm getting the same advice provided in the editorial column in* Cosmopolitan.

I couldn't help but remember the feel of Gil's mouth on mine in the park, the feeling I got seeing his arms and legs, the way the soft curve of his belly against mine in the store had felt like some great mercy. I couldn't whip myself up for Andrew's sparse, too-correct frame. Beside him, recently, I felt squashed and mangled.

"It's a rich tapestry, I'm sure," I said. There was a little *beep* and Rosenberg looked at his watch.

"It appears our time is up," he said. He stood and shook my hand in his dead-weight manner again, and I opened the door and left.

Ten

*T*he vanilla fight was one of the few times I actually heard my parents argue, really argue, not just pick at each other the way they usually did.

I was about thirteen, and we'd spent the morning taking inventory in the store and were nearly finished when she lifted her chin and said, "I have to make a cake."

Occasionally compulsions overtook my mother and she would become determined to paint the store or redo the window display, or to learn to crochet or make cheese. When she got an idea into her head it was impossible to get her to think about anything else, they could turn into manias like a cold turning to pneumonia.

"Why?" She liked to make cakes, and was good at it, but I couldn't remember anything special about that particular day.

"Just a regular cake. We can use Grandma's recipe."

"What recipe?"

"I don't know where the paper is. But I remember it."

She went to the bottom of the stairs and rang the doorbell we had rigged up to chime in the apartment. My father came tearing down a moment later with a spoon in his hand.

"What's wrong?"

When my mother explained, he didn't look pleased. "Just the store and back, right?" he said.

"You'll be less cranky when you're eating delicious chocolate cake," she said, and she picked up a cinnamon bath-ball and pressed it under her nose.

He put his hands loosely on the counter, and his shoulders eased down.

"That sounds great." To me he said, "Just the cake."

We walked to the nearby supermarket, where my mother slung a basket over her arm.

"Your grandma made the most beautiful cakes," she said, her voice going soft and wide. She had left Georgia during what she called "the War," which meant Vietnam. Over the years the slow Southern liquid faded from her speech, but whenever she spoke of her parents it returned.

When she picked up her ingredients, she used both hands and placed them carefully into the basket on the ground, before lifting it again.

"Can I carry that for you?" I reached out for it. We were standing in front of an open cooler full of eggs and margarine and I could see the fine stipple of goosebumps on her arms.

"I know brown eggs are no different than the white ones," she said, "but they're nicer somehow. We had chickens. Some of them were so grand you wouldn't believe it, fluffy as a cat; sometimes you could get them to sit in your lap."

I withdrew my hand. "In your lap? Didn't they scratch?"

We moved into the baking aisle.

"What am I forgetting?" My mother stopped, put her hand against her forehead. Two other women had to turn sideways to get by.

"Eggs, sugar, we've got flour at home. Sour milk. Cocoa. Vanilla. We just have to get the vanilla."

There was a blank row on the shelf beside the little plastic bottles of food dye and flavourings. Cinnamon and licorice, mint, banana. I wanted the banana; I didn't like chocolate cake. I knew how to make pudding, I could make banana pudding. My mother was silent beside me. I didn't suggest pudding.

"They're out of vanilla."

"No," I said, alarmed. I showed her the little dark bottle. "It's right here."

"That's artificial vanilla."

"What's the difference? It will taste fine. It will taste good, Mom."

"No one should have to use fake vanilla," said my mother, and she started to cry. "It's sad that it even exists."

I stroked her back, but I was looking wildly around the aisles. What if I saw someone from school.

We stood in the aisle, my hand hot around the plastic of the fake vanilla bottle. I said, "Mom, Mom, Mom . . ." and her head hung down as if she was made of uncooked dough, the slow, chilled flop of it. She had turned away from me and I could see the top knob of her spine, in the back of her neck, pale in the dark web of hair.

Another woman stopped and took my mother by the shoulders, turning her towards me.

"What is it?" she said. "Do you need help?"

My mother shook her head, her mouth wide open; I could see the pink flesh of her tongue, a crystalline string of spit. The woman had a bright yellow purse on a gold-coloured chain-link strap.

"It's ruined," said my mother.

The woman pulled my mother close to her and inhaled deeply. "Are you drunk?" She looked at me. "Is this your little girl?"

"She's fine," I said. "She is just upset. They're out of vanilla."

"It's right there," she said, pointing.

"That's the wrong kind." I put back the bottle I held and it teetered against the green food dye. "My mother only uses real vanilla."

The woman took my mother's hand. "Is it a guy?" she said in a whisper. She was touching her face, brushing my mother's hair back. "Can I call somebody?"

My mother's hand came up and caught the other woman's.

"You have beautiful hands," she said to the startled woman. "Thank you for being so kind. I'm sorry if I upset you." She wasn't crying anymore.

The woman snatched her hand back as if my mother's touch were hot. She didn't move for a moment, but then she hitched the gold chain of her purse up on her shoulder and went down the aisle. She stopped, looking at a tin of soup and back at us. Then she disappeared around the corner.

"Mom?"

"I'll just use some orange zest instead," she said. She picked up her basket from the floor where she had put it down.

I wiped my nose on the back of my hand and went after her.

At the checkout, she took a Mars bar and placed it on top of the carton of eggs. I looked at it and then at her, but she was staring somewhere past the middle-aged cashier, her wet face serene. I wondered if the cashier had children, if she cried when she did her own grocery shopping. Maybe she was allowed to do it at night, after the store was closed. I wanted to ask her something but didn't know what, so I pushed my greasy bangs up off my forehead and said nothing.

We walked home slowly, as if she had to concentrate to make her arms and legs do what she wanted. I offered to carry the groceries but she shook me off. It took an age to walk less than a mile.

The first thing my father said when we got back was "Where have you been?" I looked at the clock and saw it had been almost two hours since we left.

"We're making a cake," she said. He came around the counter and looked at her closely.

"You've been crying," he said. He sounded exasperated, like she'd been playing in the mud.

"Vanilla," she said, her voice faltering. "They had the fake vanilla."

"Mom," I said. "Why don't we get the cake started? We can bring Dad down a piece when it's done."

I went to take the paper grocery bag from her, but she surprised me by clamping down on it and pulling it away. I tore it without meaning to, and the eggs dropped and broke, the buttermilk and sugar thumping undamaged on the wood. The Mars bar landed belatedly after dangling for a second on the torn edge of the bag.

We all looked at it for a moment in its black glossy wrapper. I moved away, towards the stone animals. I picked up the elephant, a warm rose quartz, and closed my hand around it. My father picked up the Mars bar and went back to the counter, turning it over and over in his hands. He looked up.

"Fake vanilla set you off," he said. "But you're eating this junk. Don't you think that's a little hypocritical? A little unfair to us?"

My hand was sweating against the smooth stone. He said, "All I want is a little goddamn consistency," and he threw the candy bar at her. It hit her forehead and bounced off, leaving a tiny little red mark on her skin.

I turned and fled up the stairs. At the top, I opened the door to the apartment and stood for a moment. Then I pushed it closed and walked quietly back to the top of the stairs. I could hear them, and as I crouched down in a squat, I could see them, my father's face and the back of my mother's head.

"Consistency is being honest to yourself in the moment," she said. "Consistency is loving yourself."

My father looked like he was struggling with himself. His chin flinched forward. "You are so much smarter than all this bullshit."

"No, I'm not."

"You were."

She turned and I saw her mouth was moving strangely.

"You're an idiot," she said, without turning to him, her voice flat. "You are so scared of anybody asking you what you really think. You have no idea what you think. You're just jealous."

It was unlike anything I'd ever heard her say. I rubbed my finger down the elephant's back. I petted and petted the stone elephant until it tumbled from my hands, clinking down the stairs. Both my parents turned at the sound, but while my father turned like someone startled, my mother turned smoothly, turned while falling, her eyes going back in her head even as her body leaned towards the sound, towards me. My father jerked back and almost caught her. The sound of her head against the floor was like a door being slammed.

My father had his arms around her, sitting her up, he was both looking at her and not looking at her. He said to me, "It's okay. She's going to be fine. Head wounds bleed a lot, but she's okay." Where her forehead had hit the floor, blood appeared and covered one closed eye. It looked fake, like TV.

I ran into the apartment, leaving the elephant and my mother on the floor for my father to deal with.

He brought her back two hours later with three black prickly stitches tied deftly shut above her eyebrow. I had locked the door to the store and cleaned up the blood, throwing the rag out when I was done. You couldn't tell where it had been; most of it had been on her face, only a little on the floor. The elephant I had thrown out. It was broken into several pieces, each one a pinkish-white gem glinting from the floor. The edges were incredibly sharp.

Gil sat cross-legged on the end of my bed. He stuck his pen behind his ear, finished taking notes.

"Wait, did you hear that?" I held up my hand. "I thought my dad was on campus."

"Let's focus here," he said quietly.

"Just shut up for a second."

"Any luck with Rosenberg?"

"I said shut up."

"Darling. You are so lucky I am here, because you clearly need help staying on track."

"Maggie?" My father's voice came through the door.

Leaning forward, I grabbed Gil by a handful of shirt and hustled him under the bed.

"Just a second." I opened the door and leaned on it. "How are you? I thought you were working?"

"I couldn't get a moment of peace today. The department head is hunting for someone to chair a new scholarship panel and seems to have forgotten about my upcoming sabbatical."

He'd mentioned taking a year off before everything had happened, but I didn't know it was for sure. This would mean more of his new, constant presence in the apartment and the store. The balance of home was shifting; Andrew and my father talking over the dinner table, my mother's blue ceramic bowls gathering dust. It was hard to watch as it un-became her place, as her essence diminished, the smell of her ginger shampoo evaporated.

"So that's all settled?"

"It's been planned for a while. I'll need the time to work on the book." He stood there a moment longer, then stepped back. We hadn't mentioned our exchange in his office since it happened, nor the gun in his desk. "Well, I just wanted to see how you were."

"I'm good. Just making some notes. Store stuff." I backed into my room and closed the door slowly.

"More books," I said, as Gil slithered out from under the bed, brushing off dust bunnies. "Everybody is writing a book. All books all the time. This is a bit much."

"Academic books," said Gil, stressing the first word. "Totally different."

"Rosenberg too, though? It's like it's the only game in town."

I gathered my hair off my neck and put it up with a hair tie from my bedside table. Even though it was after dark, my room was still too hot. It was only mid-July and there was plenty more humidity yet to come. Both Gil and I were down to shorts and T-shirts. Rosenberg's Ts. *Cambridge T*-shirts. Tea shirts. I laughed to myself.

"What's funny?"

"Just—Rosenberg. Him and his book and his grand plans for research breakthroughs."

"But you didn't tell him anything about me, did you?"

"I don't think it's advisable to tell your therapist about your— whatever you are. Have you—" I looked sideways at him. "Have you ever seen those movies where a little girl in a new house starts talking to a friend no one else ever seems to come across?"

"You're worried I'm not real? Then why did I have to hide? If I'm part of your psychosis, then I'd appreciate not being shoved under your bed."

"I'm not psychotic."

"Darling, pick a side here. If you're hallucinating me, I think that counts as a gold-plated pass to Club Psychotic, no?"

"We could go out to the park. As a test. All you have to do is introduce yourself to a few strangers and I'll stop bothering you."

He shook his head. "You're wasting time."

"You know, if someone offered me the chance to prove that I existed, I would probably take it."

"Okay, then prove it."

"Me? I know I exist. You're the one who needs to—"

Gil cut me off. "Interacting with people other than you isn't of any use to me right now. I don't need to prove anything, to myself or anyone else. But since you bring it up, I'm curious. How could you prove to me, beyond a shadow of a doubt, that you really exist?"

I laughed again, incredulous. "That's completely circular," I said. "By that logic, no one could prove anyone exists." Gil didn't say anything. "Fine," I said. I knew I sounded sullen. I knew I was right but I didn't know how to talk around it. I didn't like the idea of rhetoric, of words besting meaning.

Gil came and sat beside me at the head of the bed.

"I'm sorry if I'm not going easy on you like everyone else," he said. "But I'm not really interested in your feelings. I have a job to do."

I found this perversely reassuring, and I reached out and squeezed his forearm. It was papery-skinned with a long hard muscle underneath. He was pale but unlike Andrew, who was almost translucent; there was a purplish undertone to Gil's skin, a waiting bruise. He was solid, like the dark meat of a Thanksgiving turkey. When I put my hand on Andrew's face, there was a hollow between his gaunt cheek and my palm. I knew it was unfair to fault him for it, nothing more than a fast metabolism, but over the recent weeks I'd grown tired of the hardness of his body, the bony angles and my static view of his clavicle. His blondness, tallness and paleness exhausted me. I found myself having to look harder and harder, it seemed, to see that he was there. The whiteness of his eyelashes was approaching a personal affront. But Gil was easy to see. Comfortable. He was like unfinished pine.

On the bed, he put his mouth to my ear.

"It's okay to think about him."

"I know it is. He's my boyfriend. You're the one I shouldn't think about. And anyway, I'm not. I wasn't. How did you know?"

"I understand you gave up a lot. To give up a normal relationship to work with me is—a sacrifice."

He put one hand on my hip, holding the side of my body so the bone pressed against the middle of his palm. He didn't move the hand or do anything at all. I had meant to say *What do you mean give up*, but I was suddenly tired.

"You need to go. I can't do any more today."

He looked ready to fight, but then he just got up, sliding his notebook into a canvas bag he'd brought with him. I went to check that my father was upstairs in his office, and then guided Gil down through the store and out onto the street. Then I went back inside and locked the door.

I should have stayed in the store and tidied up, or at least brought some of the newer catalogues up with me to look at, but instead I climbed the stairs to my room, where I lay in bed, thinking about what Gil had said as he was leaving, which was nothing at all, just his eyes on me, unsmiling.

Dr. Rosenberg's beard was uneven on one side. I couldn't stop looking at it.

"No new blackouts these last few days?"

"No, nothing." Each bristle was thick, like a brush stroke. The uneven edge made his face seem lopsided. He looked like a line drawing done on a flat table, lacking perspective.

"Can you think of anything that might trigger the episodes? Do they happen during times of stress?"

I didn't respond during the pause he offered. He was looking out the window when he asked, plucking unconsciously at the pleats on his pants. I continued to sit in silence.

"Do you believe in the afterlife, Maggie?"

"I don't know." I had hardly spoken during the session and my voice came out with a wheeze underneath it.

"Your mother's store."

"It's my store now."

"Of course," he said. "What I meant was, do you ever think about that sort of thing?"

"Sometimes. I like the cards. And the animals, the stone ones. I have a zircon cat, but now zircon just makes me think— Anyway, I think those things are important, that they deserve respect, whatever the answers are. Did my mother ever talk about that sort of thing when you knew her?"

Rosenberg leaned back in his chair. "Dealing with this loss and your blackouts. That must be a lot for someone your age. Confusing." I shifted to fold my feet under my thighs and the chair wobbled. "Remember what I told you about my research?"

"I remember."

"I'm very interested in the way memory can inform people's healing process. I've been doing some informal activities with some of the patients in Wooster House. But you are in a unique position." A flush was creeping up his face, as if it had originated in his now-imperfect beard. "If you would be willing to help me with my research, I would be very grateful."

"Me personally? What do I need to do?"

"When you interpret tarot cards, you're using your memory in a sophisticated way—both drawing on memorized information and synthesizing. So what I'd like is for you to let me observe you using the cards. Just observe and ask some questions. You'd be free to answer or not answer as you choose."

He was wearing a pink golf shirt, with a small bird embroidered above the pocket. I wondered if he had bought it himself. Or a wife had, or a daughter. He leaned towards me with his elbows on his knees.

"I thought we might start with a session this week, if you're comfortable."

"I'm in the store most days other than Monday. Until at least six-thirty. And I'm already here twice a week in the evening."

"Evenings are fine. Preferable, even. I'm at Wooster House during the day most of the time. If it's a schedule issue, maybe you could just stay a little while after your Thursday night sessions?"

I rubbed the curve of my basket chair with my knuckles. "I guess maybe." I inched forward. "How long?"

"Not more than twenty minutes or so."

I inched a little more. "Twenty minutes?"

"I can count on you, right, Maggie?"

I shifted my weight again and the bowl of the chair toppled

off its base, spilling me onto the floor. The cushion, surprisingly heavy, flopped on top of me.

Rosenberg hitched his slacks up on his thighs and knelt down to help me. The sun was still up and it was warm but overcast, a dingy sort of day. Rosenberg and I were both on our hands and knees for a moment and I could smell his aftershave, a thick, dark smell. He righted the chair bowl with one hand and wrestled the heavy, formless pillow back in.

After settling back in his chair, he said, "Are you all right? No bumps or bruises?"

"I'm fine." For the first time the bowl chair struck me as a bad idea in this context. Wouldn't a relaxed armchair, a couch, something less treacherous be better?

He was smiling down at me, genuinely pleased about this meeting we'd set up. I'd never seen him look so good-natured.

"Why don't we try the Journey Technique again. Do you think you can remember the cards from our last session?" His face was gentle, and I was almost relaxed by the sound of his voice. His *T*s seemed less pointed. He put his hand up in the air and said, "Just walk along the path."

I tried and got eight cards again.

Rosenberg said, "That's very good. Very good indeed. Now, there's something else I think might be helpful."

"For your research?"

"No, no. I mean to your healing process." He poured more water into my cup from a glass pitcher. Unlike Dr. Malik, he gave me a real glass, heavy and spotless. "I think you should go back to the Don River at some point if you haven't yet. Go and see it, give yourself a moment to say goodbye to your mother in the place where she was last alive. Face that place, so that you don't become afraid of it."

I got up, rubbing my elbow. It was still sore from falling off the chair. "I don't see how that would help me."

"It might help, it might not. But I think it's a worthwhile exercise, Maggie. Like the journals. You're finding that helpful, aren't you? And there's one more thing." He got up and opened a drawer in his desk. "I'd like you to use this before our next Monday appointment." He handed me a Polaroid camera. "Take photos of things that make you feel good. There's no right or wrong. And if you do go to the river, take a photo while you're there as well. I find this can be a useful tool through which to discuss things with more—private patients. You're a private person, aren't you, Maggie?"

I held the camera. "You want me to take photos of anything that makes me happy?"

He smiled at me, his mouth rising to the exact same angle on either side. "If you would indulge me," he said.

"And when I stay later to help you—"

"That's unrelated. That's just an academic exercise, so to speak. For my book. Can you stay a little longer next week, then?"

I nodded, stowing the camera in my purse. "Dr. Rosenberg, did my mother already own the store when you met her?"

"I arrived a little earlier than that. I can't recall the name of the owner before her. But it was always known as your mother's place anyway; she was always working. Everyone knew it as her place." He seemed so pleased about my agreement to help with his research that he wasn't even scolding me for asking about her.

"Do you know why she left Georgia?"

"She didn't talk about it, as far as I recall. She came on her own, I know, which was a little unusual—a lot of the women were there with boyfriends and husbands or brothers. War resisters."

"Draft dodgers?" I said.

Rosenberg frowned. "I'm sure this is all familiar to you, Maggie. We're done for today. I hope you do take my advice about going to the river."

He got up out of his armchair and moved behind his desk, opening a file of papers. "Thank you for coming," he said, and I was clearly dismissed.

$$© ©$$

I took the camera down to the store with me Friday morning, but it sat untouched under the counter all day. After closing I met Andrew and Wendy on the back patio of The Done Right Inn, a bar close to the store, where they'd ordered a round of dark beer.

I stuck my finger in the foam on top of my pint and licked it clean. Wendy laughed and so I took a photo of her but she looked slightly awkward because I'd missed the real smile and she'd posed a little. The photo developed slowly on the table while we finished the pitcher, Wendy giving her usual performance, opting for work stories rather than tales of bad dates since Andrew was there. I told them about the camera and the

Journey Technique and they tried it with their own items and locations, Andrew's at the university and Wendy's in the market, and they could hardly remember anything. Wendy laughed about it and Andrew tried to do the same, but I could see it bothered him that he couldn't do it perfectly. He asked me how many I'd gotten on my first try.

"Almost none," I said. "I'm still no good at it."

He smiled and said, "Want another one, honey?" and put his hand on my arm like I had done to Gil, and my stomach lurched.

Wendy glanced over at me and I knew she was thinking about what we'd talked about at George's. I shook my head at her when Andrew turned to talk to the server, and she shrugged—our silent little conversation.

"I think I'd better call it a night," I said. "You guys stay. I'm just tired."

Andrew and Wendy looked at each other.

"No, you're right. We've all got a lot of work to do," he said.

When the bill came we each paid the same amount. Wendy drifted off towards Kensington Market and her apartment, and Andrew walked me home, rolling his bike beside him, occasionally bashing his shins on the pedals.

"You're not just trying to get rid of me, are you?" he said after he had kissed me good night.

"Not at all. I really am just tired."

He pressed his lips together, nodded.

"Seriously. Hey. My therapist gave me a sort of assignment—he wants me to go over to the river, to where, you know— A sort of saying goodbye thing. Why don't you come with me?"

How would I explain to Gil? I had wanted to offer something to Andrew, to reassure him he was still important. But my first thought was to worry Gil might be angry, to be cut out of something so much about my mother. *What am I doing?* But Andrew was smiling, he picked up my hand in both of his.

"Of course I'll go with you. Can you get away from the store this weekend? Maybe your dad could watch over things on Sunday?"

I nodded and kissed him again, hanging on around his neck, up on my toes. I was already ruining things, things I would want so much after they were gone, and I was sorry. But not sorry enough to change, to switch the course I was on, it seemed. I had never thought I'd be that kind of person. But then I never knew what kind of person I was. I'd never thought much about it.

I let him go, and Andrew got on his bike and rode off. Before he disappeared, I took out the camera and snapped a picture of him, so small without a zoom, the straight stroke of his back above barely visible wheels. There was still enough light, the sun was barely down. The days were still so long.

Wendy came too on Sunday afternoon. I got behind the wheel of my father's car with Andrew beside me in the passenger seat and the Polaroid camera stored in my purse. It was a short distance to the river, but the idea of taking the same streetcar route my mother had taken seemed too macabre, too much like a re-enactment, and I had decided to bring the zircon with me in its glass bowl, too cumbersome for my bike basket. I thought I would put it in the river, that maybe that was the right thing to do with it. Wendy held the bowl on her lap in the back seat, not looking at it. She'd hesitated when I handed it to her.

It was an urgent, bright day, and Wendy gave me her sunglasses to wear because I'd forgotten mine. Everything was stop-and-go until we got east of the armoury. Then it was quiet through Corktown, and I could finally get above twenty-five kilometres an hour on Queen, and it felt good to be driving, to be moving so easily. The river was a little ways off yet, and I wasn't sure where we'd be able to park, how far a walk it would be to the staircase.

I looked at the bowl in the rear-view mirror, balanced on Wendy's lap. It was filled with common zircon, a brownish stone. The colour of a riverbed. I made myself look forward, at the road; we were passing Sackville Street, I could see the street sign, darkening inexplicably, green to brown to black, but we were almost there, I tried to cry out but everything was whisked away.

The wind was whipping my hair into my mouth, which was open and screaming. There was a circle of nothing around my head, my hands on the wheel, everything moving too fast and then we went up, hard, and Wendy, Wendy's body in the corner of my eye and her scream, higher than mine, sharper, cut off. And this silence from her was what made me slam my feet down, both feet stomping on top of each other on the brake pedal, the soles of my sneakers feeling like muscle pushing back against my foot. Andrew's hands on my wrists were pulling and we were tilted, half up on the sidewalk. The front bumper was crushed into the side of the Sumach Street TTC shelter. There was a tax office right in front of us; Andrew practically could have reached out his window and knocked on the door if he wasn't busy closing my mouth and wiping the snot from my face and saying "Hey hey hey" like all other words had been annihilated.

Wendy. Before I turned around I could smell the damage, or hear it; anyway I knew it before I turned around and saw her sitting upright, holding her hands in the air, tan and elegant under the blood. The panic was draining from me like the adrenalin of a nightmare.

"What happened?" I said, untangling myself from Andrew.

"Is everyone okay?" said Wendy, as if she weren't bleeding.

Andrew was in his seat where I had pushed him off me, not moving. His shirt had ridden up over his harsh flat belly, and the red welt of the seat belt looked electric on his skin. The usual downward drag on the corners of his mouth was gone; he looked years younger.

He said only, "Maggie?"

"What happened?" I said again.

"What?" I heard Wendy's voice and then my body kicked in; I could feel where the seat belt had pressed into my chest and hips, and my neck and head ached like someone had slammed my teeth together.

"I thought—Sackville Street? To the river. I don't understand." Both of them were staring at me. The impact of what had happened was sinking in. "I'm so sorry, you guys. Wendy, your hands. What happened? I'm so sorry. I'll take you to the hospital."

"I'm okay," said Wendy. "The bowl broke. I'm not cut badly."

"What happened?" Andrew asked this as if no one had yet spoken.

We were all outside the car then somehow, Andrew on his knees like he was going to throw up and Wendy sitting on a cement planter with her hands up but her body curled over so tightly that I thought I could have put her into a suitcase without much effort. Andrew got up and started pacing, and I noticed his hips, which were amazing, and I thought, *My boyfriend is a sexy motherfucker*, which made me laugh because it was the stupidest thought to have just then. The laugh made everything worse. No one wanted to look at me. I reached out and stroked Wendy's head. On the sidewalk, people were gathering, talking to each other but not to us, as if we couldn't hear them or understand English.

Andrew said, "We have to take her to the hospital."

I went to get into the driver's seat and he just stared at me.

"I'll take you home after we drop her off," he said, and he took the keys from me.

He helped Wendy into the front seat and I got into the back. The car made a noise like a construction site when Andrew backed off the sidewalk and made a three-point turn to head us westward to St. Michael's, the closest hospital. The streetcar shelter wasn't damaged at all. People were watching from both sides of the road, but no one said anything as we drove away.

Andrew parked illegally near St. Mike's and got Wendy out of the car. He came and opened the back door, petted my hair heavily and silently for a moment, then kissed my head and shut the door. I made no effort to go with them. After a while, a parking officer came by and put a ticket under the windshield. If he saw me, he didn't say anything. A while later, Andrew came back. He took the ticket and put it in his pocket. He got back into the driver's seat and headed towards home without asking me to move to the front. And when I turned my face to the window, he didn't say anything. The north side of Queen Street rolled by, the glass and concrete of the Eaton Centre, then the murder-wail of the bagpiper in front of Osgoode Hall, the squeak and lurch as we drove over the streetcar tracks.

At home Andrew opened the door for me, and we went in through the back, over the broken step because we were coming from the garage. Later I would have to clean up the glass from the back seat, find all the pieces of zircon, get a new bowl, talk to my father, find a body shop to fix the car, figure out how to pay for the damage, see if anything else had been affected, the steering or the what's-it-called—the other parts, what the fuck were those car parts called? But all that was for later.

Andrew stayed while I got into bed, again in the daylight, like after the time in the park.

"I'm going to go back to St. Mike's. I'll wait for Wendy and take her home in a taxi. I'm going to sleep at home tonight. Is that okay?"

And I said it was, and he went, and then I opened my window and popped the screen out and leaned it up against the wall and it wasn't ten minutes before Gil was there, climbing through the window the way I had years ago, only twice, when I had broken curfew with Wendy in high school. He crawled into my little twin bed beside me, and I fell asleep pressed up against him, thinking that if the worst was yet to come then I probably wasn't equal to it, I was probably going to dissolve, and I hoped Gil could keep going without me when I just fell apart, because I still wanted it to work, I wanted to get all the stories of my mother together, but there was just too much between her and me, between the past and the present.

Eleven

When I showed up for my Thursday evening session, Rosenberg uncharacteristically met me in the lobby and led me to his office. He flicked on the light after groping for the switch. The fluorescents buzzed loudly for a moment and then settled into a hum. The office was tidier than it had been the previous week and smelled of Pine-Sol. He gestured for me to take a seat.

"I got rid of that Pier One thing," he said. "I think you'll find this more comfortable." There was a second armchair, like his, with a TV table set up beside it. "I appreciate your cooperation," he said, setting his briefcase on the desk. He brought over the deck of tarot cards and put them on the TV table before retreating to his desk.

"Aren't we doing the regular session first?"

"I thought we might start with the research-related activity. Just so you're not distracted during our session. If that's all right."

"Sure," I said. After what happened in the car, I had no desire to talk about myself, and no energy to probe Rosenberg for stories of my mother. "So, I just do a reading? For who? Myself?"

"Precisely," he said. "Now shuffle the cards again please. No, wait."

He bent down and opened his briefcase again, and he fumbled for a few minutes, setting up a small video camera on a telescopic tripod. "Just a second now," he said.

When he was satisfied, he hunkered down in front of the camera and pushed the recording button. "This is Dr. Aaron Rosenberg. Session number nineteen. Patient name Margaret Pierce. Toronto, Ontario. Thursday, July twenty-third." He paused and looked at his wristwatch. "Seven oh nine p.m.," he said. Then he moved away from the camera and said, more loudly than normal, "Go ahead, Margaret. With the cards."

I shuffled and cut the deck. The cards were stiff and slick. My mother would have recommended sleeping with them under my pillow for a few days before using them for a proper reading, but I doubted Rosenberg was in the mood to wait. I emptied my mind. I didn't want to ask the cards a question. I didn't like the idea of trying to boss them around, make them perform. The blinking light of the camera was unnerving me. I hardly ever did a full reading for myself. I only flipped through the cards, laying them out one at a time to test my memory. I usually had my notebooks, just in case.

I laid out a five-card spread. They were large and unwieldy in my hands, too slippery and new. The five of cups, the queen of cups, the two of swords, the hermit, the four of wands, reversed. I bit the inside of my cheek: the queen of cups was my mother's card, but I wasn't about to tell him that.

I poked at the cards. "Twos are about potential. Things that haven't happened yet. Like two things coming together to create another thing. Or a choice. Fives are uncertain. They're not happy cards, most of the time." I shrugged. "I guess I thought I remembered more than I do," I said.

"Try a little harder, if you can, Margaret."

The inflection he put on my full name hurt my teeth. "Low numbers are personal. The major arcana, they answer big, philosophical questions. These are mostly—little things."

"Very interesting. What else?"

"I don't know. I don't remember."

There was silence for several minutes.

"Well. I need to take a few measurements," said Rosenberg, and he descended upon me, pulling on a pair of latex gloves.

"I sort of forgot psychiatrists are real doctors," I said.

He glanced at the video camera and forced a laugh.

"I'm glad we have such a relaxed relationship, Margaret," he said loudly. He took my pulse and then had me make a fist while he stung me with a hair-fine needle and took a vial of blood.

"I should have taken comparison measurements at the beginning of the sessions as well," he said. "I guess I was overexcited. Oh well." He pressed a cotton ball to the dot of blood and taped it down. "Next time." He got up and shut off the video camera.

I said, "Dr. Rosenberg," but he cut me off.

"Did you bring the photos with you?" he said. I shook my head. "You're tired, aren't you."

"I am tired." I didn't want to tell him but I knew I should. "I had another blackout."

"Did you?"

I explained what happened. "So not too many happy things to take pictures of this past week," I said.

"Again when you were travelling, I see. Crossing the street, driving, riding your bike."

"I had one in Dr. Malik's office once. I wasn't travelling then."

"Maybe you felt you were."

I shook my head. "Did you ever see my mother read cards?"

"A few times. You seem to have a different approach."

"What was hers like? Then?"

Rosenberg tilted his head, looked at me. "Let's try the park path again," he said. "Instead of tarot cards, think about things you need in order to be happy. Put those things along the path."

"Dr. Rosenberg," I said. "I need my goddamn mother to be happy. I need my brain to work to be happy. Can we stop talking about what makes me happy?"

"I think," he said, "we might break early this week. I can see what a strain this recent episode has put on you."

I got up before he could change his mind and left the cards on the table. Outside in the quiet foyer, I took out my notebook and pen. I put my free hand over the sore spot on my arm where the needle had gone in. My mother used to tickle me there, on the soft skin of my forearm and the crook of my elbow. She'd pretend she was making a hot dog, wiggling her fingers up and down my arm for the ketchup and mustard, squeezing her hands around me for the bun. Then she would pick up my arm and pretend to chomp, while I wriggled and squealed, thrilled to be delicious. Sometimes we would go ice skating on the outdoor rink at Nathan Phillips Square. If my father came along they would both hold my hands, zipping me around the ice in front of City Hall. We would get hot dogs and French fries from the trucks that parked along the street all year around, and my father wouldn't say anything about sodium for once because she was so happy. I wondered when she learned to skate. I wondered if he had taught her.

She wiped the shiny oil from her mouth and licked her fingers clean. The other hand was still clad in its woolly mitt.

"The salt stings," she said, laughing and setting her fries down on the bench. "I have to stop biting my lips."

It was just the two of us. We'd been to get our annual eye exams earlier in the day, at the glasses store across from the square. They'd put drops into her eyes that made her cry yellow tears and her pupils were huge. There was still a bit of bright yellow residue in the corners of her eyes.

"You've still got yellow," I said, and she rubbed her eyes. She did it theatrically, and then blinked at me, pulling her mouth down, silly.

"All gone?" she said.

She pulled me closer beside her and a young Indian couple sat down to share our table. We could see the skaters nearby; I still had my skates on, while my mother had taken hers off to go get us food. We had ketchup and vinegar, salt and pepper. The Indian man and woman were gazing at each other with unabashed adoration, holding hands. They both wore simple steel bracelets. I could see that the woman was pregnant. My mother was looking at them.

"Excuse me," she said. "I just wanted to tell you that you make a beautiful couple."

They looked a bit startled, as if they hadn't noticed anyone else at the tiny round table. The pregnant woman said, "Thank you. You have a lovely little girl."

My mother smiled at them. She held my hand like the woman was holding the man's.

"We live in a beautiful city, Maggie," she said. "Look at the rink. Look how pretty it is. And just down the street from our place. We are so lucky, aren't we?"

I was consumed by the pleasure of my French fries, the tang of the vinegar. I turned and looked at the rink, lit up for the holidays. My fingers were cold.

"This is such a good place to end up," said my mother. She took out the camera she had brought and took a picture of me in front of the rink. When I saw it later the soft shoulder of the pregnant woman was visible beside me, and a shock of dark hair.

We stayed until the sky began to darken, then got on the streetcar at York Street. I stood beside my mother, too hot in my winter coat amid the crush of people. It was Saturday but there were still plenty of workers in suits as well as teenagers, tourists, the usual mish-mash. I took off my toque. A young man offered us his single seat beside the window and my mother let me take it. She stood over me, her body curled towards me.

"Look at all this," she said, nodding her chin up, out the window. "This city tells you everything you need to know. It takes you in. Who could ask for more?"

When she said this, all the tired commuters on the streetcar standing nearby looked at her as if they had never heard anyone speaking before. The face of a woman behind her drew closed as if frozen, then softened. The woman looked at me. Her curls were pushed off her face under a stretchy headband. Then she turned to gaze out the window, her face still so soft, as if what my mother had said had filled her with water, with something warm in the darkening winter day. My mother stood beside me, her eyes with their enormous pupils looking outwards. Without looking down, she reached out and ran her fingers through my hair, damp with sweat from the wool hat I'd been wearing. Her touch sent a shivery pleasure shooting through me, and I looked out, trying to see what she saw.

Twelve

It was the first day of the Canadian National Exhibition. I hadn't been since my mother took Wendy and me back in middle school. My mother had filled a clown's mouth with water from a toy pistol and won me a prize. For the life of me, I couldn't remember what it was. But I could see her standing there, her feet wide apart, one eye closed and both hands on the plastic gun. Entirely serious, while all the other players laughed or missed the starting mark or got the guns the wrong way and squirted their dates.

Gil and I were wandering the fairgrounds hand in hand while I ate cotton candy, caramel popcorn, puffy baked pretzels. It was hot even after the sun went down and my hairline was like a heavy, damp cloth. I thought about shaving all my hair off, how light it would be, the way the bristles would feel. What Andrew would say when he saw.

Gil had his notebook with him, tucked into a canvas bag. I felt bad for going with him instead of Andrew, but ever since the accident, I'd had a hard time facing Andrew. The look on his face when he saw Wendy's hands. So much blood for such little cuts. A week had passed and she could type again. "As long as I can use the phone, I'm happy," she'd said when I visited her, all blustery smile, eager to forgive me. I pressed gifts on her, more rosemary soap, badly executed homemade cookies, a Frisbee I realized afterwards she wouldn't be able to play with until she'd made a full recovery. So I'd spent more time holed up with Gil. It felt safe in there, with the door closed and Gil calling me *Darling*, rustling the pages of his notebooks. He was less antagonistic, and my feelings towards him were becoming benevolent, slightly soggy, warm. He wanted to come over more and more often, and asked me to give him things to eat, crackers and paté, carrots and oranges, Skor bars and glasses of milk. He claimed he couldn't bring himself to speak to anyone else, even a cashier at a grocery store, even a streetcar driver, that he was buying nothing and speaking to no one until his book was finished. Instead of scaring me off, I luxuriated in him, in the idea of his self-indulgent silence, I wanted to slip into it myself for a moment and see what it would be like to live in his glass cylinder.

Still I felt bad about Andrew, so I forced myself to picture him, in detail, on a date with one of his dippy students, picture her gazing up at him adoringly, calling him "Dr. Kaplan" while pushing her lips out. *It's not so bad, really. I mean, it doesn't feel good. But it wouldn't kill me. It wouldn't kill him.* I figured we were even, and when a pang of guilt stabbed me now and then, I pictured Andrew in increasingly intimate situations with a series of beautiful women. I decided I was being fair. Hadn't he predicted this anyway? He must have known before I did, or I must have been in denial. I made a mental note to tell Rosenberg that—it was such a nice concrete item to toss him. *I was in denial about the demise of my relationship.*

"So we can go on as many rides as we like?" said Gil, hoisting his wrist, the knob of bone pushing violently under his skin. Wrapped around it was a neon-green strip of paper.

"It's unlimited." I fingered my own wristband. I had paid for them both, Gil standing in silence, not making eye contact with anyone. "Let's go on everything."

"I don't know. I get motion sickness easily."

"You'll be fine."

The sun had set and the fairgrounds now had an eerie quality. For the most part, parents and children had left by the time we arrived. Teenagers ringed in skunky clouds of cheap pot and college couples holding hands dominated the queues. The kids working the games called out to us with the enthusiasm of a second wind; it was the time of night when they might pass a beer around out back, when they could flirt and joke with the passersby without fearing the rage of suburban parents. I tried Skee-Ball, spending more than I had planned to, to win a small toy hedgehog. The fabric was cheap and slippery. I pressed it against Gil's face and he swatted me away, smiling, and pulled on my hand, heading towards the end of the midway. It was strange to be outside with him, stranger still to be holding hands. I felt oddly shy.

We rode things that tilted and spun, roller coasters that screeched on what looked like jerry-rigged tracks, and stumbled through funhouses with bucking floors, squeaking down playground-style slides to land sprawling on the concrete. On the last one, I slipped at the top and tumbled down face first. I threw my hands up and felt a sharp tug at my wrist. The bracelet I was wearing momentarily snagged on something and then snapped, and I fell the rest of the way. At the bottom I picked myself up. The bracelet lay in pieces on the ground.

Gil slithered down the slide, looking slightly green.

"Is something the matter with your arm?" He pointed.

I was cradling the sore wrist in my other hand. The fingers I had sprained in my bike accident were long since healed, but it seemed ominous that I'd caught the same hand on the slide.

"It's fine. I just broke my bracelet. It got caught."

"Well, we're almost done, don't worry. There's just the Ferris wheel now."

"Oh." I was feeling muddled. Gil's body had become an indoor thing, confined to my little room. It was little more than an extension of my own body, a steady breathing reminding me that I was alive; a porch light to come home to. But now he seemed more separate, more male. Across his nose and under his eyes he looked bruised; it must have been his first day out in the sun for months. Tomorrow he would be bright red. With the sun down now, he looked almost thuggish.

He kept his hands on me as we queued up for the Ferris wheel. The operator opened the door of the little cart and ushered me in after the previous cycle of riders had descended the stairs on the opposite side. Gil and I sat down, our thighs touching. He put one hand between my knees.

The operator closed the door and I said, "Thank you."

He nodded and said, "Have fun, honey," as the Ferris wheel lurched into life.

"How much longer is this going to go on?" I said. "You told me they'd stop. The blackouts."

"I said they would stop when the book is finished. It's hardly finished, is it. You have to give me more information."

"How much longer?"

He closed his eyes and shook his head. "Never ask that."

We were at the top of the cycle when the Ferris wheel ground to a halt. Gil's fingers slid up the back of my neck into my hair. I could see the Exhibition grounds spread out to the south, the lights of the fair, then the black expanse of the lake. The other way was the highway, the lights of the city.

"You're sweating," he said.

I touched his forehead. "So are you. It's hot."

It felt like we hung up there forever. Finally, the bloated wheel creaked back to life. A few rotations later, the operator released us and I went carefully down the corrugated metal steps.

"Wait," said Gil. "Come with me." He caught up to me and pulled on my hand, leading us back towards the funhouse where I had broken my bracelet.

There was no line, and the attendant barely glanced at our neon bands. Gil was pulling me urgently past the mirrored entrance. We stood on what had earlier been a square of pitching floor that had been difficult to walk over. For whatever reason, it was still now. It was open to the air on one side, but the funhouse was nearly pitch dark.

Gil came up behind me. He pushed my hair forward from the nape of my neck, up and over my face, like a hairstylist getting a feel for it before a cut. He kissed me on the nape of the neck, put his hands on my hips and knocked my knees apart with one of his.

"You look nice," he said. He drew back for a moment, and I felt as though I couldn't turn around.

I waited in the dark, and in a moment he was pressed against me again. I pulled my shirt up and off. I could feel his skin against my back.

"This isn't a good idea," I said. But everything was switched in the same direction; it was the opposite of how I'd felt picking zircon out of the back seat of the car, the opposite of how I felt sitting in Rosenberg's office, praying for time to speed up. This wasn't something to put on the park path of things that made me happy, it was more than that.

He was kissing my shoulders and back. I leaned into him, feeling his chest hair tickling my shoulder blades. He unclasped and pulled off my bra, put his hands on my waist and started kissing the edge of my jaw. My eyes were starting to adjust to the dark. *Isn't this a safety hazard? What if kids were running through here in the dark?*

Gil was standing up straight again, behind me. "You think too much," he said. He ran his hands down my chest. He laid one hand flat on my belly.

I closed my eyes and leaned back into him but there was nothing there, the sticky firmness of his skin gone. Then he grabbed my arm and spun me around.

"What the hell are you doing?"

The speaker was a dark-haired, middle-aged man. For a moment I had a wild thought that this was Dr. Rosenberg. But no.

"Where's Gil?" I screamed at the top of my lungs.

"Oh lord," said the man. "You're as high as a bloody kite."

"What? No. No. Where's Gil?" I had my arms crossed like dead royalty, covering my breasts.

The man bent down and picked up my shirt. "Put this on, for god's sake."

I didn't want to turn my back. It was the only thought I could manage. If I turned my back, this man would do something terrible. I stood with my shirt in my hand, still covering myself with my arms.

"Put it on," he said. He seemed more exasperated than anything.

I felt cold, and all I could think about was how when I was little, my mother showed me how to get my wet bathing-suit top off from under my T-shirt. For when there is no changing room, she said. I wanted there to be a modest way for me to put my shirt back on in front of this man. In the darkness, I saw that he wore a badge, a uniform. It was only information; it registered but wasn't processed. I felt like I'd had my ears boxed, I could hardly hear.

The man looked away and I pulled the shirt on. He turned to check, then took me by the arm. "Come on," he said.

He dragged me through the fairgrounds to the front gate. Two men were lounging there, chatting to each other. One was chewing gum, a huge, unrealistically giant wad of it forcing his mouth half open.

"What's this?" said the one with the gum. He too wore a uniform. The other man glared, and he had the light eyes of a maniac preacher.

The first man shook me by the arm.

"I found her stripped to the waist in the Space 2000. I wasn't going to bother you guys, but she's out of her mind on something." He handed me to the gum-chewing man.

"God," he said, taking my arm. "Better run her up to the fourteenth, then."

I was making the connection. The man who had found me had a similar uniform to the others but with some key details lacking. No name tag, no holster. No nightstick. His arm badge bore the logo of the fair. But the men he was handing me to were full-fledged, evening news, hat-wearing police officers.

"No," I said, thickly. "I'm not on drugs."

"No one said anything about drugs," said the pale-eyed cop. "Just you."

"Look, just come with us, miss." The gum chewer stopped and released my arm. He took a folded tissue out of his pocket and then reached into his mouth with two fingers. He put the gum into the tissue, folded the corners over, and put the whole thing into a public garbage can a few feet away.

I thought about bolting.

"Gil," I yelled. "Gil, where are you? Gil, you motherfucker!"

"Just stay calm, okay? Nobody is going to hurt you—we just need to take you to the station and ask you a couple questions." He turned to the security guard and said, as if I weren't there, "Maybe there really was a guy. Can you look around and call us if you find anyone else?"

The security guard nodded at both of them and left. I saw their police car parked at the curb. I was inside it. The motion of it was soothing. I slumped against the seat. We drove up Strachan, the Winged Victory atop the Princes' Gates of the Exhibition Grounds staring down, judge-like. In a moment we were waiting for the light at Queen and Strachan, right beside the store, looking north into Bellwoods. I groped for a door lever that wasn't there, but then we were moving again, west along Queen, past bars and restaurants. On the south side, the empty CAMH grounds slid by, looking forlorn. Rosenberg must have been tucked safe in bed at home, wherever home was for him. We turned north on Dovercourt, then pulled into a police station near Dundas, a flat brown Kleenex box with tall, thin windows.

What if my father is here. Impossible, how could he know, but I was frozen with fear.

The unfriendly cop opened my door and waved me out. He seemed more nervous than the other one, as if I were a maniacal drug addict who might take a bite of his arm at any minute. He took hold of my upper arm and levered me out of the car, walked me through the front door. One wall had a line of grey waiting-room chairs up against it. An older man sat in one, reading a magazine. A young girl sat two chairs from him, her head in her hands.

Behind the counter was a woman. She looked up and said, "What's this?" She wore a tag that said *Kovitch.*

"High," said the one holding me.

They took me into an almost-empty room. It had a window out to the parking lot. A fern in the corner, a folding table. There were two nicely framed, ugly prints on the walls. They sat me down; the chair was white plastic. *Pool parties, PTA meetings.* I'd expected battered metal, one-way mirrors. One officer left immediately and came back with a clipboard stuffed with papers. He thrust it into the gum chewer's hands and left again. The remaining cop wrote on it for a while, occasionally glancing at me.

"You wait just a second there," he said, as if I had made to leave. My wallet was open on the table. *How did that get there* ran along the top part of my brain, while underneath was *I'm going to kill Gil, I mean I really am going to kill him* and *There's no way I would make this up.*

He went out, taking his clipboard with him. I was alone.

Come on, do your thing. Take me home. Take me anywhere. I clenched my fists, my teeth. *Blackout. Now.* I probably looked like Carrie trying to use her telekinesis, completely crazy. *Now. Now. Now.* Nothing happened. The scene of the room just lay there, heavy and flat, like a dead end in a maze.

The door opened and the woman I had seen behind the desk when we arrived entered. She sat down across the table from me.

"You'll be home much quicker if you just tell me the truth all the way along, okay?" she said. She looked at me. "Okay, then?" She settled herself in the chair and turned her attention to the clipboard.

"You take any drugs tonight, Margaret?"

"No."

"You have anything to drink?"

"No. I don't—We didn't—"

"We? So you weren't alone?"

I shook my head.

"Were you with your boyfriend?" She made some marks on the clipboard.

"No, my boyfriend wasn't— No." The images of Andrew, the ones I'd been self-medicating with, popped unbidden into my head. *You're so strong,* said a pretty undergrad, sprawled in his lap. *She must have been a nightmare.*

"Okay. Your friend, your date, whatever. Was he there or wasn't he?"

"He was there."

"What's his name?"

"Gil."

"So you and Gil thought you'd have a little fun and at the red-hot moment he just beats it, eh?"

"I guess he saw the guard coming. I didn't."

"Why's that?"

"I had my eyes closed."

Her eyes widened a little.

"Okay." Neither of us spoke for a moment. Then she said, "If he's not your boyfriend, who is he?"

"He's a writer."

The officer didn't respond to that. Instead she put the clipboard down and became businesslike.

"Breathe out," she said. She stood up and leaned over my left shoulder from behind, putting her face down by mine. It was horribly reminiscent of Gil in the funhouse. "Big breath out."

I puffed for her and she nodded.

She picked up a silver pen-like instrument and pointed it at my right eye. It was a light. The whole room bloomed white. She had one hand under my chin to steady me. One eye, the other.

"I could make you stand on one leg and all that. I could have them test your blood, urine, the whole nine yards. But I know as well as you do that you're not on anything." She put the penlight in her breast pocket. "Wait here," she said.

After about ten minutes, she came back and got me. "We're going to my office," she said.

We followed the hallway to a small, neat office with two desks and two visitors' chairs. She sat me in one and took her own seat behind her desk. This was only the second time I'd ever spoken to police officers, the first being at the river when my mother died. I hadn't gone to the station with my father. He must have sat in a similar chair, in a similar office, alone. He'd sent me home and I'd gone.

"I need you to sign these forms," said the officer. She put an identical clipboard to her own in front of me.

I signed the forms without reading them. She took them off the clipboard and put them in the top drawer.

"You're free to go. Call someone to pick you up."

She picked up the phone, which was a multi-line contraption, and put it in front of me.

"Can't I just take a cab?"

"We'd prefer if a friend or family member could come for you. Is that a problem?"

"No." I picked up the receiver, and sat there with it in my hand.

"Do you need a phone book?"

"No."

The edges of her mouth pulled back, somewhere between a frown and a smile. If her pity had gone any further than that, it might have unhinged me—releasing tears and other things I wasn't ready for. She didn't say anything.

I dialled Wendy's number. It rang and rang and her answering machine clicked to life. I let the *beep* sound, then hung up.

I picked the receiver up again and dialled Andrew's number. He picked up on the first ring.

"I knew you'd call," he said.

I said, "Andrew?"

"Maggie?"

"Is this Andrew?"

"Yes, it's me. I'm sorry. I thought you were someone else." He paused. "Why are you calling? What's wrong?"

I had a perverse urge to laugh.

"I'm in some trouble. I need a ride home. It's okay to come in a cab. I'll pay you back."

He didn't say anything for a moment. Then he said, "Where are you?"

Kovitch had me waiting in the chair beside the girl with her head in her hands. The officers who'd brought me in seemed to have disappeared, and it wasn't long before Andrew arrived. He was wearing plaid pyjama pants and a white button-up shirt. I could see that he had misaligned the buttons. A wide triangle of neck showed at the top.

"Are you okay?" he said, but he didn't wait for an answer. "Let's go." Then, as if he'd just remembered, he came and wrapped his arms around me. He felt almost hollow-boned, and so tall he seemed to reel up away from me. I squeezed him back.

I had expected a taxi, but Andrew was driving Wendy's white Suzuki. "I borrowed it to move some new bookcases into my office," he said, gesturing to the empty back seat like it was evidence of something. At first we drove in silence. The windows were down and the temperature inside and outside the car seemed to be exactly the same. It was as if the night had no weather at all. I was trailing my fingers out the window, and then Andrew was speaking again.

"You don't have to tell me what happened. Just tell me if it was another blackout."

"No. Not like that—no."

"I don't know, Maggie. It's so hard to worry this much, it feels like, god, it feels like dying sometimes, to be so scared, you can't imagine."

"Of course I can. I'm sorry, Andrew. I really am. But you know I know what it is like to worry this much."

He nodded and I flicked on the radio. *This is* Northern Lights *on CBC Radio One.* They said it was Chopin. It sounded like glass. At the street light for Queen, Andrew looked out the window and nodded.

He said, "What happened tonight?"

"It was just a misunderstanding. I went to the CNE. I got a little disoriented."

"I've never been in a police station before," he said. Then he said, again, "Are you okay?"

The familiarity of him in the seat beside me was so comfortable. He was like fresh sheets on a bed; like warm laundry. He put his hands back on the steering wheel.

"I'm okay. I really am okay. Thanks for picking me up," I said.

He turned and looked at me for a moment. The motion was a thin crack, like light under a door. The signal changed and he made the turn. A few minutes later he pulled up in front of the store. He picked up my hand and squeezed it.

"I'm going to go," he said. "Will you be okay heading up?"

"I'll be fine. This really isn't a big deal. I know it seems weird. But it's okay."

He leaned over and pressed his lips against mine, dry. He didn't turn the motor off. I got out of the car and closed the door. Not wanting it to slam, I didn't swing it hard enough and had to bump my hip against it to get it closed all the way. Andrew gave me a thumbs-up through the window when it clicked into place. Then he drove off.

I unlocked the door to the store and went inside. Gil was standing at the back, behind the table of stone animals. He started forward.

"I'm sorry—"

"That's bullshit, Gil. You're bullshit." I rolled my neck, which felt stiff and cracked audibly. "Where did you go?"

"I got scared."

"I want you to leave."

"Darling, please. I'm so sorry," he said. "I never should have left you alone like that. I know you're humiliated. Let's go upstairs and talk about this."

"Just get out for a while. I don't want to hear it. I just want to be alone."

He walked towards me and reached out, hooked a single finger with mine. "I'm so sorry for failing you. I should have been there. To leave you like that was unforgivable. I've been overwhelmed lately, it was too many people, you're the only one I can handle right now, talk to, be with."

In spite of myself I curled my finger against his.

"A writer should always be there for his sources. It's a partnership."

I whipped my hand away. "Get away from me. I don't want to hear about your stupid book. I want you gone. You're not helping anymore. You weren't ever helping, were you." I closed my eyes but I could feel him still standing there. I opened my eyes slightly and through my eyelashes I saw him, looking lost and heavier than I pictured him when he wasn't around. His forearms seemed shorter and thicker, clumsier.

"Maggie, I'm sorry."

"I'm not listening to you any more. If there's even a *you* to listen to."

"Don't talk like that. You can't just wish me away because you're mad at me."

"Get out. I'm not kidding, Gil. I'm going to do this without you."

"Is that really a good idea?"

"I'm not asking your opinion. Leave."

After I stood there not looking at him for a few minutes, he touched my face and then left. I locked the door behind him and went to the table of animals. I knelt down beside them and cried with my mouth open, cried so hard I drooled a little. The pain of having grieved incorrectly, of having been wrong, done her wrong, was almost as bad as the grief itself. And the fear. There was no more safe warm place, no more games with Rosenberg, lying in sessions and laughing about it afterwards with Gil.

When I had tired myself out I lay on the dirty floor in the dark with a white quartz otter in my hand. White quartz for clarity, for help in reaching the spirit world. Snow quartz on my mother's table while she read the cards. She told me white quartz was unique among the stones for its receptive qualities. You could program it, get it to help with what you most needed it for, if you concentrated, imbued it. But it also absorbed things, feelings, energies. You had to be careful with it. Otherwise your head might open up and spill everything into the stone.

Did she really believe that? I did. I could feel it, humming, lifting the fine hairs on my arms like static electricity.

PART THREE

THE JOURNEY TECHNIQUE

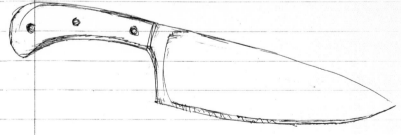

Thirteen

*A*ll stories are about my mother. All stories should be about my mother. This story is about my father.

Every Labour Day weekend until I was about fourteen I got new clothes. There would be a few T-shirts folded on my bed, in every colour my father thought a T-shirt should come in. Beside them would be a couple of sweaters and a pair of new jeans. He wasn't clueless about fashions—he was surrounded by young people when he lectured—but the clothes were always blank in a label-less way, as if he was having these things made for me by a blind but talented seamstress. My mother liked to buy me clothes but couldn't be depended upon to remember about things like the school year beginning, or what size I was, or that I broke out in a rash if I wore the lambswool sweaters she was so fond of and which she invariably shrank in the washing machine. So my father always provided, as reliable as the one beautiful week Toronto always gets at the end of August. He never forgot.

At that age you don't yet know that, at best, everything is like riding a bicycle, everything is a thing you try to do your best at and maybe you are good at it and maybe you aren't, but you do it. You don't know yet that to your father, you are a bicycle and your mother is a bicycle and his job is a bicycle and none of this means you are unloved, because everything in your life and everyone you love is a

*bicycle to you, too—a thing you do, maybe well, maybe not. Being a
daughter, a parent, a friend. But when I saw those clothes stacked
up, with the tags already removed, I didn't think that trying your
best was enough. And I never saw myself as unfair. I saw my beautiful mother, useless and effortless, offering a flower pulled up from a
neighbour's garden, the soil clinging richly, smelling of sun. And my
father, twisting a handkerchief in his hands—still using a handkerchief, before people went back to them to save the planet—unable to
do a single beautiful thing.*

A sweater lay on the kitchen table. It was the colour of wood-
smoke, a thick cotton knit with round wooden buttons. My
going-away present. I was leaving for Wooster House. Full time.
My father had posted a job ad on the English department message board. "Just temporary, sweetheart," he'd said. "A week or
two, however much time you need. Just to keep things running
while you're gone."

"Sure you don't want to come say hi to your old hippie buddy
Rosenberg?" I said to my father in the kitchen. I jutted my head
forward a little, smiled. *See? Makes jokes! Appreciates sweaters!
Definitely not crazy.*

"He's no friend of mine. I'm still surprised he doesn't consider it a conflict of interest to counsel you, considering the
way he mooned after your mother."

"I'll tell him you say hello and that you send a big hug. And
thank you for this." I picked up a limp sleeve of the sweater with
my good hand, let it fall. I filed away the new information about
Rosenberg and my mother, silently.

"It can get cold out there at night." My father picked up the sweater, refolded it.

"Port Credit isn't outer space. And August isn't exactly chilly," I said, but I felt something in my chest like a pane of glass.

He gave me a swift hug and I took the sweater over my good arm. My suitcase was down in the store with Andrew and Wendy, packed with summer clothes, my recent notebooks, the manila envelope of my mother's photos and papers I still hadn't sorted through from the third-floor storage room, and Rosenberg's Polaroid camera.

It was after six but there was a customer in the store. I must have forgotten to lock the front door before going up. When I was halfway down, I looked over my shoulder and saw my father standing in the doorway watching, and he was surprised, his hand jerked as if to close the door, but then he smiled and gave a little wave and stepped backwards into the apartment.

"There you are," said Wendy. "This lady wants to buy these candles—is it too late?" It was the woman who had bought the crystal ball just after the funeral.

"Hello, dear," she said to me. "I know it's past closing, but if you'd indulge me?"

I did the tax in my head and put the money and a scribbled note in the empty cash drawer. The till was already locked in the safe. The woman accepted the candles back, stowing them in her woven bag. She looked keenly at me for a moment and put her hand with its puffy fingers on my shoulder.

"Embrace the light," she said, giving me a hard squeeze.

It was more than I had expected from such a frail-looking woman.

"How's that crystal treating you?" I said.

"Just fine, dear, just fine. Nothing I didn't already know."

Andrew was standing beside my suitcase, silently radiating his disapproval. He was of one mind with my father about the customers, and the idea of serving someone after closing time, even if I had left the door unlocked, further offended his sensibilities. *Inelegant minds.* Wendy came around the counter and hugged me hard, picking me up off my feet. When she put me down the ropy muscles exposed by her sleeveless top were still flexed.

"Get outta here, you," she said. "I'll keep the city warm for you. Your dad will find someone to take care of the store. You'll be home before you know it." She kissed me firmly on the hinge of my jaw. She took a tissue from under the counter although she wasn't crying.

The crystal woman nodded at her, seeming to enjoy the scene.

Andrew picked up my suitcase. He took the open door from the woman, who was leaving. She stopped and chucked Andrew under the chin.

"Ease up, bunny," she said. Then she slipped out before either of us had a chance to say anything.

Andrew drove along Lake Shore Boulevard rather than the highway, taking the long way west. As he drove, I looked out the window at the little streams and wider ones, where people piloted kayaks or fished from the shore. The streams widened and narrowed, rushing south under bridges. On one reedy bank, a man stood with two children, and he pointed at something in the distance and spoke to them. Looking up, I saw a large bird disappear into the trees—a hawk maybe. We kept driving and the children on the edge of the river, with their heads twisted towards the absent bird, disappeared. I turned away, took out my latest notebook from my purse and flipped idly through it.

Our destination was a neighbourhood called Port Credit, a sweet suburban area set on the edge of the water with a lighthouse and a marina. Even with my sunglasses on, it seemed as if someone had scrubbed clean the sky between the ground and the sun. I hadn't been outside the city in a long time. The evening sunlight in Port Credit seemed thinner, like lemon juice.

After turning south towards the lake, Andrew stopped in front of a white gravel drive for a large chimera of a building. Wooster House. The front was an old house in the ranch style of the surrounding streets, but a professional-looking glass and steel extension had been grafted onto the back.

Andrew got out, took my suitcase from the trunk, and came around to let me out. He had been extra polite ever since he picked me up from the police station, ever since I had agreed to give this a try. I think he found the whole thing agreeably old-fashioned: the lake view, the little woman stuffed away with watercolours and long walks to keep her from going bonkers.

Very Zelda Fitzgerald. He would have liked that—it would make him Scott.

We headed up the short path, Andrew still carrying the luggage. It had wheels, but he refused to roll it. "Suitcases with wheels are a metaphor for what is wrong with people today," he said, hefting the strap, causing the muscles of his forearm to jump to attention, and when he said this I thought to myself that he would have said the same thing three years ago, when we first met, but he would have said it as a joke. And I knew from that thought that I would have to do something soon, or he would—that something that would be both unpleasant and a relief would happen.

The outside of the house portion was in good repair, the dark shingles overlapping like combed hair. There was a high fence of new-looking wood. I could smell it faintly, the sunny, sticky odour like a colour. Dark yellow. No one answered my knocking so we let ourselves in. The common room, which opened immediately from the foyer, was full of overstuffed couches in varying neutral shades. A wide staircase opened in the corner, sloping back over the room.

When I entered there were three people sprawled on the couches watching *Chinatown*. I didn't think this was the right movie for these people to be watching, but I didn't want to seem rude. So I said, "I'm looking for Dr. Rosenberg," and a young red-haired woman paused the video. On the screen Jack Nicholson's nose was already bandaged and he was stuck with his mouth slightly open, trying to speak.

Rosenberg came out of an office then, closing the door

behind him. "Welcome, Maggie," he said. Then he turned to the room and said, "Maggie has lost someone also."

The red-haired girl looked down at her feet and started to cry. The others ignored her, looking at me.

Dr. Rosenberg said, "Why don't we get you settled in," and he took me by the elbow.

Stepping forward, Andrew said, "I'm Andrew Kaplan."

I could hear the desire to qualify in his voice. *Andrew Kaplan, Ph.D. candidate, University of Toronto. Andrew Kaplan, normal person. Andrew Kaplan, Not Crazy.*

Dr. Rosenberg pumped his hand and said, "It's good of you to come." He moved to the bottom of the stairs and looked up. "You'll be on the second floor," he said. "You'll be in my personal small group. All the members sleep in the original wing. You'll meet the rest of them properly soon."

"Second floor," said Andrew. "Is that a good idea?" but we all went up the stairs, which were dusty, painted white with black rubber treads nailed to each step. I could see the nailheads staring up dully, trying to catch a thread of sock, a blister, a cut. I stepped around them.

At the top of the stairs, Rosenberg had to reach around me to slide the key in, and his chest was pressed for a moment against my back. We were both out of breath and warm, and I could feel his stomach going in and out for a second. I thought of George and his thigh against mine in the booth and of Gil's mouth in the park. Andrew was standing back from both of us, hampered by the suitcase. Then Dr. Rosenberg turned the knob and swung the door open, inwards. I went through and looked around.

The room was a good size with a large bed set against the wall between two bookcases. I was glad it wasn't a cot, that the blankets weren't dull and green. There were two tall windows, and through one I could see a brown metal fire escape.

"They don't open, unfortunately," said Dr. Rosenberg, seeing where I was looking. "But we have air conditioning. And there's a private bathroom." He gestured to the door in the corner. "There's no plug so you can't take a bath unfortunately, but we have lots of hot water for showers."

On the ceiling there was a blank plaster circle, as if a ceiling fan or light fixture had been removed.

"It's very nice, thank you," I said.

I had a northern view of white townhouses, weak light. A woman in cropped pants was having a cigarette on her patio. There were puffy red flowers in planters around her. I put my hand on the wall, which was cool under my fingers. It felt like oil paint. My father wasn't on the other side.

"I'll be seeing you tomorrow," said Rosenberg. "If you need anything, talk to Chad. His office is on the first floor, beside the kitchen; he'll tell you everything that's going on. There's yoga, painting, board games. Lots to do. There is a phone in the front hall. You need a quarter for that, but there's another phone in the kitchen that will connect you directly with the front desk of CAMH."

His mention of the downtown hospital made me think of Dr. Malik. Just then, I would rather have been there, sitting in Dr. Malik's chair, looking at his photograph, the sailboat, the little boy. Dr. Rosenberg didn't seem like the right person to be running a sleep-away camp for the bereaved. Slick and handsome, he looked more like he should be selling three-thousand-dollar suits in Yorkville.

He rocked on his heels for a moment and then said, "Anything at all." He took a booklet from the inside of his suit jacket. "This should help you settle in," he said, handing it over. *Wooster House Rules & Guidelines*.

Andrew put my suitcase down only after Rosenberg left. "Is there anything you need? Food? Books?"

"No thanks."

"Well, you can always call me. Of course. And I'll be out to visit, I should be able to get out on the weekend." He cleared his throat. "This is a bit surreal," he said. His hand went towards the suitcase briefly. "Well."

"Thanks."

"I had better get going. Give you a chance to get to know the rest of—everyone else." He bent down to hug me and went to kiss me on the mouth but seemed to change his mind at the last minute. His mouth touched the corner of my lips and he backed up and came in again, kissed my cheek. He kissed my forehead without moving my hair aside.

I hugged him back and stretched up to kiss his smooth, hard cheek. Then I pulled away.

"You can call me anytime at all," he said from the doorway, half turned. "I'll bring Wendy with me if you want, when I come."

I was walking around the room, touching things. "Thank you," I said again. I was hardly listening.

Wooster House took up nearly an entire block. Directly north of us was a townhouse complex made of white stone and beyond that was Lake Shore Boulevard, the main street, running all the way back into the city. Directly south of us was a park with a slope of grass and then a jumble of flat grey stones and then the lake, which seemed like a bad idea considering how prone to accidents depressive mental patients can be. But there was the tall fence around the house and a big backyard and if we wanted to leave we had to ask Chad, who ran the day-to-day operations of the House and was not much older than I was.

The next day, I met my "small group," the Dr. Rosenberg Group. All the groups were named for their attending doctor, which I thought was a lost opportunity. Wouldn't we benefit from a team name? *The Cryin' Tigers. The Bereaved Beavers. The Mournin' Mustangs.* The newer section of the House was home to about thirty or forty additional patients, sorted into a handful of other groups, with other doctors. It was hard to tell how many people there were since we were never together all at once.

Among the four of us in the Dr. Rosenberg Group, it was one husband, one wife, and one brother missing. And one mother— mine. These were the people we had lost—we would never say *dead*. The widow was only twenty-two, a year younger than me but babyish, she didn't look old enough to play the female lead in a romantic comedy. The red-headed girl who had paused the video. She'd been married for less than a year. Timothy was the only man in the group. His wife was killed in one swift instant when a tractor trailer, erratic without the weight of a load, flipped over onto her Chevrolet. They weren't supposed to drive them empty. It was a very windy day.

Because I was new, we didn't have individual sessions that day, instead we had an extended group session. It was just called Group, as in "It's time for Group." Dr. Rosenberg sat on a pillow in front of the fireplace. No fire. Occasionally he gave small, tic-like movements of his head.

"Visualize your memory path," he said, after we'd had some time to focus and empty our minds. "Your pain is a shadow on that path. Think of it flickering, evaporating. Feel the sun. Feel the warmth. And now start your memory exercise, remember the good things you've placed on the path, where you've placed them, in what order."

I wasn't picturing my mental path or my pain shadow. I was picturing the store, wondering what was going on. I was wondering who my father would find to watch things while I was gone, how badly they would mess things up.

"What if we can't remember something?" said Timothy, opening one eye. Dr. Rosenberg hadn't said to close our eyes.

"Just do your best. Try to focus on the visuals."

"My path is the drive to my office," said Timothy.

"Mine's Church Street, in the village," said Tracey, who looked to be about my age.

Tracey's twin brother had died of a brain aneurysm the previous year, three months after moving to Japan. They were of Japanese descent but had never actually been there. I'd gotten everyone's story in the morning, when Rosenberg had us share our Loss Experiences. When I was asked, I said "My mother drowned three months ago." *Three years. Three decades. Three minutes.* It was all of those things. I wanted and didn't want to be at Wooster House. For some reason what had happened at the CNE scared me more than the blackouts.

I hadn't ever actually placed anything on my path, happiness-wise, so I tried to remember the twenty tarot cards again. Tarot cards and Rosenberg were an odd, uncomfortable combination. There was something off-putting about him; he reminded me of a wooden nutcracker doll. I'd rather he had given us real work, something with photocopies, terms to learn, secret codes.

After we broke for lunch, the red-haired girl approached me.

"Hi, Maggie," she said in an "I remembered your name, did you remember mine?" tone of voice.

"Hi, Mia."

"You're really lucky to be with Dr. Rosenberg. He's the best. He really believes in us. Everyone wants to be in his Group."

"I guess we're special."

She said, "He gets the problem cases," and pushed a hank of red hair behind her ear.

When she did this, I saw that her skinny arms were ringed with puffy pink and red skin. They looked like something that had been stepped on repeatedly, the left one worse than the right. *Scissors. Kitchen knives.* I closed my eyes momentarily, emptied my mind the way we'd been told to at the beginning of Group. When I opened my eyes again, Mia was staring at me like she was the popular girl in a high school movie and I was a new transfer. *I will not cry in front of this bitch.* I looked away from her arms, but I knew what they would feel like because I'd touched skin like that before. The scars would be loose and soft, slightly raised; they would feel like polyester.

"I'm going to get something to eat," I said, and turned away.

Mia's husband was shot while sitting in his car after buying ecstasy in Toronto, not far from my store. He was a lawyer and had lived with Mia in Brampton near an apple orchard. He drove an hour and a half to the city for work every day and Mia had a horse named Socks that she had trained herself. They had tried to get pregnant but Mia was still taking the pill without telling him; she wasn't ready to have a baby, and why did she need a baby when she had Socks? Her mother got her into the program after she saw Mia's arms. The husband had been gone for only two months.

Timothy's wife was flattened. Tracey's brother with the brain aneurysm never got to see the Cherry Blossom Festival he was looking forward to. A postcard arrived from him, shortly after his funeral.

In the afternoon we watched *Aliens* and I got the impression that was the norm, like *Chinatown*: violent, sad or scary movies. Afterwards we played cards—blackjack because there wasn't any other game we all knew—and we bought in with real money, twenty dollars each. Tracey said, "I would never do this in the real world. Normally I play with quarters."

In the absence of anything to talk about, we played too seriously, bullying, and one by one we lost. Mia ended up with almost all the money, looking pleased and fluffed out, like a cat. There was no Activity Therapy planned—"You'll find out," said Tracey—so we played Candy Land and the Game of Life and Sorry! and we were ruthless. I was exhausted by the time I went upstairs.

Before going to bed the first night, I made the mattress up with the sheets I had brought from home. I took the ones the hospital had provided and folded them up and slid them under the little couch. I put on my pyjamas and got in. It was a queen bed, bigger than I was used to; the sheets I had brought were my parents' extras. My father's extras.

I tried one side and then the other. I got up to unlatch the windows for some air before I remembered Rosenberg had said they didn't open. There was a small television, and I watched a few minutes of a show where people said *damn* a lot and held their guns with both hands. When I did fall asleep, I had my dream, one I had dreamed many times since I'd gone to the river to find that my father had lost my mother.

In it I was living in a dystopian future where the ruling group had decided that viewing the natural world incited too much independent thought. All green things were forbidden; I knew this without understanding how I knew it. Huge high walls were built up all around the city, and they looked like the greying sound barriers that bracket the highway out of town. They were so tall that even the tops of trees couldn't be seen beyond them, if there were any trees left outside. I believed there were—in this dream, I believed that there were still trees out there some-where. I was in a city square, looking up at the sky. Behind me, with a hand on my shoulder, was a man who I thought was Andrew, but it might have been Gil. I never saw the man's face.

I stood in the square and looked up at the sky, and I was thinking to myself that as long as I could see the clouds, I'd be okay. But I also thought I should stop looking up before it tipped them off that they had forgotten to hide the last evidence of the natural world, of beauty. The hand on my shoulder tightened in warning or in solidarity. I stood in the square and looked at the sky and looked and looked and then the sky fell on me and it was made of dirty water and I was drowning in it. The water that was the sky rolled over me and I sat up, choking, awake. I didn't know where I was, the shape of the room was all wrong and it made me feel like I was dizzy, the distances and the light all unfamiliar and awful.

I flinched when I heard something tapping at the window. I opened my eyes and looked up and saw a man through the glass, sitting on the fire escape. There was a swinging feeling in my body and a flash of pain like a premonition, but then I saw, dimly, that it was Gil, no longer tapping, holding his hand against the glass, fingers tightly together. He said something I couldn't hear. Then he opened the window, which was heavy and wood-trimmed, sliding it vertically.

"What are you doing here?"

"We have an arrangement, darling. Don't tell me they have you all doped up and you forgot."

"I don't want to see you. I told you that. And it's the middle of the night. And I thought those windows didn't open."

He waved me away and began to climb through the window. "Don't be melodramatic," he said. "If I gave up every time you felt down, I wouldn't have written a damn page."

I saw he had a bag with him, an old-fashioned backpack like the kind mountain climbers use. It was orange.

"What is that for?"

"What do you think it's for? I'm not a bloody commuter. If you're here, I'm here. I feel like we've reached the sleepover stage, no?" He turned away and began to unpack his bag, placing his things in the dresser, beside mine. He hung his thin shirts in the little closet on the leftover hangers. I had used all the good wooden ones and left only the wire kind you get from the dry cleaner. Once he was finished, he unbuckled his belt and coiled it into a circle. He walked towards me. I had gotten back into bed and pulled the blankets up. He put the belt on the bottom shelf of the nightstand and then began fumbling with his zipper.

"Wait," I said, but he let his pants fall and stepped out of them, standing in his jockey shorts and grey T-shirt. I had trouble not looking at his pale legs, which had a lot of dark hair on them. He folded his pants and put them in the dresser.

"It's a little late for modesty, isn't it?" he said. "We're on the same page here, right?"

"I haven't forgiven you yet," I said. "I mean, I haven't forgiven you. Period." But my body was prickling and it was surprisingly pleasant. There was a curve above his knee where the muscle of his thigh smoothed out. We were both sweating in the airless heat of the second floor. I would have to ask about the air conditioning. "I haven't made a decision to let you try again."

He nodded, seemingly affable, and sat down at the wooden desk with his notebooks. He turned on the lamp and was copying loose notes into the books, scribbling away. For a while, I felt strange watching him—in what sense was this my mother's life he was writing? Did he know more than me? I'd given him more of my notebooks, thinking they might be helpful, the things I'd written down since she died.

"Why don't I just write the book myself? If you're using my notes and going ahead without my permission?"

"Not that I can hear you, dear Muse, since I'm doing very important work, but if I could hear you, I would say that you are too close to the material. There's no distance. You don't know what's relevant. Because it's all relevant to you. I'm the thing that makes it art, as opposed to just a list of events."

"What's wrong with a list? If everything is on it?"

Gil frowned and stopped. Finally he said, "A list isn't a book. That's what's wrong with it." He shook his curly head like a horse scattering flies and started up again.

I thought of all my notebooks over the years, the ones I'd given Gil, and the older ones. They were still my life, the day-to-day. Maybe they lacked structure—just disconnected scenes, hoarded, polished by my remembering and remembering of them the way water polishes stone—but they were mine.

I got up and shut myself in the little bathroom.

The shower was a modified old-fashioned bathtub with a length of flexible piping bolted to the wall and a metal frame for a circular shower curtain. While I washed, the plastic curtain stuck to me, making me claustrophobic. I resolved to change it for a clear one, so I could at least see the edges of the tub while I showered. Despite the curtain, the hot water felt good.

I changed back into my pyjamas in the bathroom so Gil wouldn't see me. Then, with my hair coiled in a wet knot on my head, I emerged and went to bed without saying anything, the light from his lamp glowing behind my closed eyes.

Fourteen

Four days a week, in the mornings, we went one by one into Dr. Rosenberg's office at the back of the house. It must have been a porch at one point but it had been glassed in. The windows were like school windows with a fine wire mesh imbedded throughout. I went first because I was the last to arrive at the House. I had to get up early and I didn't like it— after years of opening the store around ten, dawdling on Queen Street time, I wasn't used to being an early riser. *Early to bed, early to rise, makes a man healthy, wealthy and wise.* One of my father's only idioms, it somehow paled beside my mother's more colourful *You may as well hang for a sheep as for a lamb.*

We started therapy at eight and were done by noon, an hour each, back to back, and then Dr. Rosenberg left to eat lunch and go downtown to the hospital. The three of us who were not in with him at any given time sat in the common room with the patients from the new wing, who drifted in and out of their own therapy sessions with other doctors down the hall. We listened to the yoga teacher or the watercolour instructor or the woman who helped us write long disjointed poems that didn't rhyme and gave us inspiration words like *nest* and *waves* and *tower*. Activity Therapy, like Tracey had warned about.

The poetry woman was the first one I met, in the morning after my first session with Rosenberg. We all used freshly sharpened pencils to write poems in our lined notebooks and the woman played U2's "Where the Streets Have No Name" and Bon Jovi ballads while we worked, totally straight-faced. "Just let the music heal you," she said. "Get the poison out." A man from one of the other small groups was sitting beside me on the couch, and he grinned at me over his three-ring binder.

After the tape player had been shut off and we were all look-ing up from our pages, eyeballing one another, the poetry woman told us we could read our poems if we wanted. Only Tracey volunteered.

"There's a neighbourhood coalition," she said at the end of her poem, which had included rocks that bled and horses that jumped over dried-up streams full of fish bones and long-lost lures, which may have been a nod to Socks, who was being cared for by Mia's mother and a hired man while Mia was in Wooster House. I thought at first that the coalition was part of the poem.

"I heard about that," said Timothy. "I went down to the gro-cery store; those women in line were talking about it right up behind me."

"I heard it at the park," said Tracey. "They want us to wear special T-shirts."

"Who does?" I said. "Who wants T-shirts?"

"The neighbourhood. They want to know who we are. They're worried we might do something crazy. They want us kept in, behind the fence."

"Orange," said Timothy.

"Yeah, orange. They all want orange T-shirts."

"Why orange?" asked the man beside me.

"It's the craziest?"

"Did they all discuss this?" said someone at the back of the room.

Everyone was there except Mia, who was still in with Rosenberg. This conversation was not bitter or even dismissive. It was impish, and also indulgent. We felt indulgent towards these neighbours, who were known to grab their small daughters by the upper arms when they saw us walking down our gravel path, when they saw Chad unlocking the front gate. We felt amused, mildly irritated. But none of us had been there very long yet.

When I went up to my room after therapy and poetry were over, Gil was not there. This was the time we had arranged to meet and I had to be back downstairs for croquet soon and didn't want to be late and raise suspicion.

I straightened up the things on my dresser, already neat. The envelope of photos and papers from the third-floor storage room was squared beside my notebook, with my hairbrush, my pens lined up perfectly beside. I reminded myself that I still needed to check through the manila envelope sometime, once I'd gotten what I could from Rosenberg.

I checked the washroom to make sure Gil wasn't there, thinking I might find him in some compromising and undignified position, pissing with his eyes closed, cock in hand, feet bare on the floor. Or peering into ears or nose, checking for an over-abundance of hair. Gil had the serious, slightly ridiculous dignity of a child. After a few minutes of sitting on the bed, feeling stupid, I went downstairs, out into the bright sun of the back-yard, and claimed a green ball with a white strip as mine.

The croquet went the same as the blackjack had the day before. We never took the extra stroke when we bumped into each other, we always sent the other person into the shrubs, where the base of the fence disappeared—except Mia, who could not be counted on to take part in this invigorating sav-agery. It became apparent that nobody liked Mia, who was beautiful and cried all the time. She cried when she knocked her red ball into the shrubs and asked if she could have a do-over. Tracey rolled her eyes and said, "How is that fair?" But Timothy said one time wouldn't hurt and everyone listened to Timothy because he was a doctor, although he was actually a dentist. He had very small, square teeth in two perfect rows and you could see the lower ones more than the top. They looked very white in his dark face.

Tracey showed her gums all the way around when she smiled but when her mouth was closed she looked elegant. While she whacked at her ball, she said she had grown up with very strict parents who expected her to be either an accountant or a lawyer but instead she worked as a copywriter for the Canadian Cancer Society and they looked away when she talked about her job. Tracey said that her parents were being stereotypical first-generation immigrants, putting too much pressure on her, and she could care less. She didn't seem to think it strange to talk like that, even though one of the other small groups was playing checkers in pairs on the back deck and could hear her. She stood like someone with very good feet, high arches, healthy knees.

"Don't let them get to you," she said, looking straight at the other patients, who dropped their gazes. "They're crazy anyway."

After the game, the four of us sat around a table in the kitchen and Tracey taught us to play euchre. When we got bored, Timothy made a pot of tea with some Lemon Sunshine leaves I had brought, and when we were done, he got us to turn the cups upside down on the saucers, wait seven seconds, and then pass them to him.

"My aunt taught me," he said. "It's silly, but obviously none of us are exactly scientists, right?" And he laughed and I thought, *I'm not sure I would want him as my dentist.*

"I'm pretty sure that's an acorn right there, Mia. It's on the future side, but near the bottom. That's health—so, good news." He turned the cup back and forth and said, "Maybe." Pulling Tracey's cup to him, frowned. "I think that's a loop, that skinny leaf and this one. Like a roller coaster. That means you shouldn't do anything impulsive. But that looks like a shell there—good news. Again."

He took my cup last, turned the handle towards himself. "Does that look like a sailboat to you?" He pointed. "That's good—protection, I think. Or a visit from a friend. Maybe both. Unless it's an iceberg. It's kind of pointy. Iceberg is danger." He looked at me and said, "Let's say it's a boat, yeah?" Then he said, "The car was less than eighteen inches high. In some spots. After the truck rolled over on her. God"—he looked at me—"it's so good to be around people who understand."

Timothy said he went to work the day after his wife died because he couldn't think of anything else to do, and he slid his big latex-covered fingers into the mouths of people who would never know what it's like to be told their wife was in eighteen inches of crushed car. He said that he felt once, just for an instant, like ripping a man's jaw off his face.

"Because, why me?" he whispered, and he put his hand out on the table like he hoped someone might take it. "Right?"

And I wanted to tell him I knew just how he felt. But my own grief didn't make his more attractive to me. Instead I wanted to bolt upstairs. I put my head down and looked at the tea leaves, and Tracey said, "I think I need some fresh air."

The next morning Gil was back in place, writing at the desk before I went down for my therapy session with Rosenberg. We did the Journey Technique again and then Rosenberg had me turn over the tarot cards, talk about what they meant and what emotions they brought up. He sat there, looking at me with his hand on his jaw, covering his mouth.

"Strength," I said, poking the card like a dead fish. "I can't remember what that one means." I turned another card over. The Wheel of Fortune. "What goes up must come down," I said. "Or vice versa."

"What does that mean to you? Changing fortunes. You're experiencing an enormous change now—do you feel you're going up or down?"

I turned over another card. The magician, reversed. All major arcana. Had I shuffled properly? In the image, the table in front of the magician held one of each of the symbols of the four suits. A lemniscate floated over his head.

I stared at the card. Rosenberg leaned forward.

"Did my mother ever tell you anything about where she was from?" I said, and he slumped back into his chair.

"Have you been doing your mental walk exercise? You can do it on your own, you know, not just during our sessions. In bed at night. Why don't we talk about the things you've placed on your path in the park. Are there people on the path? People who contribute to your happiness?"

I said, "I had a dream last night. I've had it before."

"What kind of dream?"

"There's a man I can't see. I think he wants to help me. But then there's water everywhere, and I can't— Then I wake up."

"How do you feel when you wake up?"

I thought of the woman who bought the crystal ball. I thought of the ball, the breath of air caught in the glass.

"Confused, I guess." I turned the magician card over. "Tell me something about her. Please. Just anything about what you remember. What sort of person was she back then?"

He shook his head. "I don't want you to think I have some special information I'm withholding, Maggie. My impression of your mother was very positive, but I didn't know her very well, I didn't have any unique insight. She was a person who was good at what she wanted to be good at. There's something special about that."

I turned over the next card in the deck. It was the hanged man and his saintly glow. "Thank you," I said. I cleared my throat. "I think maybe the memory exercises are helping. With the blackouts. Maybe we could try again? With something simple?"

Rosenberg took me on my mental walk a few more times, and I did a little better with a list of twenty numbers and then a list of twenty countries than I had with the cards.

"I'm pleased to see you embracing the Journey Technique so enthusiastically," he said.

"It is nice. To go there in my head." This was true, I liked thinking about the park. But mostly I'd just wanted to distract Rosenberg after he'd told me what he thought about my mother, turning it over in my mind. *Good at what she wanted to be good at.* I looked at my watch.

"Time's up," I said, and the little bell sounded.

Our Activity Therapy for the day was cancelled because the Pilates teacher had called in with a pulled groin, so the Rosenberg Group was stationed outside, in the backyard, enjoying the morning sun. Even though it was only 9 a.m., Tracey was laid out on a towel, sunbathing. It was late August, sunny and hot. There were greenish bruises on her thighs and she told me that the pay phone had fallen on her when she pulled it off the wall two days before I got to Wooster House.

"I was talking to my parents. I have some issues with anger-and-or-impulse control," she said, as if reciting. "I broke a bottle over someone's head, that's why I had to come here. This was the touchy-feely option, instead of community service."

"Oh," I said. "What did he do? The bottle guy?"

"You know," she said. She had a tube of sunblock and was rubbing some on her shoulders and in the V of her tank top. "He was an asshole."

She offered the sunscreen to me and I rubbed some over the bridge of my nose.

I'd been sitting on the swinging bench for a few minutes when Timothy came out with his arms full of grocery bags. He was wearing a bright orange T-shirt. We'd all gotten them that morning—Hanes and Hanes Her Way, too tight in the hips, too loose at the collar. We had to wear them when we left the House.

"I thought we could make some picnic things," he said. "Just for fun."

Tracey and I followed him into the kitchen. He had bought ingredients for breaded chicken, coleslaw, brownies and egg-salad sandwiches. There were pickles, olives and cookies. "We have to sign out knives with Chad," said Tracey. "Thanks to our little red-headed drama queen." She twiddled her fingers up and down her forearm.

I went to Chad's office to ask for a knife to cut up the cabbage and bread. He brought one in and watched while we chopped.

Timothy said, "Chad, you're a good-looking young man, I bet you have a girlfriend."

Chad blushed, almost seeming to glow. "No," he said. "Not right now."

Tracey was beside him, her tank top still rolled up under her breasts from tanning. She was mixing the bread crumbs and spices for the chicken.

"I'm not supposed to ask," Chad said. "But what made you go to town on the phone like that the other day?"

"Oh," she said, shaking her hands in the air. "You know parents."

When we finished cooking and the chicken had chilled in the fridge during Timothy's and Tracey's sessions, we brought everything outside and sat on the blankets we'd found in the hall closet, and Chad showed us how to twist the corners under to keep them from flying away without weights. He sat outside with us and didn't take any food for himself until Tracey insisted, piling a plate and passing it to him. I ate some of everything, even the olives, which I normally avoided. They were black olives, loose around their pits, and they tasted like a bitten tongue, like pennies. The sun was bright and I was sweating under my arms and down my back. Occasionally I would peer up at the top floor of the House even though I couldn't see my own bedroom from the backyard. But Gil was in there. He was so solid the House could topple over under the weight of him and the notebooks.

It occurred to me I should bring him something to eat. He had been writing all day. I could make a plate up for him; he'd be grateful, surprised. I would be useful. It was a version of love.

I felt guilty for thinking about Gil that way. I should be thinking about my mother. I hadn't even gone through the envelope of things I had brought down from the storage room yet. I was memorizing lists for Rosenberg, trying to improve my memory, when it was her I should be memorizing: her clues, her habits, her small rotten spots that I would check and check again. I tried to make sense of her history, the little Georgia town that I could see on a map but which revealed nothing, her journey to Canada, the dirty draft dodgers—including Rosenberg, no less—who she slept beside in our apartment, when she was all of eighteen years old, playing her guitar on the streets of Yorkville and then, just a few years later somehow, unimaginably, choosing my father, his auburn hair cut to come to a point in the front, his upper lip without indentation, blank beside her perfect cupid's bow. I listed all these things as if every person made sense if you could only find out enough, as if no one was illogical in the end—it was something I'd always believed without knowing I believed it, something my father might say, come to think of it. I wanted to remember the details because the problem with love is that it obscures what is underneath it, what is being loved, and you don't notice until later. We like to think of it as a light we're shining, strategically, but maybe it's more like a blanket you throw around someone who is on fire, to smother the flames. Love extinguishes. But afterwards, when you're left holding it, trying to remember the person who was wrapped up in it, you're stuck remembering the love instead, the scratchy feel of it in your hands, and what was underneath is just a vague person-shaped thing that could be almost anyone. Nice. Funny. Strong. Good. Who wasn't, at least some of the time?

The problem with dead people is that you can't get any new information out of them; you have to use what you already have. In five minutes I could have asked my mother a dozen questions. I had years and years and I hadn't asked her; I hadn't wanted to pry, like she was a stranger in line at the supermarket. Also I didn't want to upset her. I just threw the love around her and held on, and figured that was enough, that she would tell me, sometime, everything I needed to know.

Fifteen

At night, in the room, I sat in bed and watched the news while Gil scribbled, occasionally asking me to clarify something from one of my notebooks. I was tired and hot, sick of his questions. There was a cut on my foot where one of the nailheads on the staircase had nicked me and I'd had to throw out my bloodstained sock.

"So, just to be clear, you never gave the zircon cat to that Elaine girl?"

"No. Isn't that what it says? I figured you would at least be literate if you're trying to write a whole book."

"Aren't we a grumpy girl," said Gil, looking up from his notebook. "Don't you know girls are supposed to be nice and sweet?"

"Don't you start with me," I said. "I'm not in the mood to be talked down to."

Gil looked up at the ceiling, an angelic expression blanketing his features. "Ending a sentence," he said quietly, as if against his will, "with a preposition. And you want to write the book yourself—"

"Seriously, stop it."

"Apologies," he said, grandly.

I moved to the little couch and turned on the radio. I couldn't find a comfortable position even there. "Gil?" He turned to me. "I'm trying. But I'm—" I stopped and shrugged.

"Just a little longer," he said. "I think."

"But—"

He waved a hand in the air. "Darling," he said, "exactly what would you be doing instead?"

I got up and crossed to the bed. I lay down. I heard the chair scrape the battered floorboards. Gil stood beside the bed.

"I've been saving this," he said. "I wasn't going to give it to you yet. But."

He put a small package on my belly; it was clumsily wrapped in cheap, shiny paper, the Scotch tape snarled in several places. I unwrapped a box, removed the lid and turned it upside down.

"Careful," said Gil, as the little jade angel fell out.

I picked it up. The price tag was still stuck to the underside of the base, smooth and circular.

"You bought it for me?"

Gil took it from my hand and put it on the nightstand beside me. He leaned down and kissed me. "I just need a little more time," he said. Turning away, he went into the washroom.

After a moment, I heard the shower running. I got up and approached Gil's desk, standing motionless for a few minutes. The steam rolling out the bathroom door made me feel like sneezing.

I'd resisted up to that point reading any of his work. Gil had put me off with promises to edit them soon, or declarations that reading the manuscript in its unfinished form would ruin the final work. "I can't have someone involved in the source material offering editorial advice," he'd said. "It would just create a wormhole of self-censorship."

Picking up the notebook was an impulse, like putting your hand on a hot stove. I had to do it quickly or I would lose my nerve.

My eyes scanned the page, jumping from one sentence to another without attention to narrative.

I envied the secretive allure of wild horses . . . shambled down the wide shallow steps . . . vague, Gypsy knowledge . . .

"Are you kidding?" I said, throwing them down. I crossed to the washroom, banged on the door. The shower screeched off.

"What are you doing?" said Gil, coming out moments later with a towel hitched around his waist. His chest and face were mottled red.

"These are my notebooks. You stole all of this."

"I'm using your source material, that's true. But it was hardly in publishable form, I think you'll agree."

"But you're just copying them! You're not adding anything. There's nothing in here I didn't write."

"I'm expanding upon them. I'm creating a narrative structure using your raw materials. I'm creating order. I didn't think this would matter, you're the source, I'm the writer, so there's a little overlap. What's the problem?"

"You're stealing. These are mine and you're stealing."

"I'm a writer."

"Why do I even need you, then? I don't need you. I'll do it myself."

"Will you? I highly doubt that. You need me. Don't think for a second you could do this without me."

"You said you were *writing* me, not *being* me. You're pretending to be me."

"Does it make a difference?"

"Of course it does. It makes a difference to me. You're saying things I said, you're—"

"I'm sorry," he said, impatient. "I thought I had explained things in a clear manner. It never occurred to me that the narrative perspective would be an issue."

"The narrative perspective?"

"First person, third person, and so on."

Reddening, I said, "I know what it means."

"Well, you seemed not to." He rubbed his hairline. "Let's all calm down," he said.

"I'm not calm," I said, "I'm fucking un-calm." I was clenching my fists so hard my nails were denting my palms.

"Maybe this is just a waste of time," he said. He took a long step and swept the stack of notebooks off the desk. Then he sat down. "Do you think this is easy for me?"

One curl of dark hair was sticking straight up, askew from when he'd put his hand through it. Suddenly I hated that curl. I wanted to rip it out of his head. I wondered for a moment where Chad kept the scissors locked up.

"I don't really care if it is easy for you, Gil." The sound of his own name made him wince. "Who cares? If it's the way you say, then you're just a record press. You're—a Dictaphone." I gasped when I finished, loudly. I had run out of air while speaking.

Gil stood up quickly, sending his chair skidding backwards. For a second he didn't move and something washed over my body, pricking and cold. I thought he was going to hit me. I almost wanted him to. I remembered the first time I'd seen him in the store, his hand around the jade angel, his body unknown, unmapped. But now he spun on his heel and went back into the washroom, pulling the door closed. He came out a moment later in a white T-shirt and loose pants. He had done a poor job drying himself and his clothes were sticking to his chest, his crotch. He went out the window without looking at me. He didn't make a sound going down.

It was late when he came back and though he entered as silently as he had gone, he woke me. He picked the notebooks up from the floor and went back to the desk as if nothing had happened. There was a hesitant scribbling for a few minutes and then silence.

The floor creaked as he crossed to the bed and the mattress sagged a little when he lay down. He rolled onto his elbow, hovered above me. Then he pushed my hair up and off my face and was very close. He put his whole mouth over mine, put his mouth on my closed eyes, slid down to my chest and then pushed his head up under my chin. Our hands and elbows got in the way. His weight was more than I was used to, and for a moment my breath wouldn't catch and I bucked a little and he said "Sorry" and shifted. He had to get up out of the bed to take off his pants and socks. I thought I must look different now, older, worse, but Gil didn't seem to notice anything. I thought my blood might leak out the cut on my foot, there seemed to be too much of it in my body, I could feel my pulse at a dozen different points.

After it was over, he wouldn't let go of me. When I pulled a papery tissue from the box on the nightstand, the box toppled and hit the floor. "Last one, I guess," I said.

Gil said nothing, but pressed his face to my shoulder. He was shaking like someone lifting a heavy weight.

The air through the open window was cool against my damp skin. The sheet was kicked and crumpled at the bottom of the bed. What had Rosenberg called it? *Body confusion.* The way we feel about sex after someone dies. I didn't feel confused, though. Instead I felt suffused, full of light, as if I were a prism, reflecting and absorbing something beautiful. What was the word? *Diffuse.* I put my head on his chest.

"You're not upset, are you?" he said.

"No. Or maybe I'm upset that I'm not upset."

Gil shifted, put an arm behind his head. "Women," he said. "You're a crazy bunch." But his voice was soft and he reached down, stroked my hair.

We lay in silence, overheated. I closed my eyes. *This city tells you everything you need to know. It takes you in. Who could ask for more?*

Two days later, I was making my way downstairs when Chad stopped me in the common room.

"You have a visitor," he said, and I trailed him to the front door.

Andrew was there, holding a bouquet of daisies. I went hot and then cold all over, like a flu.

The first thing he said was, "Are you allowed to have these?"

"No, they're worried I'll build a daisy chain and climb it out the window."

He stepped into the House and I hugged him close. He kissed me and I went overboard, mouth open, kissing him back. *Everything's normal, I love my boyfriend.* I felt nauseated, like Gil's handprints were fluorescent all over my body.

Pulling him by the arm, I said, "Let's get those in some water."

People from the other small groups were sitting in the common room, watching reruns of *The Simpsons* and chatting. When I crossed to the kitchen, they stared openly. Visitors were pitifully infrequent, always of interest. Some of the younger women were looking at Andrew. *I know I've got a spare stashed upstairs, but that doesn't mean I won't scratch your eyes out, ladies.*

I put the daisies in a vase and brought Andrew to the swinging bench in the backyard.

"You didn't tell me you were coming."

He looked surprised. "Your therapy is during the day, isn't it?"

"Well, yeah. But I mean, I have other stuff to do. Not that I don't appreciate you coming, I do. It's just— I actually have a session with Dr. Rosenberg tonight."

"At night?" Andrew put his arm around me, jerkily, as if on command. His legs were crossed, his foot fiddling in the air.

He gave me the things my father had sent with him: a box of crackers, two tubes of toothpaste—*how fast did he think I went through it?*—a reading light.

I wished I had something to send back, some small well-made thing.

Andrew said, "How are you feeling? Are things okay here? Any blackouts?"

"Things are okay. No blackouts lately."

We sat and talked, Andrew telling me about the classes he would be teaching in a couple of weeks, me looking over my shoulder and then telling him about my small group. I didn't say anything about Rosenberg.

"Scarlet, the girl your dad hired, she came to the bar with Wendy and me the other day. She's actually pretty bright."

"Really?"

"She moved here from Vancouver, to do her master's."

His voice itched to add more, but I didn't ask. Instead I said, "Oh. How is the store?"

"Good. I think she's keeping everything running smoothly."

The sun set while we talked, disappearing behind the back fence. When the darker blue of early evening had spread across the sky, Andrew said, "I should get back to my reading lists. Trying to get everything ready for the term. Do you mind?"

I shook my head no. "Thanks for coming." Then I turned and kissed him, my hand flat on his chest. "If I'm not home yet next week, maybe you could come again? You and Wendy could drive out together."

He looked away, back towards the house. "That's a good idea."

When I escorted Andrew to the front hall to say goodbye, Rosenberg was standing there beside the pay phone with his hands in his pockets. Chad was there too.

"Is it eight already?"

Rosenberg shook hands with Andrew, who said, "Take good care of her." Kissing me on the top of my head, he jiggled his car keys and said, "Better hit the old dusty trail."

Once he'd gone, Chad escorted us somewhat formally to the sunroom-office. He gave me a small wave after Rosenberg had turned away, towards his desk, then he pulled the door shut from the outside.

After I'd gotten comfortable, Rosenberg asked me more specific questions about the blackouts, the few seconds of gathering darkness that seemed to mark their coming, what I'd been doing and feeling and seeing and smelling and touching each time, until I wanted to take a page out of Tracey's book and rip something off a wall. I answered mechanically, shutting off my mind as best I could. When it was over, Rosenberg sank back, then roused himself to shut off the camera. He took my blood and then took his usual measurements—my pulse, my pupils—and his hands were soft, hardly touching me, like an insect landing only briefly on my skin.

Sixteen

"We look like crossing guards," said Tracey. We were standing in front of the foyer mirror, plucking at the orange T-shirts. "I feel like I should be directing traffic."

"Sorry," said Chad. "It wasn't my idea. People are ignorant."

I wondered what Chad must think of us.

We walked down to the Second Cup and bought cowboy cookies and drinks from the girl behind the counter. Tracey got an Italian soda and spilled part of it down her shirt while she put the lid on. The clerk was very quiet when she gave us our change, and as we left the store I turned and saw her picking up the telephone.

"When do you think we'll go home? I mean, I know we can leave whenever we want, but when do you think we'll get the stamp of approval to rejoin society?" said Tracey.

She had on her cut-off jean shorts and I could see the soft skin of her inner thighs when we sat cross-legged on the grass by the yacht club. I slid my notebook and a pen out of my shoulder bag, clicked the nib up. I doodled idly on a blank page, drawing the sailboats as a series of triangles.

I said, "Next week, maybe?"

She laughed. "My family doesn't think I'm ever coming home. Did I tell you they mailed me my clothes and books? They even sent my old photo albums. My poor parents," she said, and her voice was harsh. "Oh-for-two. A dead son and me." She put her hand on my arm. "Sorry. I kept forgetting it's your mom. I shouldn't complain about parents to you."

"No, it's not like that. Go ahead."

"When she died," she said, "could you feel it? Like, in your body? I felt my brother. I felt like all the blood disappeared from my body. Or like it all turned into something else, something wrong."

"No," I said. "I didn't know until my dad phoned."

"Oh. Maybe it's a twin thing."

"Maybe," I said.

Or maybe I was missing something, something that could have helped my mother. Some small switch in the brain that was supposed to be flipped. There were times she tried to explain it to me, the thing that made her different.

"There's a place I can go inside my head," she had said, pulling a scarf from her hair, or twirling a bone ring on her finger.

She had said that sometime, and now I had a thousand questions, things I hadn't thought to ask then. Maybe I hadn't been listening; I thought I was listening, hard and carefully. But now that she was gone, old conversations would open back up, wider than before, and I would hear things that had slipped by me then, while I was bent over a cash register or a basket of laundry, as if the range of my hearing had expanded after she was gone.

"Sometimes it is hard to get back, and it's getting harder. Do you know what I mean?"

I didn't know. I wanted to know. I tried to dredge up such a place inside myself and relate somehow. But while my mother had an ocean inside her to look into, I had a stream, a puddle. I couldn't help but stand there looking outwards, looking at her.

She could see on my face that I didn't understand.

"I'm sorry," she said. "I shouldn't say these things to you. I am a bad mother."

"No," I said. "Never."

All this with my father in the kitchen, listening around the corner, or in the store with an old woman waiting with her arms full of incense.

Back then I would lie in bed at night, Andrew with his knees hanging off the side of the bed, me with my hip and thigh pressed against the wall. It was hot but the paint was always cool, slightly tacky. My mother, lost inside her head. My mother, on the other side of the wall, ten seconds away. And my mother, miles away, in places that I couldn't go.

Maybe that's what living was, though—not a series of moments, but a set of places. Even after memory fails and the context—how old was I? what year was it?—is gone, the places stay. Andrew's bed with its thick, slippery sheets. The store at night, after closing, the brass of the ladder rims catching the street light. Bellwoods in the spring, with the south lilacs blooming. Which spring? Being oriented in time doesn't matter in the end, because once something has happened it will never un-happen, it will only go on happening forever in the place where it happened, and the mere mention of places will bring people and events to life, not again, but still, because that's what they are—still happening, continually happening. The

Don River will always be full of my mother's body. George's diner will always be stuffed to the walls with Wendy's wheezy laughter. My father's bedroom will always hold him sitting up in bed, in his white-white T-shirts. It's easy to get out of time, to slip sideways out of it, to find it's gone missing, but there's only one way to get out of space, and that's in the river, with your pockets full of zircon.

Tracey's hand closed around my wrist. I took the pen off the page.

"Let's talk about something else," she said, and her dark eyes were reflective, wet.

Her hand on my arm was soft and small, square-palmed. The tips of her fingers, though, were dry and rough, with shards of skin poking up, scraping against my wrist. She pulled her hand away.

"I have skin problems," she said. "They crack." She rolled her hands into fists.

I put my notebook back into my purse and we walked to the park. The shore smelled like rotting fish but the breeze was fresh. Summer was winding down. We skipped rocks and squatted near the water's edge. We walked back up to Lake Shore and looked down at the docks, where tanned people stepped confidently onto boats tied up with just one or two little ropes. We leaned there, looking out from the bridge, and people put their heads down and walked in a wide berth around us, like we were asking them for money.

"We ought to start drooling," said Tracey. "Give the people a show."

But our hearts weren't in it. We returned to the House and rang the bell. Chad came out and let us in, smiling at Tracey.

Inside, I said, "Have you tried almond oil? For your hands."

Tracey held them out, palms up. There was a jagged series of cracks on each finger-pad, little dots of blood and white, dead skin. "I've tried everything," she said. And then she reached out and pulled me to her and I could feel her body, soft legs and firm torso. I was much taller than her and she tucked her head under my chin and her black hair was hot from the sun and slippery against my damp neck. It was so thick I could feel each strand of hair like the whorls of a record.

"Why haven't we ever done this before?" she said. "Fuck yoga."

And we stood there for a minute like that, before heading into the backyard to sit on the swinging bench.

I could only imagine what we looked like to the people outside the fence. There were narrow gaps between the wooden slats. Our bright T-shirts would wink at them through the spaces as we moved, doing nothing more interesting than getting up for a glass of water, or to get a deck of cards. How distracting the flashes of colour would be to the people walking by, keeping them twitching, looking for something from the corners of their eyes.

When I went upstairs, Gil was standing in the middle of the room. I looked at him and opened my mouth and then everything was wide open, there was no light, and a gust of wind nearly knocked me off my feet. The darkness dissipated, fuzzy and fading until it was gone. We were on top of a tall building and I could see the city around us.

"Where are we?"

"We're on top of the Royal York Hotel."

The roof was long and narrow, with a waist-high wall where the familiar mint-green copper scrolls continued. There were planters full of green, rows of wooden stakes and covered lights. Small trees were tied to support poles to encourage them, and the usual collection of odd-shaped industrial metal contraptions littered each corner—cooling units, storage sheds, stairwells.

The hotel was a landmark. Wendy had an art deco poster reproduction tacked up in her apartment: *Royal York Hotel Toronto: The Tallest Building in the British Empire.* I guess it was, once. Wendy had stayed on at the Royal York while we went to university, working as a room-service attendant, gleefully relating to me the various states of undress she had witnessed while delivering champagne, cheeseburgers, crustless cucumber sandwiches, fresh-squeezed orange juice, and every other request the rotating cast of guests could dream up. Sometimes I would meet her in the foyer, her requisite black slacks stained with stories for later, the lobby clock sticking straight up from the spiral staircase like an eyeball that had been plucked out and left dangling, defying gravity. I had never seen the roof before, though.

"How the hell—"

"You trust me, don't you?"

I didn't say anything. The wind was warm, almost wet, and the sun was dim and colourless in the sky, swaddled in cloud. Gil approached me and opened his coat like a flasher. He was wearing worn navy corduroy pants and a white shirt with a button missing in the middle.

"Come here," he said, and he pulled me against him, wrapping his coat around the both of us.

I wasn't wearing my orange T-shirt; instead I had on a light dress. I remembered buying it the summer before. It had been in my Wooster House luggage. Against Gil's body, I was warm.

"Maggie," he said. "The book isn't working. I tried to keep going without you. I couldn't do it. And even now, back with you—"

I could see the CN Tower off to the side like a defiant erection, and the smooth hairless ball of the SkyDome beside it.

"Well, I'm not getting better," I said. "At least, the blackouts haven't stopped. And I don't think I trust you."

"We're going to have to do something extreme," he said. "That's why we're here."

The wind was whipping my hair around my head. I felt my head was in the eye of a storm. I felt calm, pressed against Gil.

"We have to jump," he said.

We were standing near the edge and I could see over the barrier. The city below looked rumpled, as if it had slept in its clothes.

"Did you hear me?"

"I heard you."

"I know suicide is a touchy subject, but I think we're against a wall here. Dead writers are always more successful."

I tried to look up at Gil, but we were too close together. I was still wrapped in his coat. I put my cheek against his. I could feel his hair against my face, his curls longer than when we'd met and none too clean.

"You want to jump?"

"I want us to jump."

I snuggled closer to him. "What if I don't want to?"

He didn't speak for a while. "I don't know," he said finally.

I took Gil's face in my hands and kissed him. "Well, if that's how it has to be," I said. Then I pulled away from him and turned to the wall. I started to climb onto the edge.

"Wait," he said. "I don't know if I can do this. I am actually pretty fond of being alive."

"Don't worry," I said. "After you're dead everything will be easier."

"I think maybe we should do something else, though," he said. "I may have been too hasty. Maybe we could overdose on pills?"

I replied by straightening up from my crouch on the edge. It was dizzying to look down at the street, full of cars heading to the expressway like someone had flicked a finger against them at the top of the hill. Straight below, hard to see, there were balconies, terraces, step progressions of lower levels of the hotel that would need to be cleared on the way down.

I called, "Are you ready?" I was having trouble keeping my balance.

"The sun is awfully bright, isn't it?" he called back.

"It's overcast. You can't even see it."

"Bright in an absent sort of way, though."

"Would you just get up here?"

Gil moved slowly, using the scrollwork for handholds. I had to pull him up most of the way; he was surprisingly heavy. I grunted a little as I strained.

"Your visceral noises are, I must say, less than romantic," he said. Then: "I don't think I want to do this, darling."

I shook my head. "No, you're right. It's got to be this," I said. "Maybe it would help if we closed our eyes? We could say one, two, three, and hold hands."

"All right."

I took his hand. He closed his eyes. I looked west over the city, and thought I saw a scrap of grey-green that could have been Bellwoods. My park with its lilacs and dog shit and bike paths, its steep little valley in the north end, its stately limestone gates. But surely I couldn't see it from where I was. We weren't high enough. It must be some other green space I was seeing. I dropped Gil's hand so I could push my hair behind my ears.

"One, two, three," I said. Then I pushed him off the roof.

He was utterly gone. I couldn't bring myself to lean over and watch, but the air where he had been standing felt charged, like it would give me a shock. For a moment I didn't know what to do. I got down carefully and walked along the rows of the roof garden. It felt colder than before and I wished I were wearing more than the flimsy dress.

"It's because the sun's gone behind the clouds again," I said out loud. Then I said, "Talking to yourself. Definitely the hallmark of an insane person."

I pushed and pulled at handles on various industrial metal things until I found a stairwell. My legs as I went down felt like they might give out before my feet found each step, as if I'd been running for too long the day before.

I tried the door at every landing I came to until one opened into a plush corridor. The doors were unbearably smooth. I thought of skating rinks, bruised knees. Then a wide, silent space before banks of elevators. Intricate carpet, dark wooden furniture, expensive mirrors.

I pushed the button, waited, dropped, made my way past the grand spiral staircase and the blue-eyed businessmen drinking in the lobby bar. Just like that, I was on the street. The doorman with his burgundy coat and brass buttons tipped his hat to me and his white glove had three straight, sewn pleats on the back like bones.

I stood on the sidewalk on Front Street, streams of people jaywalking to Union Station, the long lines of competing taxis. I still had transit tokens in the bottom of my wallet. Where should I go? The store, of course. Or Bellwoods, to sit under the trees and wait for the night to drape itself over me, put me peacefully to sleep like a parrot in a sheet-covered cage. Or I could call Wendy, go to George's.

But then what? Go to bed, get up. Blackout. Walk around the city like I'm being followed, like the sidewalk is rolling up behind me.

Still. There was something about what I'd done, the violence of it. There's something sort of celebratory about pain, about causing pain, even your own, something parade-like, explosive, expressive. Was that how she felt when she hurt herself? I was buoyed up. Why couldn't I leave Wooster House? Why couldn't I kick the blackouts?

I crossed the wonky double intersection at Front, University and York streets, heading north and west. I turned on Queen, walking through the mall-ish strip of stores, the wide sidewalks clogged with people, the ankle-turning tangle of streetcar tracks at Spadina. I passed the throng of teenagers smoking outside the Big Bop and jogged to catch the light at Bathurst. I could almost smell the park, the stillness of it, the cloudy glow of electricity, garbage and hot cement, wet grass.

It wasn't yet six, so the store was still open. A few customers milled around and there was a new girl sitting behind the counter in the store, holding a rolled-up five-dollar bill between her thumb and forefinger. She let it unfurl on the counter, then rolled it up again.

"Hi," she said when I entered. "Let me know if you need help or anything."

The tables were a mess. I went to the back and waggled the ladder on its rail. There was a crunching noise while it rolled over the unswept floor. A little ametrine fish was sitting on the edge of a shelf of books. I put it back with the other animals.

"I'm Maggie," I said to the clerk.

"I'm Scarlet," she said.

"Oh," I said. "I mean I'm Maggie. Dr. Pierce's daughter."

"Oh." The girl unfurled the bill and slid it back into the register. "Hi. What's up. That's right, they said you crashed your dad's car." She nodded as if agreeing with herself.

"So how do you like it here?"

"Yeah, it's good. Bit dull, working alone, right? But it's fine." Her hair was shaved close up the back, spiky and black, with long straight bangs that she tucked behind her ears. On one side, a bright white stripe.

"Well. I just wanted to introduce myself. It's nice to meet you. If there's anything I can help with—"

She nodded, the white streak flopping out from behind her ear. "Yeah. Well, it's pretty straightforward, right? But thanks."

I was itching to fix everything. Different scents of lotion were mixed together in the Natural Beauty section, everything stacked all higgledy-piggledy. Necklaces were snarled together in a basket. A bottle of sulphate-free shampoo was lying on its side. I put my hands at my sides, wishing for pockets.

Scarlet was watching me. "They said you were in the hospital."

"They?"

"Dr. Pierce and the younger guy. The skinny guy."

"Andrew."

"Yeah."

"Well. Is my dad home, do you know?"

"No, I don't think so." She took a package of ginger candies from under the counter. "I paid for these, I promise," she said. "Do you want one?"

I held my hand out and she put a twist of paper into it. I popped the candy in my mouth, tasted a spicy sweetness that was more like a smell than a flavour. My mother's ginger shampoo. The candies looked like drops of amber. Amber for stomach and spleen; arthritis and headaches. I could hear my mother saying it. I swallowed the ginger drop, and coughed.

Scarlet frowned. "You're supposed to suck on it," she said. "Aren't you?" She turned the package over to read it.

I looked out towards the park. The front window looked dull, dirty. Thanking Scarlet, I went up the back stairs and let myself into the apartment, but no one was there. I was starting to feel foolish, like I'd shown up to a party no one told me had been cancelled. I went back down, nodding goodbye to Scarlet on my way out. The sandwich board looked like it hadn't been re-chalked since I left, it was faded so badly.

I made my way slowly towards Wendy's, going out of my way up Spadina, past fur coats and banks, then windows framing skinned and hanging rabbits and ducks, heaping displays of paper umbrellas and peacock feathers, carved wooden boxes, two-dollar T-shirts, miles of shoes. The streetcar went by and then another and another, like synapses, like the city thinking of itself. My hands tingled at my sides; I could still feel Gil's back and shoulder, the way the muscle gave just a little when I pushed him.

In Bellevue Square, I followed the diagonal path, past the playground employed by a group of goth kids passing a bottle around. Kensington Market was strangely quiet. None of the restaurants or stores had their lights on. Even with the sun still up, everything seemed dim. I was headed to Wendy's apartment near the north end of the Market, near George's. It was very different from the glittering financial district down by the Royal York, where even a little sunlight was multiplied, reflected in a thousand mirrored windows. I let myself spread out, mentally checking the city like a tongue running over the empty socket of a tooth. The wonderfully wretched bars and tall row houses of the Market, now strangely dark. The university up to the right— elegant, imposing limestone buildings towering over ugly 1970s Brutalist additions. It was like doing the Journey Technique with a bigger version of the park—organized in my head, laid out on a grid, each neighbourhood a path or picnic table on my mental walk, full of things I wanted to list and remember. Behind me was the store itself, south and slightly west, not a beating heart but alive somehow, capable of changing the quality of light. I thought of my mother's sun lamp, how it turned the pale blue bathroom dark orange and buzzed faintly. I could hear the store the same way, a frequency too low to register.

When I got to Wendy's door, I stood for a moment. I tried to remember the last time we'd spoken. There were no lights on, not in Wendy's third-floor apartment nor in the rest of the house. I rang the bell for Wendy's unit. Nothing happened. I waited a moment, went to ring again and stopped myself. I stood and counted to fifty as slowly as I could. Then I knocked, loudly and for a long time. I was about to leave and then the door opened.

"*Maggie?*" said Wendy. She was wearing a long black T-shirt and striped boxer shorts, the white and blue just visible beneath the hem of the shirt.

I felt shy to reach out for her harsh little body until she grabbed me into a hug. "What are you doing here?"

"I left the House."

"Now? Today?" She stepped back. "Come in, sorry, come in."

We went up the dark stairs, turned at the landing and continued up. In the apartment, Wendy didn't turn on the light, but instead rummaged in her kitchen drawers and produced four white pillar candles and lit them. Hardly any light came in through her northern exposure.

"We lost power about an hour ago," she said. "The whole Market, I think."

The light was soft and flattering and Wendy looked so utterly beautiful in it that I reached out and touched her face.

She put her hand on top of mine and said, "I'm sorry I haven't been out yet." She dropped my hand and looked down. "But don't you need to go back? Or call someone at least?"

"No, it's fine," I said. "And don't worry, I haven't been gone long." When she didn't say anything, I added, "I know you're busy. Were you napping? Sorry if I woke you up. I wasn't even sure you'd be home."

Wendy pressed her lips together. "Well, here I am," she said.

"Right," I said. "So what have you been up to?"

She shrugged. "Work," she said. "The usual. Nothing special." Her face fell. "Oh," she said. "There's something else."

"Something else?"

"I don't know how to tell you this," she said, "so I'll just say it. Andrew and Scarlet—they have a thing, I think." She shrugged but her shoulders didn't come back down. "They bonded, I guess."

"Bonded? Andrew?"

"I'm sorry, hun."

I felt strange. "But," I said, and then I had a quick and unbidden film reel go through my head of Andrew sitting at the dinner table with my parents, Andrew running his hands through his hair before a university party, Andrew's flat white belly with the red seat-belt mark, Andrew with his buttons crooked, coming through the door of the police station. And I heard his voice reading from *The Lion, The Witch, and The Wardrobe* after my blackout in the park, with his thin, hot, dry body pressed against my back like a warm stone. And then there was nothing. That was what I'd had of him, and my brain had felt the need to run through it with me, as if for approval before letting it go. An almost administrative impulse of the memory. I got the heavy, tight feeling in my chest that came with tears, but didn't need to cry. I felt like I'd been standing outside in a high wind, like I had on the roof. Buffeted.

I said, "Do they have power on College Street? Want to go to George's?"

Wendy twisted the hem of her shirt in her hands. "I don't know," she said. "But shouldn't we call somebody? Your doctor? Or your dad?"

"I don't know if I'm going to go back."

"Um," said Wendy. "I guess we could go see George."

We hadn't sat down, but were standing in the room that served as Wendy's living room, dining room and kitchen. Wendy had been in the same apartment since we started at U of T; she was a pack rat and had stuffed the small space to the ceiling with low shelves and giant Rubbermaid containers, all filled with old Halloween costumes, Koosh balls, promotional Frisbees, broken tubes of lipstick that she was meaning to heat up and melt back into one piece, and scribbled notes that no longer meant anything to anyone. But although I knew every ceramic cat and cracked photo frame, I felt strange, as if I had brought in an unpleasant smell to which Wendy was too polite to call attention. There was B.W. and A.W.—Before Wooster and After Wooster. And After Wooster Maggie was not to be trusted with all of this, this endless catalogue of stuff that Wendy had accumulated so easily.

"Well," she said again. "I better get dressed."

She stepped into the little nook that was her bedroom and let down the curtain. It unrolled from above the door frame and had horizontal bamboo rods to flatten it out, like the battens in a sail. It was perfectly audible when Wendy said, "I'm sorry, I know. But she's here. I know. I don't know. What am I supposed to do?" There was a pause and she said, "Okay."

I went and lifted the bedroom curtain, pulling on the little strip of fabric that tugged it smoothly up, level with my face. I didn't say anything because I didn't have anything to say. Wendy looked at me. The bedroom window was covered. She had lit a single candle on her bedside table so I could see her only dimly. She was standing up but she closed her eyes and kept them closed, like it was too bright to look past the curtain.

"Was that my dad?"

Wendy shrugged. "What do you do, what is a person supposed to do?" she said. "There's nothing to do. I just can't handle it."

"I'm only asking for one night," I said. "I don't think it's so much to ask. I'll go home in the morning. I'll go out to the House and work things out with Rosenberg."

Wendy wasn't the type to cry. Instead her face was like ·a shut-off television screen, her hands resting on her bruised legs, pale below the hem of her boxer shorts.

"I'd give you a hundred nights if I knew how," she said.

Neither of us said anything for a minute.

Then she said, "You know you don't really have any other friends, other than me. That's not easy. For me."

The bed moved slightly and Andrew sat up, his pale chest aglow in the candlelight. Then I could see his white feet sticking out the bottom of the sheets. He didn't say anything.

Wendy looked at him briefly, an incredulous *why did you sit up?* look, and then back at me, her eyes watery, her mouth pulling to one side.

"I said Scarlet, just to see how you were feeling. How you'd take it."

Her misery clung to her, a miasma that kept her separate. I thought it would bend if I touched her, keep me from making contact. I didn't want to touch her.

"I'm so sorry," she said. "I didn't expect you to be— I mean, I didn't know. I wanted to wait for a better time to talk. That's stupid. A better time than now." She said more things. She said *I'm sorry* a lot more.

Andrew said he was sorry too, fewer times than Wendy. He looked at me and said, "We knew things were winding down, but—" His voice broke, like a teen, and he didn't go on.

I thought about all the unflattering things Wendy had ever said about Andrew. But she'd also said, *Don't leave him*, she'd also said, *What else is there?*

"So there wasn't anything with Scarlet?" I said. I was finding it hard to keep my brain in the moment, from slipping backwards and forwards: how this had happened and how things would have to happen from now on. I thought I should be able to do that television trick where you freeze time for a moment. You wander around the room and peer into motionless faces, pluck stationary objects from the air before they can shatter on the floor.

"She runs this little magazine. She threw a launch party. I went, and I heard him reading. I heard him reading the poems he'd written." Wendy was wiping her nose. Andrew stayed in the bed, looking like someone I knew but being a person I didn't know. Andrew writing poetry. Andrew reading his poetry aloud, in some bar somewhere in the city, on Queen Street undoubtedly, my city, my Queen Street, and Wendy sitting at a sticky table with a bottle of beer, listening. None of this was realistic, was likely or believable. More information that didn't make sense, that I'd failed to see coming, to understand.

Wendy said, "I wanted to go see you. I wanted to go, I wanted to. But you know I'm not a good driver. You know how nervous I get on the highway." Even while she was talking she looked astonished, as if she were listening too, standing beside me, as if she were on my side.

I nodded and let down the curtain. I went into Wendy's little bathroom. Andrew would be too tall for the showerhead. He'd have to crouch to shave in front of her mirror. I put the toilet-seat cover down and sat, with my hands resting on my knees, lightly. I thought of Gil's back and shoulder, the way they felt under my hands, again, but this time I thought what it must have been like for him. The firm, quick pressure, the word, *push*, like the thing itself. Then just air.

My stomach heaved and I got on my knees, smacked the cover up and vomited in Wendy's toilet. It kept coming up until it was just liquid, burning my throat, nothing of substance. When it finished I knelt for a long time on the linoleum floor. Then I rinsed and wiped my mouth and left the dark apartment, and the sound *Maggie, Maggie, Maggie* was the only thing that followed me down the stairs.

I walked up to College Street. I could see George's was dark as well, locked up. He must have gone home when the power went off. Here and there girls in tights and boots took tiny steps beside baby-faced boys in jeans and sneakers. I was close enough to the university to catch the students who were back in town, or here for the first time, about to start classes, talking loudly about the blackout.

Fucking mayor should fix that shit.

Oh my god, I hope nobody, like, falls down the stairs.

What about the food—will restaurants give stuff away, do you think?

Some of them could have been my father's students, might have notes in their particleboard desks with my father's descriptions of *Paradise Lost* and *Utopia*. I envied them.

I crossed the street and hailed the first taxi that came by. The driver agreed to take me the whole way for forty dollars. It was all the money I had in my wallet. The cab did a U-turn and pulled into traffic, down Spadina, past the power failure and back into the functional, black-and-white, electric city, and then out onto the highway.

When I got back to the House, the sun was down. How many hours had I lost before Gil and I got to the roof—I hadn't had a blackout this long in a while. I scaled the fire escape, and the window opened like it was oiled and closed with a homey little click. I undressed and put on my comfortable pyjamas, the ones with the blue mice printed all over, and I got into bed. I found the remote under the pillow and turned on the little TV. Reruns of the old *Batman* show were playing and I laughed to myself, mouth closed, at the *Biff!* and *Zap!* and *Kablam!*

The toilet flushed and I sat up in bed. The washroom door opened and Gil walked out.

"You do not want to know what I did with your toothbrush," he said, zipping up his pants.

I got out of bed and stood on the opposite side, putting the bed between us.

"The look on your face," he said. "I just used it to brush my teeth. It could be worse. You can always get a new one."

"What just happened?" I said.

Gil approached and stood against the side of the bed, directly opposite me.

"I'm not mad," he said. "I deserved it. But let's not dwell on this."

I backed up until I was pressed against the bookshelves that lined the wall near the door. "I want you to go now. I'm—unmaking you. I'm done. Go."

Gil shook his head. "You didn't really think it would be that easy, did you?"

Pow! went the TV. *Zonk!*

"You're in this," he said. "Rosenberg and your family might not think much of you, but I know what you're capable of." He held out his hands like a magician showing his audience. *Nothing here, nothing up my sleeves.* "Get back into bed," he said.

"I'm tired," I said. "I want to go home. I don't want you anymore." My head felt like it had been inflated with a bicycle pump. I felt my hands on Gil's back, on the roof, again. The solidness of him. Andrew's feet sticking out of the bottom of Wendy's bed. The dim Market. The bamboo curtain rolling up and down. Everything was coming undone.

Gil sat down at the desk, took out a pen. "I'm not going anywhere," he said. "Not unless it's with you."

At a loss, I got into bed and curled up. I'd been here for almost two weeks, in a mental health facility, and I'd worried—just *worried*, what a luxury!—that I was going crazy. But now, now. What now?

What if I had two minds, one running on top of the other? One solid and logical and flat, like the Gardiner Expressway running above the city. The mind underneath was the one that told me things I didn't want to hear, like that Rosenberg was trying to steal all my memories of my mother for himself. Or smaller things: that the man from the other small group beside me on the couch would find out about me and make me stop trying to remember my mother if I said anything to him, or if I declined his invitation to play checkers.

The lower mind told me that my father hadn't visited because he thought it was my fault that she died, that he couldn't stand to look at me. It told me that only Gil could be trusted, that I could get my mother back, in some small way, through him, if only for a minute.

And most of the time I knew that this voice was not something I should be listening to, that Dr. Malik would have told me not to pay attention to it. But somehow, this lower mind was the one connected to my body, the one that told it to do things and got it to listen. Like with Gil. My upper mind didn't want to sleep with him, it wanted to sleep with Andrew. It wanted to get things back to normal.

Gil sat at the desk, watching me look at the TV. Into the silence, Adam West said, "The joke's on you, Riddler!" There was frantic music and an explanation of how the villain's nefarious plan had been flawed. I changed to a cable network that had aired a documentary I watched earlier in the summer about how people could perform feats of inhuman strength if their family was threatened or if they were about to die or something like that. That was the lower mind, saying, *Pick up that car right now* or *You're going to have to chop your leg off to get out of this bear trap—get to it*. Most people can't hear it, or they hear from it once or twice in their lives and maybe not even that if they're lucky. The real me was the one above, saying, *You've got to be kidding*, but then there went my body listening to that other voice, happy as a clam, *Oh sure, whatever you think is best*. Maybe that is what insanity is. When your body jumps tracks, changes frequencies from one mind to the other.

Seventeen

Our assignment in Group was to write a letter to our lost person. Mia to her husband, Tracey to her brother, Timothy to his wife. Me to my mother. Chad handed out loose-leaf paper and sharpened pencils and Mia pressed the tip of hers against her fingertip and looked at it hard.

"I wouldn't bother trying," said Tracey. "Chad's a pro."

Mia looked up fast, her pale face flushed. "I wasn't," she said. "I wasn't anything."

Tracey rolled her eyes at me but I didn't join in. I didn't want to write to my mother. I didn't want to be downstairs at all, with Rosenberg sitting on a cushion in front of the dead fireplace. I didn't like to see him sitting cross-legged, it was too chummy, too false, like a youth pastor with gelled hair and a puka-shell necklace.

"Go ahead," he said. "There are no constraints. This is an activity to help you achieve a sense of closure. There are always things that go unsaid, that we wish we had time to say or to ask. You need to absolve this sense of guilt, of unfinished issues. Why don't we chat a little bit to get the ball rolling?"

"Chat how?" said Tracey. She was rubbing the lead graphite

onto her fingertip and dragging it across the back of her hand, leaving silvery smudges.

"We can share some things we'd talk to our loved ones about, if they were here. Imagine that your person is here for an hour."

We all shifted nervously and looked at each other's chests and feet.

"Timothy, why don't you start?" Rosenberg fixed him with a beady stare and the rest of us looked down, relieved.

Timothy's soft, rectangular face went slack. "Uh, to Mary?" he said. "Say something to her?"

Rosenberg adjusted his cushion. He didn't speak.

"Well," said Timothy. "I'd tell her how pretty she is. I didn't say it enough maybe. I'd tell her she was a terrific wife?" Timothy's tone was interrogative, and he looked at Rosenberg for approval, his shoulders drawn up, giving him a turtle-like look.

"Go on," said Rosenberg.

"I'd tell her— I'd tell her—"

"I'd tell my brother that his leather jacket made him look totally fobby," said Tracey. "I never had the heart to, but I should have. And I'd tell him he was wrong about our dad. I'd tell him that his expensive cologne smelled cheap."

"I'd tell Michael that I liked it when he drove too fast," said Mia. "I was faking it when I pretended to be scared."

Rosenberg looked at me. His face was smooth and impossible to read.

"Do you have anything to say to your mother, Margaret?"

I shook my head no. Did I have anything to say? I had everything to say. Every day I had new things to say, and in the mornings when I was still living in my apartment I'd be halfway to her room before I remembered she wasn't in there. I started to write notes on the scrap paper under the cash register before I remembered no one was going to read them but me. Back in June, two girls had passed me on Queen Street and one of them said to the other, "A guy called me beautiful on my way here. Or pitiful. I couldn't hear him that well," and I wanted to tell my mother that. I wanted to tell her that I was sorry for calling her homemade flax bread "hippie bricks," that she could make a thousand loaves and I would eat every one with a smile. I could almost taste them. I could see her in the kitchen with her rooster apron on and her dark hair tied back, a lock escaping. And there were other things, harder things, sludgy black angry things that lived on the back of my lungs and that I tried not to think but that made it hard to breathe sometimes. The *Why* things, the *Why couldn't you* things, the *What about me* things. And Gil. I wanted to tell her about Gil. Even if she didn't believe, she would have known—what he was, how to get rid of him. *If* I could get rid of him. What would she have said? I should have kept her talking every day; I should have asked about Georgia; I shouldn't have settled for half-answers. I wanted to say, *Have you ever gotten lost in something you thought you could control? Have you ever gotten in over your head and wanted and not wanted to get out?*

"No," I said, and Rosenberg inched away from the fireplace.

"Nothing at all?"

"I don't know."

"Why don't we," he said, "try the letters now? Just write whatever comes to you. You might be surprised. Mia, Tracey, Timothy, you all did a great job brainstorming." He was fussing with a cufflink, not looking at us.

I picked up my pencil and started to write. We all sat there, quietly shifting the lap desks Chad had given us, occasionally murmuring for more paper or a new pencil. It was hushed like an exam hall.

Right off the roof, I wrote. *It was the strangest feeling.*

Rosenberg had stood up and was circling the room. I was bent over my paper, still writing. After a few minutes, I realized he was standing over me, behind the wing chair, looking. I curled my hand over the text like I'd caught him cheating off me.

"Very good, Maggie," he said. "A slow start isn't the end of the world, is it?"

I moved my lips but didn't say anything. Eventually he moved away, putting a hand on Mia's shoulder and nodding to himself.

"Why don't we try to wrap things up now," he said a half-hour later, after he had circled to each person. "This is an excellent start."

"What do we do with them now?" said Timothy, folding his fat letter over a second time.

"We're going to dispose of them," said Rosenberg as Chad came around and collected our letters. "The point is we're releasing these thoughts. Think of this as a cleansing process."

When I handed my letter over, my hand brushed against Chad's and it was rough. Sometimes I saw him smoking on the porch.

"Thanks," I said to Chad, and he looked at me and then at Tracey. He handed the letters to Rosenberg.

"Close your eyes," said Rosenberg, who was shuffling the letters together. "Think of the words you wrote down, the things you want to say to the person you've lost. Your words are released. When you externalize, you cleanse." In a flourish, he ripped the letters in half, and proceeded to shred them into dozens of tiny pieces. Then, in a flatter tone, he said, "I have to go to the hospital this afternoon, I will see you all tomorrow."

Timothy and Mia got up and wandered into the kitchen. Rosenberg went into the foyer and began assembling his city ensemble, a suit jacket of good quality and ridiculous movie-star sunglasses.

"Take care, everyone," he said, and left.

Once the door had closed, Tracey crossed the room and sat beside me on the couch. Chad had disappeared into his office.

"I need to talk to you," she said.

"Why?"

"I just do."

I shrugged and nodded my head at the kitchen. "Let's go out back," I said.

On the porch, Tracey said, "I think I'm going to leave."

"Leave? Where will you go?"

"Do you know how much they pay Chad? It's pathetic. And he's so smart too." She touched her neck in the V of her cotton shirt. "We're going to hitchhike to B.C. It's almost harvest, and Chad has a friend whose farm we can work on."

"Chad?" Reflexively, I pointed in the direction of his office. "Our Chad?"

"He's great, isn't he?"

"Are you guys in love?"

Tracey smiled. One of her front teeth protruded enough that I could tell she had never had braces. Her pale pink gums showed almost all the way around.

"I wish you'd come with us," she said. "But I know you won't. You can't stay here, though."

I lifted my hand a few inches and she reached out and took it. Her fingers were still cracked and scratchy.

"I'll write to you at your mother's store once we get settled."

"Just write me here."

"No."

"You're really going? You guys talked about it?"

Tracey looked out towards the fence and squeezed my hand a few times. "Oh yeah," she said. She was silent for a moment and then she said, "I feel brave. And I feel like a coward. I feel like I should knock Chad out with a sock full of pennies and try to do it on my own, get out of here. But I just can't. And he needs my help too." She let go of my hand. "That sounds like I'm making excuses."

"If you leave," I said, "you're still gone. Who cares the reason?"

"I care," said Tracey, leaning on the porch railing with both hands. Then she turned and pulled me into a hug. "I'll miss you. Give Rosenberg a good one–two from me. Tell him you see his death in your tarot cards. Tell him you see the stock market crashing and he should get out now."

"I'll go down fighting," I said.

Tracey tucked my hair behind my ear and the motherly gesture made me jerk away. She said, "Don't go down at all." And then she kissed me on the cheek and shrugged.

I'd seen her and Chad exchange a few furtive glances, nothing more. But this?

Tracey got up and walked back into the House, her beautifully arched feet somehow silent on the boards that always creaked. I stayed on the porch after she'd gone inside.

In the morning they were gone. Mia and Timothy and I stood in the kitchen eating Special K.

"What do we do now?" said Timothy.

"Where did they go?" said Mia, and I felt proud that Tracey hadn't told anyone else. Then Mia smiled and went to Chad's empty office. She came back with his key ring and immediately opened the locked knife drawer. "Anyone for fruit salad?" she said.

We chopped up kiwis and oranges and Mia moved the knife slowly but properly, rocking it back and forth against her knuckles. I had almost gotten used to the sight of her arms by then, her bright green henley rolled up past her elbows, the stripy patchwork of scars no longer as jarring.

"I wanted to be a chef," she said, "When I was little. Before I got married."

"How old are you now?"

"Twenty-two."

"Twenty-two," said Timothy. "Dear, you've got loads of time."

Mia put the tip of the knife into the crook of her elbow and blood came out in a sudden steady stream, dripping on the floor. Timothy yelled, "Jesus God," and got the knife away from her. I had my hands in the air, palms up and out like someone saying "Stop!" but I couldn't say anything. A clear, spicy smell came up, so strong it made me dizzy. Timothy was wrapping her arm in a towel, yelling at me to call a fucking ambulance. She was small in his arms and her blood was all over everything, Timothy grabbed her face in one hand and gave her a little slap and there was blood on her cheek from his hands. The sight of the bloody cheek seemed to unstick me from the ground, and I ran to the front hall and called 911, something I had never done before. All I could think of was a show I'd once seen on television about a baby that dialled 911 by accident, how the emergency workers had berated the parents for taking them away from real emergencies. That was what I was thinking, a gush of nonsense in my mind that I couldn't seem to turn off even as my fingers and voice were steady.

"There's a girl here and she's bleeding, she cut herself," I said. "Wooster House on Peter Street, south of Lake Shore. Please send someone right now." While I was still on the phone, I heard the crunch of tires in the drive and Rosenberg came through the door, sliding his stupid sunglasses into his breast pocket. I threw the receiver at him and ran. I heard him say "Hello, who is this?" before I rounded the corner to the kitchen.

Mia and Timothy were struggling, she was trying to scratch him, and he had his hands around her wrists. For a moment it looked like he was yanking her around by the arms, but then I could see he was just trying to keep her from digging her fingers into his eyes.

I yelled for them to stop and called Mia a bitch and I banged my fists on the laminate of the kitchen island. Mia turned and looked at me and tried to lunge, and when Timothy yanked her up and back she came right off the floor and kicked her feet. She spit at me badly, all in a spray. Rosenberg came in opening his jacket, taking out a small bottle.

"Chad's gone?" he said, and to Timothy: "Hold her tight." He pressed on the hinges of Mia's jaw. He grabbed her nose and held it until her mouth opened, then he shoved his fingers into her mouth. She bit down but he didn't cry out, then he pulled his fingers away and held her with one hand on top of her head and the other under her chin.

"Swallow, Mia," he said. "Swallow. Swallow. Swallow it." Between the two of them, he and Timothy held her another minute or so until her movements slowed. All three of them had blood on their clothes and faces.

I stood with my arms up, my hands on the back of my neck.

When Mia finally went limp, Rosenberg said, "Put her on the couch," and washed his hands in the kitchen sink before he went out to examine her arm. The towel Timothy had wrapped her in peeled off slowly.

"Same as usual," he said. "Nothing fatal." He got gauze from

Chad's office and wrapped her arm properly, his hands small and deft. "They'll just need to fill her back up."

I stared at him.

"It's fine now," he said. "There's nothing to worry about, Maggie."

I turned and ducked out of the common room, heading for the stairs. I missed the doorknob to my room, fell against the door, got it open, slumped onto the bed. Gil was there, sitting in front of an open notebook, not writing. He looked at me, his brown eyes floating up from the page. We hadn't spoken much since the roof. He had fallen asleep beside me the night before and been there in the morning, but until I saw him there, I wasn't entirely sure if I would find him still in the room.

After a moment he came and knelt beside the bed. His face seemed to flicker, as if lit from within. But I wasn't sorry he was there.

"I didn't help," I said.

"You called for help."

I curled onto my side, turned away from him.

"Tell me," he said, and I shook my head.

The jade angel sat on the bedside table. I picked it up, my hand wrapped around the uneven surface of carved stone. The face was blank, thin and elegant.

"Are you sure you want us coming?" asked my mother. "Twenty-three—you should be out raising Cain." She didn't say, When I was twenty-three, I already had you.

It was my birthday, and we were heading out for dinner. She was standing behind the counter of the store, just closed for the evening.

I was holding a citrine turtle, wiping the table below where the four tiny stone feet had left clean circles in the dust. Uses for citrine: laying on the stomach for digestion issues; sleeping with it to eliminate sleep disturbances, nightmares; good for thyroid issues; help in overcoming addiction. For protection and dream recall.

She was singing tunelessly to herself, tapping her fingers in no particular rhythm on her leg. She looked the same as always: the twist of black hair threaded with grey, a white cotton skirt. Flat eyebrows like quick brushstrokes, knotting now over her eyes. The right incisor, still too sharp, too prominent. She was smiling.

"You don't want your old mom and dad there."

My father came down the stairs, his dress shoes hitting each step like a series of knocks, his head down while he skewered his cuffs with gold-toned cufflinks.

"I'm not feeling well," said my mother. "You should go without me. I'll lie down a little while, come for a glass of wine in a bit."

My father and I exchanged looks. "It's fine, Mom. It's just on the corner."

"It's too warm for May, I think there's a pressure system. They said there is a pressure system." She put her hand on her head.

My father took her by the arm and steered her out from behind the counter. "You love Italian," he said. "Andrew and Wendy are meeting us there."

We went out the front door, and I locked up. My mother stood on the sidewalk beside my father, her gauzy scarf wrapped around and around her neck so that her head looked balanced on it, a cloud of fabric.

Wendy and Andrew waved to us when we came through the door,

and the waiter led us over to them at a table under the window, looking out over Queen Street. Andrew jumped up and pulled out my
chair. There was wine on the table already, and my father rotated the
bottle so he could see the label, then smiled and nodded at Andrew.

"I'm not very hungry," said my mother, looking out the square-
paned window at the passersby. "I'll just have something small."
But she was already eating a piece of bread, tearing little pieces off
and tucking them into her mouth between words. Her mouth was
greyish, like someone about to be sick.

Wendy reached across the table and squeezed my hand, said,
"Happy birthday."

After we ordered, Andrew and my father chatted about the university, using names of people I'd only heard about from them and
never met, until our appetizers arrived. We all had small, elegant
salads, except for Wendy, who ordered shrimp. My mother watched
her eat, pushed her own food around the plate.

I got up to go to the washroom and when I came back I saw that
my father's hand was light on the back of my mother's neck. I
watched the hand, spindly, the wedding ring loose. She hadn't said
anything since our food arrived. I stood there until a server behind
me said, "Excuse me," softly, but in a way that I knew meant he'd
been waiting for some time. My mother looked back over her shoulder and she saw me staring. She pushed herself up with her hands,
sat up straighter in her chair, her shoulders squared. She reminded
me of a peeled potato, slightly wet to the touch.

We got halfway through our entrees. We'd finished the first bottle
of wine and Andrew had just raised his glass to make a toast when
there was a smash and clattering noise, my mother's plate and

utensils falling to the polished wood of the floor. Other diners turned to look, a few people clapped and laughed.

"I'm not hungry," she said, as if no time had elapsed since she had spoken when we first sat down. Then she got up and walked out of the restaurant.

My father stood up, looked down at the broken plate. Andrew's hand was still on his glass. Through the window, we could see her go by on the sidewalk, moving quickly towards home.

My father said, "I'm sorry," and handed me his wallet.

Our waiter came over with a broom and dustpan. "Don't worry," he said. "Don't worry at all. Happens to the best of us." When he straightened up, the dustpan full of china shards, he said, "Is there a problem?"

"We're finished," I said. I put my father's wallet in my purse and took out my own credit card. The waiter looked at the table.

"Do you want any of this packed up?"

Andrew said to me, "Oh, don't pay for this, I'll get it" and went to reach for his own wallet, but I shook my head. After looking at me for a moment, he said, "Okay. I'll walk Wendy home," and Wendy said, "I can walk myself." But after they both hugged and kissed me, they left together, looking over their shoulders, walking far apart from each other.

The waiter came back with the bill for me to sign. "Is everything okay?" he said. "Is there anything I can do?"

His hands were folded in front of him, loosely. There was a plain silver ring circling his pinkie and a gold band on his index finger. I had an irrational impulse to take his hand; his skin would be smooth, firm. I signed my name and wrote a tip on the blank line.

The waiter smiled and waited for me to hand the receipt back. Instead I sat back down at the table.

"Stay as long as you want," he said after a moment. He touched my shoulder, lightly, and his hand was very hot. "I'll bring you some coffee."

I sat for a minute, looking out the window. You could see only the corner of the park from this far down the block, a scrap of tennis court, dun-coloured spring grass under the street lights. I didn't know it would be the last thing we ever celebrated. Tried to celebrate.

The waiter came back a moment later, carrying a flat box.

"There was a birthday cake," he said. "It's already paid for."

I stood up and accepted it. He brought me my coat and then I had to put the cake down while he held the coat open for me.

He said, "Do you still want that coffee?"

I picked up the cake and shook my head. "Thanks anyway," I said.

"I'm sure everything will be okay," he said. "Hope the rest of your birthday is happy." He stood there and watched me walk out.

There were lots of people on the sidewalk, even just in the short walk from the restaurant to the store. The weather was unseasonably warm, a fluke spell that would last until after they pulled her out of the river a week later.

I went into the unlocked store and my mother had the box-cutter in one hand. Her arms were covered in long shallow cuts. My father was struggling with her, and when I walked through the door, he turned her around and got his arms around her, holding onto his own forearms below her breasts. He was saying, Stop please for god's sake stop Maggie's fucking in here don't you even give a shit stop Carol Carol Carol please please please, *and all of this was strung together in his mouth like he was trying to get it all out at once. We should have known, he should have known, I should have known, that it was a terrible idea—even a small restaurant, even close to home. On a bad day.*

All those people on the sidewalk, in the restaurant, were like little electric shocks to her, over and over and everywhere around her. For a moment I felt like the shop was full of them, zap zap zap, *no wonder she had the box-cutter.*

What happened after that? My father's sleeves above his cuff-links, streaked with red. I put the cake on the front counter, crossed to the back of the store, passed the Natural Beauty section where my parents were, picked up the citrine turtle. What did I do after that—did I help him? Did I lock the door? Call for help? She slumped against him, her back to his chest. Neither of them was crying. My mother's head hung down, her face obscured by the dark netting of her hair, but my father's head was thrown back. He looked like a man who had been punched in both eyes, one after the other. The box-cutter was on the floor, it must have fallen.

It was worse than usual, and the next day wasn't a good one. Usually the day after a bad one would be good; she had a way of looking me right in the eye, her smile coming up slowly, sharing a joke. There would be good food, appearing as if out of nowhere: waxy gooseberries, thick egg custards, fresh bread. She would massage my palms, dissolving tension, her own raw arms hidden under long sleeves; she would talk about what we would buy in the next season.

But after my birthday she was grey and draggy, she circled the store aimlessly. I was afraid, I should have known. But even the fear was too familiar, too comfortable a contortion. I didn't really believe.

Those marks were still on her arms at the funeral, like a tangled net, like veins on the outside. They put her in long sleeves; the casket was closed. But the marks were still there, underneath everything.

Eighteen

I was curled on my side in bed, the paper of my notebook damp and sticking to my fingers. Gil was lying beside me, his hand heavy, resting on my back. I lay there until it was time for my evening session with Rosenberg.

It was odd to go down without Chad, my usual escort. Two patients from other groups sat knitting in the common room, one coaching the other through the stitches, a long shank of woollen stripes hanging from her own needles. When I went by, they turned their heads in unison, not towards me but away.

When I asked Rosenberg during our session about Mia, who hadn't returned, he said she needed a more stable environment than Wooster House could provide.

"Not everyone," he said, "works as hard at recovery as you do, Margaret." He leaned back and tented his fingers. "Now tell me what you see."

I looked down at my spread; I was reading cards for him again. I let my eyes go out of focus.

"The stock market is going to crash," I said. "You should get out now."

"Let's not waste each other's time here."

"That's what I see."

"Really."

I laid my hands on the cards. "It's not a science," I said.

"Maybe I've been pushing too hard," he said. "We can talk about something else if you like."

"No, it's fine."

"But maybe we should."

"No, I'll do a new spread. Maybe this one is just unfocused."

"No, Margaret. No more spreads."

I didn't know how he'd managed to get me begging to read more cards, but I wanted to. He was making me nervous. I didn't want to know whatever it was he really wanted. I picked up the cards and started to shuffle.

"Let's talk about Gil," said Rosenberg, and instead of rippling into each other in a neat stack, the deck flipped out of my hands and landed everywhere.

For a moment I didn't do anything and I thought about the tip of the knife as it went into Mia's arm, how it disappeared for a second, a good quarter-inch. The crook of my elbow ached all the time now from Rosenberg's measurements, the little needle dipping in once a week or more. It had been a month since Andrew's visit. There were three cards face down in Rosenberg's lap.

"Who?" I said.

Rosenberg opened his jacket and took out a piece of paper.

"'He's got that kind of curly hair like Grandpa had in your photos, Mom. He wears a cap like that too sometimes,'" he read aloud.

I could see the back of the paper showed indents where I'd pressed so hard that the words were embossed into the page. My letter.

"You're violating my privacy," I said, and I tried to grab it back.

Rosenberg put it on his desk near the window and positioned himself between the letter and me.

"It was an exercise. I am your doctor. I took only one page. I wasn't going to say anything. I wanted you to tell me yourself."

"You tore them up."

Rosenberg smiled a little, as if he couldn't help himself. "I used to do a little magic," he said. "When I first moved to Canada, before I went to school. I worked as a busker. That was when I knew your mother."

Rosenberg-as-busker was so impossible to picture that for a moment I forgot about the letter. First Andrew as a poet, now this. Was there anyone I knew at all?

"A busker?"

"We all have to start somewhere," he said. He picked up the cards in his lap and made them disappear. "I guess it's all muscle memory," he said, letting them slide out of his sleeves. His smile, almost pleasant, faded. "If you're pushing people off buildings, Margaret, I think there's a burden of responsibility on me, your caregiver, to know about it. Whatever you've told yourself—I wasn't aware how far your delusions had gone. I don't even know whether we're dealing with delusions or hallucinations. I don't think it's inappropriate to tell you that I'm worried. What you've written here. It's a convoluted coping mechanism. A bizarre one, a fascinating one. But a mechanism."

This made me picture Gil as a machine, metal joints bending on well-oiled hinges just under his skin. A faint whirring noise while having sex. The occasional *ca-clunk* hidden under a snore.

I stood up. "I am leaving. I want to leave now. I'm going home. This is a voluntary program and you can't make me stay."

Rosenberg grabbed me by the forearm and for a moment neither of us moved. Then he gave me a yank. "Sit down," he said. "You're going to sit down and tell me what is going on." In the past weeks he had lost weight. The thinness didn't suit him, though; he looked pinched. "I need to know." His hand was still on my arm and he squeezed me hard. "I want to know," he said. "Tell me about him."

"No."

Rosenberg sat back, his hand on his beard. "Then tell me about your mother," he said.

I looked up. I had my hand on my arm where he had grabbed me.

"What would she think of Gil?"

Rosenberg's hand hadn't left a mark but I felt it should have. I could see the veins in the soft underside of my arm like a topographical map. Rivers and streams. Blue-green and blue.

"Is Chad in trouble?" I said. Rosenberg took off his glasses and wiped them on his shirt.

"Chad had to move home to Ottawa to take care of his father," he said. .

"I don't believe you."

He looked surprised, a moment of genuine expression. "Why would I lie to you?"

I shook my head back and forth, my hair swinging slightly in front of my eyes.

He said, "Your mother wrote you a note, didn't she." He waited and then went on. "Your mother's suicide note. You haven't mentioned it at all."

"What, was that in my file? Have you read it?"

"I haven't read it. But Dr. Malik referenced it in his notes."

"Well, I don't have it. The police had it. They gave it back to my dad. It took a long time."

"How did you feel when you read it?"

I leaned back in the chair. "I tried to take care of her. I thought the real her was the good one. That the other one was just like a storm, or something, some sort of bad luck that stuck to her sometimes. But reading the note was like watching her hand the reins over, and I just couldn't—" Here I stopped.

"What did it say?"

"That she was sorry, that it was getting harder. I bet they're all pretty much the same, right? You're the expert. *I love you. Please forgive me. It's not your fault.*"

"You said 'the real her' and 'the other one.' Do you think of your mother as two people?"

"Maybe everybody is. Two people, I mean."

Rosenberg sat back and smiled. "Oh, at least. At least two," he said. "Are you angry at one of those two people—the real her or the other one?"

I wasn't crying but my nose was running. "I haven't been thinking about it that way."

Rosenberg's voice was soft, higher. "Tell me about Gil. How do you feel when he's—around?"

I put my hand into my pocket, where I had the jade angel, and felt the smooth glass of the base against my fingers. Then I reached over and plucked the cards off Rosenberg's lap, the three cards he'd palmed and released. I turned them up on the TV table. They were all cards I knew well.

"The two of swords. The chariot. The six of swords."

"What do they mean?"

The two of swords pictured a blindfolded girl, seated, holding two crossed swords. It was a funny card. It could mean indecision, because of the precariously balanced swords, but could also be read as resolution, balancing contradictory things. Two swords. Two sharp edges. The girl was balanced but the card needed direction. Behind her the sea was rough. It was a card I'd always identified with and I didn't like finding it in Rosenberg's lap.

"That's indecision," I said, pointing. I didn't elaborate. "And that, the chariot, that's triumph through hard work. A comfortable journey, sometimes, because of the chariot. The sphinxes in front are mercy and justice—they want to go in opposite directions, but the charioteer controls them, see? It's a good card. Bold. Boldness."

"What about that one?"

In the six of swords, a man ferried a woman and her child across a river. The water was rough on one side and smooth on the other. Six swords stood straight up in the bow of the boat.

"More travel," I said. "You planning on going somewhere?" Rosenberg shook his head. He was silent. "That's not the main thing. It's movement. Away from pain, going somewhere better, more peaceful. Some people think it can mean letting someone else help you or speak for you, because of the ferryman."

"Maybe I'm your ferryman," said Rosenberg. "That's certainly what I'm trying to do."

"Maybe they're your cards. You were holding them." My nose was still running.

We sat and looked at each other for a minute, until Rosenberg dropped his eyes. I slid the cards across the TV table towards him, and when I did, a fourth appeared, unsticking itself from the back of the six of swords. The world. A naked woman was surrounded by a green wreath, floating in the air. We both looked at it.

"That's the last card in the major arcana," I said, and the timer rang, making me jump.

"Time's up," he said, still looking at the final card. He stood up, I thought to open the door and usher me out. But instead he knelt on the floor in front of me so we were eye to eye. "I want to help you," he said. "I don't know why you don't believe that." My hand was still on the world card, and he put his own on top, running his finger over the bones in my wrist. He put the other hand on the back of my head; I could feel each of his fingers. "Why do you shut me out? Why won't you tell me anything? Why are you here if you don't want my help?"

I pulled away from him, my shoulders drawing up nearly to

my ears, but he pulled my head forward, closed his hand around my wrist. His face was much too close. I could see the shadow in each pore where he had shaved, I could see his cheekbones smoothing out under his skin, making me too aware of his skull, like he was solid bone all the way through, no heart or lungs or blood. It made no sense, but it was all I could think.

"You're not even that pretty," he said, without taking his hand away. "But there's something about you." A dry heat vibrated all through my body, so hot it hurt. How was his hand not igniting? My mind felt too slow and he was talking, still talking, but somehow his mouth remained very small. "I mean you're pretty, you're twenty-three. But you won't give an inch, you're like a one-way mirror."

"And that does it for you?" I said this instead of *Get your filthy fucking hands off me*. How did that happen? I meant to say *stop*, to stand up and run. I pulled my hand away, but he pressed forward at the same time that I tried to get my arms between us and push him away.

He put his mouth against my ear, I could feel his lips, he said, "Your mother," in a voice like someone had been choking him. "I know she was on SSRIs, even back then. She had a brother who died, did you know that? It must have been bipolar II, or PTSD, or both, and I wanted to know. You think you want to know? You wouldn't even understand, it wouldn't mean anything to you. What have you got in your pretty head but that New Age bullshit? You know that by the time I could go home to see my parents they were dead?"

I bashed the side of my head against his and he dropped back, right onto the floor, and then stood up quickly, smoothing his clothes.

"I'm sorry," he said. "I've been inappropriate. Let's move on." He sat back, his face neutral, as if nothing had happened.

I got up, my hand over my ear, which was sore from connecting with Rosenberg's face, and walked out, past the other group members and all the way up the stairs. *A brother? SSRIs? Bipolar what?* And then it was as if I'd gone deaf in my head: my mind had run out of ink, and the thoughts, though pressed in, were blank. I put my hand on the doorknob, completely calm, opened the door.

In the room, Gil was writing.

"I'm leaving," I said. "Not later. Now. I'm going. To Georgia. I want to talk to my grandparents."

Neither of us spoke for a moment. Then he grinned. "Yes, ma'am."

I went to the dresser and found Gil's orange mountaineer backpack in the bottom drawer. I tossed it on the bed and started to pack. Out the window, someone turned on a light in the townhouse complex, throwing the street into relief. I had a shirt in each hand, slowly unfolding. I stowed Rosenberg's camera in the backpack, and tucked the envelope of photos from the storage room on top. I still hadn't gone through it.

We left as soon as we were packed. On a theatrical impulse, I arranged some pillows under the bedclothes to approximate a sleeping figure. If we hadn't had the fire escape, I might have tied sheets together and shimmied out. I wanted a long white nightgown, hair down to the middle of my back. Leaving—I thought of it as *escaping*—felt somehow Victorian to me, and a combination of panic and euphoria coursed through my veins, like the feeling you get right before having sex with someone more attractive than you. Gil was crossing the room with a handful of underpants when he dropped them on the floor, grabbed me by the hand and spun me around in a manic waltz.

"Yes," he said. "Yes, yes. Yes indeed, darling." He dipped me low and my hair hung down on the floor. The underwear was in a pile beside my ear. He zipped me back up and recovered the underwear, stuffing it into the orange backpack.

Gil opened the window and a plume of fresh, warm night air swept immediately into the room, making it look darker despite the moonlight. I climbed out first. The weight of the backpack and shoulder bag I was carrying made it hard to go down the steep metal steps, and once or twice I scared myself into overbalancing. I cried out the first time, and accidentally bit my tongue, raising a smooth little ridge near the tip. After that I was silent. Gil was whistling softly behind me, apparently unperturbed by the angle, or the possibility of being caught.

On the ground beside the House, I looked around. There was no window directly under my room; the closest was the kitchen window twenty feet back or so. No light came through, but I could see the ambient light in the backyard, surely coming from Rosenberg's sunless sunroom. I didn't want to go out the front gate, where anyone watching would see me. I rolled my lips over my teeth once, then threw the backpack over the fence. Then the shoulder bag. I shoved the rubber-tipped toe of my sneaker into the cross slat of the fence and grabbed the top beam. I couldn't get up, so I stepped down and backed up. I looked over my shoulder at the House. Gil was at the bottom of the fire escape.

I took a running start from a few metres back and tried to time it: jam toe into hold, push up, grab crossbeam, swing sideways and up. I made it most of the way over, the top of the slats digging into my stomach and ribs in a diagonal punch. I fell in the direction of my momentum and landed on my hip in the wet grass. I was out.

A light flicked on in the townhouse complex and a woman's head emerged from an upstairs window. I froze, with the damp seeping through my jeans and a little cool lick of it right against the bare skin of my stomach where my shirt had ridden up. She looked down at me, my red top unmistakable on the black canvas of the grass, the same red as the peonies that this very same woman grew on her patio. She put her hand out and did something in front of her mouth, a small glow. She was smoking a cigarette. When she blew the smoke out, her rounded mouth looked like she was blowing me a kiss. The hand with the cigarette hung limply, but then I saw her wiggle her ring and pinky fingers, the ones not holding anything. The merest suggestion of a wave.

There was a muffled noise, like snow falling from the overwhelmed branches of a pine tree. Gil was there, over the fence, beside me.

Together we walked through the quiet streets to the bus stop. It was thirty minutes before an orange and white bus lumbered into view to take us to Long Branch, and the adrenalin was wearing off. Maybe I should have waited till morning. I could call CAMH, get Rosenberg in all sorts of trouble. His lips on my ear.

At Long Branch, we got off the bus and transferred onto the streetcar, where Gil took the window seat and started writing in his notebook. My ribs ached. I'd never climbed over a fence before.

Looking up from the page, Gil grinned at me and said, "Do you want to be Thelma or Louise?"

"I don't know. Which one of them got Brat Pitt?"

"What a one-track mind," he said, and I swatted at him.

We were on Lake Shore Boulevard approaching Kipling, still ages from home, but I was already thinking of the store, of Bellwoods glowing under the street lamps. How the limestone gates looked like clouded ice from across the street. Across the aisle an old man was playing a battery-operated radio, holding it in his lap. Gil looked down at his hand on my arm as if he were going to remove it. Instead he gave me a squeeze.

The old man's radio was playing *Northern Lights*, the CBC classical music program. A woman's voice murmured softly between numbers.

"Mahler," said Gil, leaning back with his eyes closed. "I like that 'ah' sound. Very expressive, those wide vowels."

For a moment there was only the music and laughter from some girls behind us. Outside, Lake Shore emptied and filled as we passed through neighbourhoods and the gaps between. New pink brick townhouses had cropped up near Humber College, cheek-by-jowl with Caribbean restaurants, sports bars and suspicious-looking dental practices. The streetcar stopped, picking up people bound for downtown, then sped up again, swaying slightly, passing old lakefront mansions on our right and discoloured modernist apartment complexes on our left. In the dark it was hard to see the streams and creeks I'd observed on my initial journey out with Andrew. There are so many little rivers in southern Ontario, the waters ranging in colour from white to blue to brown. Some of the streams were as wide as the Don River. Any of them would have done the job. It wouldn't have mattered where we were living—suburbs, city, outer space. There is always a river, sooner or later, if you're looking.

On the hillside, just outside the city, there were a series of corporate logos made of white rocks and grass, strategically arranged. They changed from time to time, depending on who was paying. They looked grey in the ambient light of the city. Quartz, I bet. The cheap stuff was often used for gardening purposes. White quartz for clarity, for help in reaching the spirit world. It was either that or gravel.

I was slumped against Gil's shoulder, nearly asleep, when he said, "I'm getting close. I think it's almost done."

I straightened. "It's almost done?" He'd filled a dozen of the black-and-white notebooks. Now they were crammed into the bag at his feet. "No more blackouts once it's done," I said. "A deal's a deal, right?"

He nodded.

Then he said, "So what now?"

I turned up my hands. "I thought you would know."

"All I know is the book," he said. "All I know is you." He paused and then said, falsely casual, "Do you have any more of your notebooks?"

We were almost at Ossington, which meant the store was only three stops away. On the sidewalk people were hurrying to the corner to catch the streetcar, directly outside of CAMH. A young mother picked up a lagging child without pausing in her stride, hitching the little girl up high on her hip while she walked. The little girl put her head on her mother's shoulder and immediately sagged into sleep. I nudged the bag of notebooks with my foot.

"No," I said. "I've given you everything.".

"There's nothing else?"

I remembered the things I had taken from the storage room. The envelope of photos I'd never opened. The streetcar whined to a hard stop, and several of the people who were standing stumbled. The orange mountaineer backpack was on the floor between my feet. I looked up from it and saw Scarlet, the new clerk from the store, coming down the aisle, looking for a seat. Her eyes were red, her face flushed. She turned and looked at herself in the window, the white stripe in her hair brushed forward, obscuring her features.

Gil said, "What's wrong?"

"It's that girl up there, with the black and white hair. She's the one my dad hired to work at the store. Quick, let's get off and walk. We're almost home."

I grabbed the bag and Gil, and we went down the stairs, out the rear doors, just before the light changed. I looked back and

Scarlet was looking out the window, right at me. I couldn't tell from her face if she recognized me, but she made eye contact, and her pretty face was pulled into an expression I'd never seen, a naked misery that was almost boastful.

On the sidewalk outside the hospital, Gil said, "Are you sure you don't have anything else?"

I stopped and propped the orange backpack on a bench outside the main doors and began riffling through it. After a moment I found the envelope.

"There might be something in here," I said.

Inside were the photos my mother had turned into slides, from her trip to Georgia when I was ten. The Spanish moss, the bird-girl statue that they used later for that movie. It was nothing new. There was a map of Georgia, badly folded, that made up most of the bulkiness of the envelope. There was a small page with my mother's handwriting on it, the writing I'd so longed to see—part of a letter, but no other pages that matched. I found a lined sheet folded up in an empty playing-card package, and all it said, back and front, over and over was *Gabriel,* again in her handwriting. I'd done the same thing in a notebook in elementary school about a boy I liked. And who was Gabriel? Someone from before, from home, part of the reason she'd ended up here? Some old, dull-throbbing, red-faced story about errors in love? Or was it worse, from later, a man, not my father? Or the brother Rosenberg had mentioned or, for all I knew, made up? It was too much to think about after everything that had happened, I kept digging.

Underneath were more snapshots, older and vaguely familiar,

black-and-white. The first one was my grandparents again, younger. I thought they might be under forty, but it was hard to tell with the old-fashioned photos. I noticed again how my grandfather's cap looked like the one Gil had been wearing when I first met him. Then there was my mother, a teenager. Her hair was shorter and curlier, and she had a fringe that didn't suit her. There were half a dozen photos of her, beside my grandmother, my grandfather, the house with an expansive veranda, a horse whose nose had been cut off by the photographer. There was a picture of her in a line of girls, arms around each other, grinning like they'd been told to behave for the photo. Then there was one of her smiling wide with her arm linked through the arm of a dark-haired young man beside her, who was unmistakably Gil. My blood roared in my ears and for a moment I thought, *Blackout*—but nothing happened.

"Uh-oh," said Gil.

"What is this? What the hell is this?"

Gil shook his head.

Looking at it, I knew I'd seen it before, in a frame, somewhere. I couldn't remember where but I remembered the frame, wooden with gold corners. Up on the wall—when? Before Elaine, before Georgia. I remembered the smile on my mother's face, which was so big that her teeth didn't quite meet; you could see a dark sliver of mouth. I didn't remember Gil. Of course I didn't or I would have asked him. But seeing it now, I knew I'd seen it before. The photos she'd taken down when she got home from her parents'. I sat and put my head down between my knees.

"Who are you?"

"I'm someone who wants to help."

"Give me a straight answer." When he didn't say anything, I said, "Then I'm going to ask them, ask my grandparents. And if you've been lying—if you know anything, I swear to god I will kill you."

"I'm coming with you."

"Not a chance."

"Try and stop me. That's where I'm from."

Turning away, I said, "I need to call the bank. Tell them I'll be using my credit card in another country. I don't want them to think it's been stolen."

"What if they blocked your card? Rosenberg?"

"I'm an adult. And Rosenberg isn't the fucking CIA."

He held up his hands in surrender. "You're acting crazy."

I stuffed the offending photos back into the envelope and put it in the backpack. When I did, my hand touched hard plastic. I took out the Polaroid camera. Gil stood up and backed away from me. I stood up too and lifted the camera.

"I thought you liked being in pictures," I said, every sound in it hard against my teeth and tongue.

"Maggie."

I turned at the sound of my name. Dr. Malik was adjusting the collar of his jacket with one hand while trying to balance a file full of papers in the other.

"Dr. Malik." I stepped forward and then stopped myself. I realized I was still holding up the camera and I lowered it slowly.

"How are you?" he said, looking very directly at me.

"I'm okay. I just left Wooster House," I said. "I don't think

Dr. Rosenberg's methods are for me after all." I paused, unsure whether to say anything more. Then: "I'm sorry I stopped coming to see you."

Dr. Malik looked uncomfortable. "Wooster House? I can't address the methods of my colleagues, but I can tell you that if you feel as though the dynamic between you and your doctor is counterproductive, that is a legitimate complaint." I brightened, but he added, "Sometimes, though, we find problems because the process is uncomfortable, in order to give ourselves a reason to stop. That's also something to think about."

Rosenberg's mouth on my ear, his fingers on my wrist. "I really don't think that is the case here," I said.

He shifted his papers and said more quietly, "What about the blackouts?"

"I had one. A little while ago. But less than before."

Dr. Malik put his hand on my shoulder. He wore a long camel-coloured trench coat; it hung straight from his square shoulders. Even in the warm night, I was caught up with a desire to get inside it, not with Dr. Malik, but with his warmth still lingering, get into that dense, carefully tailored coat. A man's coat. The weight on my shoulders.

"I'm no longer your doctor, Maggie, but I do care about your well-being." He shifted again. "Well, I'm running pretty late. I lost track of the time."

I nodded. "I know just what you mean," I said.

And he looked at me again, with that sad little crease between his eyebrows. Then he dipped his head, briefly, and trotted across the street before the light changed.

I turned and looked at Gil, skulking in the shadows of the building, who said nothing but looked tense as I walked to him. His mouth was flat and he was swallowing repeatedly—I could see the tendons in his neck jump each time. I raised the camera.

"What would happen," I said, "if I took your photo right now?"

"Think about what's important," he said.

He cast a shadow on the sidewalk. If anything, he was more finely rendered than the city around him, each little line on his lower lip drawn as if in ink. Everything else faded in and out while he remained absolute, the sound of his voice wrapping around me like a hand around an arm, stopping me in place.

"You're so close," he said.

I raised the camera and he held up his hand. There was a flash that seemed very bright on the dark street and Gil staggered backwards as if shot. One foot went back to balance, and I went towards him, almost touching him.

We were in my bedroom at home, above the store. It was still dark. Gil was sitting on the edge of my bed, with his head down. I stood in front of him. I had the photo out—not a Polaroid, but the photo of Gil and my young mother. I thought about crumpling it up and throwing it at him. But I would want it back. I'd want to smooth it out again. I wondered if that was how she had felt. If she was sorry at all in the last seconds, if she wanted to get out, dry off and get warm, smooth herself out again. If she thought about me, how I would have to live from then on. From now on.

I looked at her young face in the photo; she was looking at the camera. Gil was in three-quarter profile, looking at her. You got the impression he turned at the last moment, as if she had said something.

I felt tired, like I'd donated blood and forgotten my cookie. I went to my nightstand and took out a blank notebook and my passport. Under my passport, in an olive-wood tray, were odds and ends: pens that didn't work anymore, business cards, promotional pins. In one corner was the zircon cat I had taken from the store as a ten-year-old, meaning to give it to Elaine. I'd never taken it back and instead had kept it with me like a talisman. It was cool against my fingers. I picked it up and slid it into my pocket, where I was holding the jade angel.

"I'm leaving in the morning," I said.

I went and checked my father's room, which was empty and dark. The clock on the stove said it was just before midnight. I wondered where he was, had a vision of him laughing over a glass of wine with Wendy and Andrew, the three of them discussing some book I'd never read.

"Don't make any noise," I said. We got under the blankets, holding onto each other. "I should hate you."

"Maybe. Maybe things are more complicated than you think. Or they have to be complicated because to get them the simple way would be too much."

"Why did I have a blackout tonight? If the book is almost finished?"

"Because it's not finished. Not quite."

"Is it really going to be?" He was silent. "Don't come with me tomorrow," I said. "Let me go alone."

Gil shifted, his chest against my back. "I can't do that," he said. "You know I can't."

I didn't say anything else. I fell asleep with his arm thrown loosely over me.

PART FOUR

GIFTS
&
ODDITIES

Nineteen

*M*y mother's mother once beat her with a wooden spoon. Only once, even though it was the South in the fifties. My mother left the door to their barn open and my grandfather's horse escaped. He was a good horse, and he would probably have gone out and eaten for a while and just walked back home, his large head with its prey eyes nodding in that ponderous, dignified, horsey way. But one of the neighbours decided to be helpful and bring him in, a teenage boy who mounted up with his girlfriend watching, no saddle, and kicked the horse, whose name was Quincy, into a gallop through the country roads of my mother's hometown in Georgia. Nothing is known about the girlfriend—whether she was impressed and clapped her hands or whether she looked away, determined not to lend approval. Whether she was beautiful or plain. Whether she married the boy. What is known is that Quincy, an old horse my grandfather never would have jumped over so much as a puddle, tripped over the fence the boy tried to make him clear. Boy and horse broke a leg each, and all of this unwound like a spool of thread and travelled through time and town to find my mother holding the other end.

"She cried the whole time," my mother told me. "She cried until the spoon broke."

"Did you cry?"

My mother broke a pencil point in the store ledger. We were sand-wiched in the little backroom taking inventory. "I want you to know," she said, "that I would never hit you."

But she had, and she did. What she meant was she didn't want to. Or that it came from a place she couldn't get out of, that she had no control over it. She would never think about it, is what she meant; she would never walk into the kitchen and take a wooden spoon out of the blue ceramic jar and think, I am going to hit my daughter. She would never plan, or aim. She would never give warning.

I said, "I know, Mom."

And she put her hand on my face, underhand, like she was hold-ing it up. "You're so soft. That reminds me," she said. "Skin cream." She got up and took down the basket of office things, rummaging for the pencil sharpener. "Should we order rose or eucalyptus?"

"Both," I said. "And aloe."

She sharpened the pencil and made a note in the margin. She said, "What would I do without you, Magpie?" and swept all her hair over one bare shoulder.

My own hair was short, tucked behind my ears, dyed an inadvis-able, flat Crayola orange.

Her arms still had faint, smooth pink lines from a recent bad time, almost pretty compared to the bark-like welts that had healed first. A few weeks later Wendy and I would wander down St. George Street, following a crowd of clapping and chanting upperclassmen at the University of Toronto during our first week of school. Four years later Wendy and I would graduate. I'd meet Andrew. And so on, up until Wooster House. But the thread could always be rolled back up, one end in my mother's hands. She sat there, letting the

*end of the pencil drift unconsciously into her mouth now and then,
making little notes and flipping catalogue pages, oblivious. I tried to
picture her at the barn door, wandering dreamily away, or in the
farmhouse kitchen after the vet had gone, his smoking rifle slung
over his shoulder, I tried to picture the spoon, but none of it fit; I
couldn't let my mother be anything more than I could see. I'd never
been to Georgia. I couldn't get the backgrounds right.*

The flight cost four hundred dollars, plus it had set me back
another fifty to get to the airport from the store. I felt a little
reckless buying the ticket. "I need to go today," I said to the man
at the airline desk, and he said, "Today? And you don't have a
ticket?" He seemed thrilled rather than irritated by the idea.
There was still room on the early flight to Savannah, connecting
in North Carolina. When he handed me my boarding pass he
said, "Don't eat in the pub," as if sharing a special secret.

I had never been on a plane before, but I didn't want to tell
anyone that or ask for help. I was embarrassed. We'd never
flown anywhere on family vacations, and once I was old enough
to go by myself, I didn't want to leave for that long, didn't want
to leave her alone. I'd gotten a passport, talked to Andrew about
a trip to Paris or Rome, but nothing had ever come of it.

This morning I'd left while it was still dark; I wanted to get
away as soon as possible. My father's late and noisy return had
woken me up in the night, but I left in the morning while he
was still sleeping. He never knew I'd been home. Gil, I had left

asleep in my room, easing out of the bed with the greatest of care, my heart beating loudly in my ears.

I waited two hours at my gate without speaking to anyone. By the time the attendants announced my boarding call, I felt glassy and thin, like the waiting, the not-talking, had bleached me out. I'd been talking so much lately.

The seats on the plane were plush and claustrophobic. The actual takeoff was anticlimactic. I held my nose and popped my ears the way Wendy said she always did. It was a jolt to remember where I'd last seen Wendy—thinking of her was still normal and initially painless, and then the little curtain rolled up and I saw her standing over Andrew. In my head she held her nose, popped her ears. Smiled.

Out the window, the sun was so bright glinting off the Great and little lakes below that they looked like metal, not water. It was almost painful to look at. It didn't feel like a long time before they announced we were approaching Charlotte, where we landed and went through the process of shuffling from one plane to another, like a class trip, and then we were up in the sky again. I slept then and by the time I woke up, we were dropping smoothly towards another runway in the grey nothingness of early evening.

I drove a rental car to the hotel like I was taking a driver's test, moving well under the speed limit and eliciting honks and curses. I did not want to drive into a Savannah bus shelter before I had a chance to ask a single question of my grandparents. If I found them. If they were still alive. I should have spoken to my father, called them first at least. My throat seized up and I took my foot off the gas, prompting the driver behind me to pass, shouting, "Learn to drive, asshole" through the open window.

I made it blackout-free to a hotel that the car rental clerk had recommended, where I asked for a phone book at the front desk and took it to my ground-floor room, trying not to think about the money I was spending. In the movies, when people went searching for things, no one mentioned the bill. Then, for a split second, I couldn't remember my mother's maiden name. I sat on the edge of the slippery bedspread, my throat tight and aching. Finally it came to me, and I wrote down the numbers I found in the book and told myself I'd call tomorrow, that the flight had worn me out. I returned the phone book and set out walking.

Savannah was laid out in a series of city squares. Pretty, hushed green spaces opened up suddenly, centred around a statue or monument, some of them so high that I would have had to struggle just to climb onto the supporting base. Street lamps like something from a movie set leaned over me as I walked aimlessly through the downtown area. Candy-coloured buildings seemed like they would be soft to the touch. All of Savannah seemed good to me. I wanted to reach out and put my arms around it. Overhead were the tops of the monuments, the Spanish moss hanging in the trees—*oak trees?*—and then other, tall trees that looked like spiky, feathery palms. And the crooning street lamps. It was like there was a loose web woven over the squares, a net of protection.

As I headed towards the water, everything was hot and dimly colourful. It felt like Toronto in July but it was September. An electronic sign on a hotel I walked by said 81 degrees, but I didn't know what that meant in Celsius. It said 7:56 p.m.

I had the map from the storage-room envelope in my purse. I took it out and spread it open, then folded it so I could see where someone had circled *Savannah Beach* in black ink. Near where the city sloped down to the river, I went into a convenience store and asked the girl behind the counter the best way to get there.

"Savannah Beach?" she said. "Doesn't mean anything to me."

A man turned from the back cooler, two beer bottles held in one hand. "You want Tybee Island," he said. "They haven't called it Savannah Beach in, what, thirty years. You're too young to have been around—where would you have even heard that?"

"I'm from Canada," I said, and this seemed to be enough for them both.

"Well, Tybee's easy to find," said the girl. "You're only twenty minutes away or so, driving. You want to take President Street to the 80 East. There's signs."

"Thanks." I nodded to her, turned to the man and said, "Thanks," feeling foolish. Of course things had changed. The map was easily twenty-five years old—older than me.

"Have a good one," the man said, adding another beer to his handful. "It's a nice night for it."

Back outside, I walked down a cobblestone slope to the water, where enormous riverboats with names like *The Georgia Queen* were draped in American flags and huddled at the piers. They were covered in signs promoting their various cruising options. Opposite the water was a line of shops, including a candy store beside the riverboat ticket wicket. Set into the cobblestones there was a single set of tracks, like the streetcar ones at home. I looked up and down the tracks, then crossed to the candy store.

It was quiet in the shop. Most families had returned to their hotels for the evening and couples were already out to dinner. I wondered when the store closed. A contraption like a miniature grain elevator deposited saltwater taffy into large barrels. The walls were covered in every kind of candy imaginable and in a stall in the centre of the store, two teenage girls held court over a small universe of fudge, pralines and chocolates. Candy stores and fretting about my VISA bill—I knew I was doing this whole thing wrong, this trip that was supposed to be different, poignant, revelatory.

In the mirrored wall, I caught a glimpse of myself. My face looked thin, hollowed, even though I'd put on weight since I got to Wooster House and stopped riding my bicycle. I tried to see myself as my grandparents would, if I found them, if I managed. That first glimpse, searching for her in me. I attempted a smile. Sickly, toothy. False.

"That's what we like to see," said one of the girls. She was beautiful, with a short afro dyed red. "Happy people." She was smiling and looking me in the eye. She was the kind of girl who was going to spin this job into something impressive on her college applications. *Leadership potential*. The girl beside her lacked her intensity, smiled vaguely at me.

I bought some saltwater taffy. Banana, golden pear, lemon meringue, mango. The little ovals were freshly made, soft in their waxy paper. What would it be like working in a candy store? You'd keep things neat. Direct people to what they wanted. It wouldn't be so different.

I thanked the girl when she rang me through.

"You're welcome," she said. She smiled beautifully, professionally. "Enjoy Savannah."

Twenty

The house was a different one than in my photos. It was a compact white house on a small street without sidewalks, a blue Dodge in the driveway. The tall feathery trees were everywhere. I parked on the street and got out, moving slowly. The ocean was visible over my shoulder, grey and puckered.

I knocked on the door and they answered right away, like they'd been standing in the foyer, waiting. My grandparents, older than I'd ever seen them. He wasn't wearing a cap and I felt a little cheated. Instead he had on an aqua golf shirt.

I searched for her in their faces, but they looked like any old man and woman. I wanted to push and pull at their faces until I could see her.

"I'm Margaret."

They stood aside and my grandmother said, "Come in, child. It's so nice that you're here."

It was the same voice I'd heard on the phone when I called that morning. She didn't look surprised to see me, just like she hadn't seemed surprised on the phone. My grandfather reached out and shook my hand.

The house was neat and a little cramped, full of things without being messy. There was a lineup of milk-glass vases on the hallway table, and hanging above them, right there, was a photo of my mother and Gil. I thought I was going to have to hunt around; I'd been plotting and it left me off balance to so easily have found what I'd been looking for. It wasn't exactly the same as the photo I had, but it was so close it must have been taken at the same time. The clothes were the same. My mother had better control in this one, her smile was big but decent. Gil was looking at the camera straight on, composed.

"Well," said my grandmother. "You've come an awfully long way. Are you still able to stay for supper?"

I pointed. "Who is that?"

My grandmother looked at me like I was being cruel. "That's my son," she said. "I suppose he would have been your uncle."

"What was his name?" I knew I was being rude. For some reason I felt betrayed by these people. Their very existence was a betrayal. So far away, so long withheld.

"Gabe. Gabriel."

Gay-brill. The vowel sounds were not lost on me. How funny memory was. The way children hear things without hearing them. Mis-remembered. The way the photo had seeped in. I plowed ahead. "I thought you couldn't have any more children. That's what she said. That the doctor said your back—" I didn't know how to finish.

"He did say that. After your mother."

"But what about the horse? She let the horse get out."

My grandmother stared. "Oh. Oh, Quincy." My grandfather looked down at the ground the way people do when you've said something rude. It was directed at me, not my grandmother.

"Was she sick then? Did she ever forget things? Forget where she'd been? Or hurt herself?"

My grandfather reached out and put his arm around my grandmother's shoulders.

"She's come on a plane, Lawrence." *Luh-rinse.* Their voices, yellow-gold, like warm lake water.

He said, "Carol had some trouble but she was a good girl."

"Trouble?" I stared again at the photo. "What kind of trouble?"

My grandmother's hair reached almost to her chin and she was twirling the end of a lock around one finger, behind her ear. It was strangely schoolgirl-like. She was over seventy. She looked me straight in the eye, not in a showy way, but in a way that made me think she wouldn't have stooped the way tall girls do sometimes. She would have stood up straight.

She said, "We did the best we could. You must know what that's like."

After a moment, I said, "Do you still have chickens? The ones that would sit in your lap?"

"We've got chicken for dinner," said my grandmother. Her face had lost its sharpness, seemed misty around the edges. "If that's what you mean."

I was wearing jeans and a T-shirt. It occurred to me I should have dressed more nicely.

We made our way into the kitchen. There was cold chicken and a salad and fresh rolls.

During dinner my grandfather barely spoke. He drank glass

after glass of some dark yellow liquor, neat, from a glass with flowers painted on it. I looked at his Adam's apple, which was sliding around in his neck as he swallowed, and I had trouble getting my knife to work through the chicken.

"Don't worry about him. He can drink like he's got ten pairs o' socks on."

There was a pecan pie for dessert. When my grandmother served it she said, "Seeing as you've never been down here, it seemed like the thing to do."

"Mom always made cakes," I said. Then I added, "But this looks nice too."

After a few bites I put down my fork. "What happened to Gabriel?"

My grandfather had his mouth on his glass, and his voice came out the side. "He died in Vietnam. So they said."

"Who said?"

"They said he was having—said he was going off. In the head. And then he deserted while on patrol. They thought he deserted. But when they gained a bit ah ground they found him. Shot. In the chest."

My grandmother said, "As if he'd just wandered off into the jungle. That's what Colin Sieslak said he heard."

My grandfather said, "Another boy from town. Went over there. Said Gabriel was forgetting to air his feet." He said this as if it explained everything.

My grandmother took the glass out of his hand and went and put it on the counter.

"Your mother left right after. For *Canader.*" She sat down

again. "We thought the army would straighten him out. Not that he was bad. He wasn't bad."

"She was so young. Why did you let her go? Why didn't you come get her?"

"In *Canader?*" My grandmother's already slack face came completely undone. Without seeming to look at her hands, she served me another piece of pecan pie. The cooked pecans were pliant, fleshy.

"We wanted to come up for the funeral," she said. "But we're not— It's just too far. We can't drive too long any more, and your grandfather can't go on the airplane. Gabriel's funeral was in town." She had a little smear of oily dressing on her mouth. "You don't expect to outlive one of your children. You don't expect to outlive both of them."

"She came down to visit, after she got married," said my grandfather, who had recovered his glass somehow and was drinking again. "Your father came down. Very pleasant fellow. She was taken care of. She seemed all right that time. And she had the— She had you."

He put his cup down. I set to work on the second piece of pie. I should have tried to make normal conversation. But what if this was the only dinner I would ever have with them? They seemed unmoored in time—Gabriel's funeral, my mother's. What if they were losing it? Was anyone checking on them? What did dementia look like?

"What was she like when she was little?" I said.

The two of them were still on their salad; they ate unbelievably slowly.

"What was she like?" I said again.

"She was bright," said my grandmother. "But soft." And after that she would only talk about the weather.

After dinner, we sat with sweet tea in the living room. "I made it this morning," said my grandmother. "Figured you should have the whole Southern experience." Then she abruptly walked out of the room, leaving me with my grandfather. He said nothing and I was trying to decide where to begin when my grandmother came back with a pack of cards.

"Do you want me to tell your fortune?" she asked. There was no introduction to this.

"Those are playing cards."

She nodded and sat down on the end of the couch. She handed me the cards and I shuffled, cut the deck. She laid out a simple three-card spread, right to left. Past, present, future. The nine of clubs, the three of spades, the four of spades.

"You're not like her, you know." She fiddled with the cards, making the edges line up straight. "There were always hearts in her readings."

"What does the spread mean?"

"That's reserve there." She pointed to the nine of clubs. "Strength held back, or stubbornness. Preparation, you could say. Readiness." She pointed to the three of spades next. "Confusion. Three's a crowd, so to speak. Maybe sorrow." She laid her hand over it.

"What about the four?" I was trying to figure out how the suits corresponded to the tarot. The number matched the numbers on tarot cards. I needed my notes.

"Rest. Logic. Decisions. The world."

"The world."

"That is, the actual world, the physical world." She grasped the couch as if demonstrating.

"Did you do this for her?"

She nodded.

"Do you believe in this?"

My grandmother slotted the deck back into the cardboard package and tucked the lip in place. "I thought I didn't believe in it. But I thought I didn't believe in God either."

We sat and sipped our sweet tea and at one point my grandfather cleared his throat loudly, for a long time. After a minute he got up and went into the washroom, and I could hear him spitting into the sink.

"So my parents came down? After they were married and I was a baby? Did I come with them?"

"You stayed with the other grandparents. You were too little for flying."

"I didn't know if I'd ever been on a plane before. I guess not."

She said, "It's hard to know sometimes, what we have and haven't done. I have to look at the photo albums, but sometimes even then—" She stood up suddenly. "I hope you don't think we're hard," she said. "It's not even that you look like her, so much. You look more like your father. It's just been such a long time, and in our situation—You'll understand when you're our age." She paused, and turned the pack of cards over a few times. "She was always delicate, but after Gabriel, well. She talked to him after he was gone; she thought he was still here sometimes. When she came down in '85, she thought he was going to be here; she was in a state, talked like he had been here all along. After a couple of days she calmed down and got back to herself, but it was awful the first time she came in—she called out for him—" My grandmother stopped talking and looked straight ahead, just silent. "But he wasn't here, of course," she said after a moment. "And after a while she went back to Canada. I knew she wouldn't be back here, but I never— I could understand her leaving, though. A country that wouldn't fight. But it was in her, she was no Canadian; I could see it just as bad when she come back then, when she saw he wasn't here. She fell down outside. We sold the house and moved into the new house after that." It took me a moment to realize that she meant the house we were in. The *new house* that they'd been living in for more than ten years. Then she said, "You know, when she fell down outside, she was calling for your father."

My grandmother stood looking past me like she hadn't just given this speech. It was too much to think of my mother falling into the dirt, realizing again and again that her brother was gone. I saw then how my father might have looked to her, how safe, how constant, past the age of recklessness, if he'd ever had one. He was a man with one old gun in a drawer somewhere, balanced by a balustrade of books and knowledge—a man less likely than any other to go to war, to leave, to fight. A man who would think carefully and move slowly, deliberately, who beside the dramatic rhetoric of the draft dodgers would have seemed almost zen-like.

I reached out and hugged my grandmother, and she held onto me for a long time. My grandfather came out of the wash-room and saw us there. She let go of me and then he hugged me briefly, his face held away from mine, but he put his hand on the back of my head, cradling it for a moment. They walked me to the door.

"Have a good flight," said my grandmother. "Thank you for coming."

My grandfather cleared his throat again. He said, "Be safe."

I got back to the hotel around nine and lay down on my bed. I closed my eyes. Out loud I said, "You can come in now."

"Thanks, darling." Gil lay down, the mattress sagging under him.

We lay on the low, hard bed with its requisite burgundy flowers-and-vines comforter. We held hands, chaste like an elderly married couple on the shiny, crinkling fabric. He pushed his free hand into his hair, unconsciously, and mas-saged his scalp. I touched my sock foot to his.

"You know the summer's almost over at home," I said. He didn't answer. I said, "We had a deal. You said you'd give me what I needed to stop the blackouts."

I expected him to protest that he wasn't finished. But he said, "I did."

"You said you would and I want you to make good."

"No, I mean I did give it to you. I already gave it to you."

It was like being in school, looking at little black print on a paper and knowing you know the answer, just out of reach. I stood up and as I did, darkness bunched itself up in the corners of the room and spread through the air, quickly, the same clouds of black sand that were now so familiar. The room dimmed and when I took a breath even that small space seemed to darken. I put my hand in my pocket just before the light was drowned and took out the jade angel.

It glowed. Not steadily but in a flickering way, like a candle, and it was warm to the touch. The dark subsided a little, only a little, and I could just see Gil's shape, still unmoving on the bed. I reached down, groped for his hand, found it. We left the hotel room, and the hallway was dark too, dark as a power outage. Twice people passed by us; I could only see them the moment before I bumped into them. The light cast by the jade angel, which I held in my upturned hand, wasn't strong, but it was enough to illuminate a few steps ahead. The other people in the hallway didn't seem to notice anything strange and blundered by at top speed.

We walked back the same way I'd been earlier, to one of the bigger squares off a street called Congress. None of the street lights seemed to be working, and now and then I would stumble and pull on Gil's arm to steady myself, like a clumsy ice skater. Being outside made the dark worse somehow; the openness, instead of being a relief, was a terror. Everything except the small circle around my moving hand was swallowed. It was much, much darker than night.

When I spoke it felt like an hour had passed. It was as much to steady myself, some desperate attempt at sonar, as anything. I said, "Why didn't you tell me when you gave it to me?"

I had to keep my hand open to maximize the light from the carving, and it was hard to resist closing my fist around it for safety. What if I dropped it and the blackness erased us? Where would I end up?

"Miracles aren't wishes. They aren't the answers to prayers," said Gil. His voice didn't have its usual grandstanding tone, its brittle-glib protective coating, and I could tell he didn't like this darkness any more than I did, but he kept talking. "They're fantastic things that happen to prove or teach you something. The word has lost its meaning; people talk about miracles like they're lottery winnings."

"You're being obtuse," I said, and the bickering tone in my voice seemed to beat away the fear.

He didn't speak for a moment and then said, reluctantly, "I didn't tell you because I didn't know how it worked. There are different kinds of blackouts. There are different kinds of help. Your mother. She had what she needed too. Just having it isn't enough."

"She had this?" I closed my hand reflexively, and the small, jerking light whooshed inwards, only my fingers illuminated. I stopped, opened my hand again and we kept walking, side by side, untouching. I had dropped Gil's hand when I stopped.

"No," said Gil. "But she had what she needed."

"What was it?" I was thinking of the store, the other carved figurines. What could it have been? A needle in a haystack. Not that it mattered now.

Gil took my hand. He didn't say anything and I turned to look at him, realized I could see his face. The darkness was draining away, and street lamps were flickering rapidly, and then more slowly, and after a moment, they burned steadily orange in the dim and glowing city night. The light of the jade angel was hardly noticeable now. Closed-up shops could be seen through the trees, off in the distance.

"I'm here," I said. "We're here." I pulled at Gil's hand. He wasn't holding on and his hand slipped out of mine. I tucked the jade angel away.

"I don't feel well," said Gil.

"It worked," I said. "We made it through."

"I guess," said Gil. He didn't sound afraid anymore, nor did he sound happy.

"Why are you being like this? We should be celebrating." I spun on one foot, the grass slick. I took a running start and turned a sloppy cartwheel.

"Quit it," said Gil. He was hugging his arms around himself.

"Bet you can't catch me."

"Come on. Let's go back."

I turned another cartwheel, more neatly, the world orienting just a moment later than my body. Then I took off along the path. I heard Gil call, "Hey," and I rounded the far side of the monument, feeling an electricity around my head that spurred me on.

"Come back," he called, his voice laboured.

He appeared at a run, and I took off again. I circled a tree and headed back to the centre of the square with Gil following, faster now. I turned back and saw that he was closing in. He reached forward, made to grab my arm, and I stopped, stepped sideways. He kept moving, tangled in himself, and fell onto his knees. Instead of getting up, he stayed there, his sides going in and out. Then his head jutted forward and he vomited spectacularly. I went over to him and put a hand out.

"Are you okay?"

He retched again, then spit. "No, not particularly," he said.

He stood up and when he went to wipe the dampness around his mouth, I saw that it was dark, much too dark, black in the dim light. I took him by the hand and led him under a street light. It was blood, and there was a thin trickle coming out of his nose as well.

"It must be bad," he said, "for your face to look like that." He was breathing with his mouth hanging open.

"We have to get you to a hospital," I said, but he was shaking his head spasmodically, continuously. "You need a doctor."

There was a lengthy inscription on the base of the monument, illegible. Gil's face was passive but there was an animal noise coming from him. He sat down on the paved path. I got down beside him, stroked his back.

"Can you pinch my nose?" he said. He had his head tilted back. "My hands feel heavy."

"Why don't you let me take you to a doctor? We're in the middle of a city, we don't need to act like field medics, fuck."

"Cursing doesn't become you."

"How can you just talk like that? There could be something seriously wrong."

"I'm well aware of that, thank you."

"Well," I said, "at least let me take you back to the hotel." I got his arm around my shoulders and pulled him up. He didn't start walking; he had his eyes closed.

Then he said, "Okay," and we started off, slower than slow.

In the hotel room I went through my toiletries bag, looking for anything useful. What stopped bleeding? American cranesbill, shepherd's purse. Heliotrope gemstones. Zircon. Was any of that true? In my jewellery bag, where I had stored the jade angel, was the zircon cat figurine.

It was all I could think to do. Gil was lying on the bed, but I stood him up and unbuttoned his shirt, the fabric cheap and slightly shiny around the cuffs and collar. Light blue, like a workman wears. I opened his pants and slid them down so he could step out of them. His legs were very white and hard, especially for a man who did so little walking. They felt more like bone than muscle. I folded his clothes and put them on the dresser.

I helped him into bed and he lay on his side, trying to find a comfortable position, the skin on his chest creasing a little. He seemed older to me then, as though his skin had come loose from the layer underneath somehow. Lying there, he was fragile, damaged, but I felt healthy and unnaturally awake, like the blood had been emptied from my body and returned to me purified. When he rolled onto his back I sat up, hovering over him.

"This is probably bullshit," I said. "But it can't hurt." I held the zircon to his closed mouth while he looked at me, silent. He didn't protest.

Through the window I could see the trunk and lower branches of a tall tree, black in the darkness, and I had the impulse to climb it, the way I'd climbed trees in Bellwoods with Elaine as a child. I could almost feel myself at the top, even past the limbs that could support a person's weight, perched in branches no thicker than fingers, and then higher, impossibly high, with the cool Savannah leaves barely grazing the soles of my feet.

Twenty-One

W̶hen I got out of the cab on Queen Street, the store looked the same as always, the indigo paint on the sign peeling slightly, just right. The flowing white letters of *Pierce Gifts & Oddities* were less shiny than the background, like it would feel velvety, dull, if you touched it.

It was evening and the store was closed. I put my hands on the glass of the window. The display inside was dismal, with boxes of letter-pressed stationery turned in every direction and recycled glass carafes left wherever curious customers had replaced them. Apparently Scarlet was still working her magic. She'd forgotten the sandwich board outside too. I was irritated, and then I remembered her face through the streetcar window, her red eyes and that aggressive sadness, her expression so different from the studied, bored one she'd had in the store when I visited.

Letting myself in as quietly as possible, I reached up to dampen the bell over the door. I got the broom from the little backroom, which still smelled of dust and vanilla, and the warm tobacco undertone we'd never been able to get rid of. How I'd expected my Georgia grandfather to smell. Instead he'd smelled like Dove soap. A letdown.

It was a little lonely to be in there when the store was closed, especially with the sun setting earlier now as summer wound down. There was a neon-tube sign on the wall for the Fortune and Foretelling section; it was red and said simply, FORTUNE. My mother had bought it from a strip club in the east end that was closing up, years ago. I wondered if there'd been more words when it was at the strip club. Or maybe it was a dancer's name. It stayed on all the time and glowed, and in the dark it made everything red-black; it cast a tawdry, flattering light.

I untangled scarves, hung up bags, re-shelved books, always putting my feet down carefully. There was no sound from above.

On the counter was a stack of unopened mail, behind the horoscope scrolls, several of which had obviously been opened and re-rolled. Amid the usual bills and junk was a letter addressed to me, which I opened. It was from Tracey.

Vancouver is so pretty, it's as pretty as people say with the mountains and all that. I love Chad so much but we tell people we met on the Internet because no one ever asks anything else after we say that. In a weird way I feel like I love him with all the love I had for my brother that was just hanging around after he died. That sounds sick, I know, and it's not the same kind of love of course but, well, what can they really expect from us Wooster House alumni? Sorry I didn't tell you about Chad and me until the last minute. Anyway I'm writing to you at your mom's store because I know in my heart you'll be back here by now. I'm feeling good about everything these days. It's still the honeymoon stage with Chad, I guess—I feel like a cartoon animal. Something pink. I feel dumber and happier. You should come out here. They've got a bunch of stores near our place that I think must be like Pierce Gifts & Oddities, all that New Age—y and organic stuff. I'm doing okay and I hope you are too. If you ever come to Vancouver, look me up. I don't think I'll be back to Toronto. But who knows, really.

    Lots of love from the West Coast,

    Tracey

I went to the drawer under the cash register and dug down to the very bottom. Gil's cards were still there. As I slipped Tracey's letter in, I wondered whether any of it was true, or whether Rosenberg had been telling the truth about Chad moving home to Ottawa. I saved the envelope too so I could write back to her, sometime, later, if it was even a real address. I believed that it was.

I took out Gil's cards and put them in my purse. Then I went outside and brought in the sandwich board, making the bell ring and accidentally letting the door slam closed behind me. I put down the board and locked the door and then went to the animals, found a cloth and began dusting them, picking each one up and going over it gently.

A moment later, I heard footsteps and looked up to see my father standing at the bottom of the staircase with a baseball bat in his hand.

He said, "Maggie? You're home." His silver hair feathering over his ears, untidy. "I heard the door," he said. "You didn't tell me you were coming."

"I wanted—to surprise you." My voice cracked as if I hadn't

spoken in a long time. I cleared my throat. I saw from his face that he didn't know anything that had happened, that Wendy hadn't called him, that Rosenberg hadn't ratted me out. "I'm feeling a lot better," I said. "I left Wooster House. So I can start working again."

"That's wonderful," he said, and, "You sound croaky. Are you getting sick? I have some cough medicine upstairs, I think. It's just the drugstore brand but it should help."

He was in one of his white T-shirts. I couldn't believe the baseball bat. I'd never seen it. Where did he keep it? He leaned it against the wall at the base of the stairs and came over to give me a kiss on the cheek.

"Is there anything I can do?" he said.

He reached past me and picked up the closest of the stone animals, a chrysoprase eagle. Chrysoprase, for healing wounds. One of the stones I'd thought of for Gil, but hadn't had with me. Chrysoprase shouldn't touch the wound, it should just be held over the afflicted area. Indirect healing. Also for safety, in doorways, and as a cure for restlessness, and protection in or on water. For bringing together the conscious and the unconscious. So many things for such a small stone, the eagle's wings dwarfed in my father's hand.

"You always loved these things," he said. "You played with them like dolls."

I nodded. "I like the citrine." He looked at the green eagle in his hand. "Citrine's the yellow one," I said.

"I never could keep it all straight." He patted my arm. "Did you want to come up? Where is your luggage? I could make some tea. Or coffee, if that's what you like. Or I could get some. Tim Hortons will be open."

My father's face in his hands after the funeral, his voice breaking, saying, *Maggie's in here* to my mother when she had the box-cutter, his slow steps the time he carried her up the stairs. The gun upstairs, the baseball bat I'd never seen. My mother believed in auras, colours that could bloom in and around you. But most people couldn't see them, most people missed it. My father was nodding at me, wanting me to say something.

I hadn't gone back to the river. I'd flagged a cab on Queen Street with Wendy fluttering beside me and left my father standing there with the police officers. He had told me to go, to go home, to get some rest. It never occurred to me he might want me to stay, to put a hand on him, his shoulder, his arm. To treat him like I would have treated her.

He put the eagle back on the table. I gave him a kiss on the cheek.

"I put your mother's old shoes away while you were gone," he said. "I hope you don't mind. It was just difficult to look at them. I don't even know where you dug them up, I hadn't seen them in twenty years."

"Mom's shoes?" And I saw in my mind the brown canvas shoes I had found myself wearing after the first blackout. The ones that had pinched. "I guess—I mean, I got them from the attic. I'd been looking through some of her old things."

"I know you had. If it helps," he said, and then put his hand on the back of his neck. "Well, if it helps. I don't even know what all is up there, what all she kept."

"We'll have coffee soon," I said. "I'm going to George's for a little while, but I won't be home late." I pointed to the eagle. "You should put that by the apartment door. It's supposed to protect us."

"You don't really believe the mumbo-jumbo, though, do you?"

I pointed to the baseball bat. "You wouldn't really use that on a robber, would you?"

He looked into the shop behind me for a moment. "I don't know," he said. He was a man who gave a serious question serious thought. "If it was a matter of survival, well. I suppose I don't know." Then, "Are you sure you want to go to George's? I can make you something here. And I got some of that cereal you like, with the little bits, the little sugar—" He made a pinching motion with his fingers. "You know the one I mean. You don't have to go out."

I said, "I just have to get something off my chest, Dad. I won't be out late."

He hesitated, then, "Well, tell Wendy I say hello."

As I went out the door the bell rang again. My father locked it from the inside and waved through the glass before I turned to walk away.

I took the streetcar east and got off at River Street, walked across to the staircase. The stairs were just in front of the clock sign with the RIVER I STAND IN text, a little past the spot where King and Queen streets ran into each other in a kind of crooked elbow. Below was the Don, flowing like a great vein. If the city were a body, this was where you would draw blood.

Near the bottom of the stairs at the water's edge, Gil was waiting like I'd asked, hugging himself despite the warm, humid night.

"So why here?" he said.

"I wanted to talk to you about our project."

"Our project?" He was grinning at first, but as he looked at me his expression slipped away. "Darling, please," he said, reaching out for me.

I kept my body away from his. It was hard not to lean into him. I wanted to press my cheek against his furry one. He'd been clean-shaven in the photos with my mother. Where had the beard come from?

Instead of hugging him, I said, "You're not my uncle, are you." I took the cards he'd sent me out of my purse and handed them to him.

"Ah," he said. "No souvenirs, I guess. And I thought you were the sentimental type." He slipped the cards into his back pocket. "No, darling. I'm not your uncle. You'll undoubtedly be relieved to hear."

Even now, even here, it was hard not to check him over for blood and bruises, hard not to ask, *Does it still hurt?* Instead I said, "Are you going to tell me? Who you are? What you are?"

"There's still more to find out. About her," he said. "Don't you care anymore?"

I reached into my purse and took out Rosenberg's camera. Lifting it to my face, I said, "Smile," and he was so surprised that he did. I pressed the button flat and there was a flash. The photo slid out of the camera into my hand and I tucked it into my sweater pocket, then took off the sweater and laid it on the ground. Then my sandals. I put my purse down with them. A pile of things on the bank again. I walked forward, barefoot.

"Let's not be too hasty here," he said, but he was backing up while he spoke, as if he didn't notice himself moving. I pressed towards him, facing the water. He backed up until he was standing on the concrete ledge above the river.

"I can still help," he said. He stopped, stubborn for a moment. "I'm not a well man," he said. "You should be gentle with me." When I kept walking towards him, he said, "Aren't I more fun than everyone else? Who will call you darling if I'm gone? Do you really want to be alone?"

"There are millions of people here. I'm not alone."

"Hundreds, millions, dozens, it doesn't matter. Without me, you're alone. I don't want you to be alone," he said. "She wouldn't want you to be alone."

"I need you to go away," I said. "You can go be with her, if that's how it works. I don't know."

"I am with her." His voice was even but his eyes were wet. "Darling, come on. An ending isn't the same as an answer, you know. Not always. Don't you want answers?" He had started to bleed again, out of both nostrils. "Maybe you should move away," he said, conversationally. "Vancouver. We could see Tracey." He reached out and grabbed me by the wrists. "Come with me, please," he said, and then, "It's only fair. You pushed me off a building."

And he stepped off, pulling, and we went in and it was a farther drop than it had looked like and there was a second to think about being in the air before crashing through and down into the water, noise going inside out.

We surfaced together, Gil's hands still on my wrists, now tightening as he pulled me up against him and kicked off from something, the wall maybe, and we went down again, the dirty water in my mouth and eyes and everything was deaf and manic as I kicked, trying to get my feet under me, getting a breath that was half water, rolling under with him again. Rocks scraped my knuckles, my knees. And then I was submerged with him on top of me, his jutting bones like heavy zircon, my back on the bottom, and the black and white of light bending and snapping how far away, beyond the surface. There was no more air, just the high muffled note of my own closed-mouth keening and the dark outline of Gil. It was like being in the MRI.

I kicked and pushed, something was poking me in the shoulder, pressing into my back. I was still struggling, my lips pressed tight, when I came up into the air and was able to move too easily, I fell, got up again, fell, got up, slipping on the bottom. And then I was breathing, and every cut and scrape took in oxygen too, and I was walking and swimming to the edge, looking for a place to get out, the wall far too high and flat and I'd never be able to climb it. I tried not to think of bacteria, three-eyed fish.

Just there, where the great green supports of the Queen Street Bridge ran into the concrete, there was a collection of flat rocks, a kind of step up to a dirt ledge. Things were scattered on this outcropping: a new-looking duffle bag, a bicycle pedal and several shiny wrappers that seemed bizarrely pretty, catching the faint light under the bridge. I was moving, the river falling away behind me. It didn't even feel hard, getting out, slipping past the guardrail, circling back to the staircase. I stood at the bottom, looking up, dripping. A man walked by on the path, stopped, pissed in the river where I'd been flailing just a moment ago. He didn't say anything or look at me, just continued up the path, past the stairs. There were cigarette butts on the ground. The river was perfectly still. There was no one else around.

I started squeezing the water out of my dress and hair and it smelled like clothes left in the washer for a month. It puddled on the bank. I transferred the photo to my purse, then rubbed myself dry with my sweater and slipped my sandals back on. Only my hands felt cold. Over the train tracks to the west I could see cars sluicing north, following the river. I thought I could move like that now, easily and focused. I climbed the stairs.

Up on the bridge, more cars were going by under the *step in, stand in* sign and clock. The city was glittering; it was brighter up on the street than on the dark path. The streetcar went by with a noise like bone on bone and I followed, heading west along Queen, crossing over to the north side to walk beside the westbound traffic. The streetcar was soon gone in the distance, but I walked on ponderously, looking around like a tourist or a castaway. I was seeing everything at once. I couldn't let myself turn around—what was the myth, about walking away from the underworld and not being allowed to look back? Greek was it, or Roman? There was another one like that, from the Bible and the Torah, where you'd get turned into a pillar of salt. All for looking back. We had books of myths and religious texts at the store, but they weren't popular. None of the books were.

It was a long walk and the night that had felt warm left me chilled now in my wet dress. I stumbled crossing Parliament and a car honked. At Sherbourne, I sat down on the cement edging around the base of a tree. Moss Park and the armoury glowed under the stadium-style lights behind me and a group of men sat nearby, yelling across the road to a man in front of a convenience store. I couldn't tell if what they were saying was friendly or not.

I was shaking a little, more like a vibration. Every joint in my body was a screw tightened too much but my hands were loose in my lap. I reached out again, in my head, to feel the city, the mental walk. As if the vibration in my bones were something civic, the power grid looping through my chest and back up into the streetcar wires. I didn't ever want to leave again. Almost due west, past the Roncesvalles Bridge and the streetcar yard, miles away, were the quartz logos on the hillside, the same ones I'd seen on my way back to the city. The quartz that could absorb what spilled over, when there was too much. I heard Elaine's formal voice after coming back from sailing, how she would say *did you not* instead of *didn't you*. The new school clothes every fall, the projector he borrowed for her photos from Georgia. The chocolate cake she so wanted to make for him. Not on a whim, like I thought, but to show him something she could hardly see herself, something that was skewed and mishandled but also desperate and true.

At the corners of my vision, black sand gathered. I took the jade angel out of my purse and it flickered innocently in my palm. With the street lights and bright shops it was hardly noticeable. If it hadn't been for the warm, orange quality of the light you might have missed it altogether. I closed my hand around it. The blackness at the edges of my eyes wavered, then dissolved, leaving only the city to fill my view, the men on the corner; the storefronts; a great, hanging harvest moon.

Pocketing the jade, I got up and started walking again, my bag hanging from my shoulder, my scrapes and shallow cuts tiny gasps against the air. When I passed them, the men on the corner looked at me but said nothing.

I walked for a long time, along Queen Street and up through the Market, past Wendy's apartment, where I didn't stop. Instead I continued up to College and smoothed my fingers through my hair before heading into George's and settling myself into an empty booth. I put my notebook and pen in front of me, lined up carefully.

A few minutes later, without my saying anything, a cup of coffee slid across the tabletop, steaming slightly and bringing George's hand into my field of vision.

"Looks like midnight out there, eh? You know summer's gone when the light starts to go like this. And that moon." He was holding a cup himself, and he sipped from it as he looked out onto College Street. "Mind if I sit?"

I slid over to the window and he settled onto the bench beside me. His slacks were grey, heathered.

I said, "It only took us, what, ten years to work up to sitting while talking?"

"Well, I'm old-fashioned. Just wait until you're sixty, I'll be kissing you on the cheek and asking you to afternoon tea. Va-va-voom."

"Be still, my heart."

George smiled, eyes crinkling up, less handsome than he had been but nicer to look at somehow. "Your hair's wet," he said. "Coming from the gym?"

I shook my head.

He looked at my dress, not yet dry, but all he said was, "What are you writing? Diary?"

"Sort of." The corner of the photo from the river was sticking out from between pages of my notebook.

"What's that?" he said.

I shook my head. "Nothing." I pulled it out. There was the river, and the boxy buildings past the Don Valley Parkway in the background, the bright round puncture mark of the moon. George put his hand over mine on the table.

The corners of the photo hadn't developed perfectly, they were still shadowy, black-orange, the aura of an ill person, lighter than the darkened skyline in the background. In the square frame of the photo, Gil's face flickered in front of my eyes, his dark beard and curls coming in and out of focus, a sliver of the bridge visible over, and then through, his shoulder. He was captured there, and then as I watched him fade completely out of the image, he was still present in his absence. Gone but not forgotten, caught up in what would be, to anyone else, just a badly composed shot of one small corner of the city, empty of life.

A wash of light arced over the booth in George's, headlights of a car turning south into Kensington. George pulled his hand away, picked up his mug and sipped from it. His wedding ring had disappeared.

Another car went by, throwing shadows. I wasn't looking forward to walking home in my damp dress, and I sipped my coffee slowly. Maybe I'd take the Bathurst streetcar, stay warm a little longer. In the meantime, though, George and I sat in the booth, the diner empty save the dark-haired clerk—*the same girl? a new one?*—and two tired-looking paramedics eating sandwiches and drinking coffee. The warm light bumped up against the windows, inflating the room so that the whole world fit inside, just for a moment. Then the door opened, and it was gone. Two couples entered, looking around. One woman took off her glasses and wiped them on the hem of her shirt. George stood up, both hands wrapped around his cup.

"Let me know if you need anything," he said, and he headed back into the kitchen.

I opened my notebook but didn't pick up my pen. Instead I sat, looking out through the window, watching the dim street. People walked by, their mouths complaining about the cooling temperature, the end of summer, even as their lungs took in the clean air, their bodies cursing and praising the city at once. I let myself sit for another half hour or so. Then I put my money on the table and went out to join them.

Acknowledgements

Many fine folks made this book possible: my agent, Martha Magor Webb, who calmly performed a miracle; my editor, Michelle MacAleese, who is a lioness and lucky star for her writers and who has been guide, champion and friend; Louise Dennys, who founded the New Face of Fiction program and has pulled many astonished writers up on stage, Springsteen-style; and the rest of the amazing team at Random House of Canada, especially Anne Collins, Allyson Latta, Amanda Lewis, Ruta Liormonas, Andrew Roberts and Susan Traxel.

In the beginning there were my early readers Jessica Westhead (my literary guardian angel) and the brilliant Robert McGill; Zoe Whittall, Tanis Rideout and my dear Vikki VanSickle, who offered writerly advice and sympathy; Steve Heighton, a source of kind encouragement and insightful advice on titles; and beautiful Vanessa Matthews, who opened the first door and believed.

Two texts were particularly helpful in creating Pierce Gifts & Oddities and Maggie's world: Eden Grey's *Mastering the Tarot* and *The Illustrated Directory of Healing Crystals: A Comprehensive Guide to 150 Crystals and Gemstones* by Cassandra Eason.

Also, I am deeply grateful to the Ontario Arts Council for the important support, both emotional and financial, of the grant I received while writing.

I am indebted to Carolyn Smart of Queen's University, who provided me with helmet, map and compass, and to the faculty of the University of Guelph MFA program, with special gratitude to Catherine Bush and Lisa Moore, who drew Maggie's story out of me like magicians with scarves.

My deep thanks to those who have done the less tangible but no less important work of the heart, especially: Anne, Claire, Lisa (and Mike and Irene), Mark, Ryan (and Beau), Sam and Sara (and Hartley, Ruthie and Gord). Special thanks to Tina, who reads aloud to me.

To my family, whose lively dinner table made me love stories, I am eternally grateful for a childhood full of books and make-believe and frequent trips to the library.

Finally, to Evan: my thanks and thanks and thanks. It's good because it's good with you.

GRACE O'CONNELL holds an MFA in Creative Writing. Her work has appeared in various publications including *The Walrus*, *Taddle Creek*, *Quill & Quire* and *EYE Weekly*. She has taught creative writing at George Brown College and now works as a freelance writer and editor in Toronto.